"Victoria, I told you I loved you," Michael said,

"and I asked you to remember it no matter what came later."

"Oh, I haven't forgotten. And neither will you, because you're not normally a liar. Just this time."

"I meant what I said," he protested. "But speaking of liars..."

"Yes, I lied to you. It's the only protection I have against the users—people who have no idea how much misery they expose me to, people who wouldn't care, even if they knew, as long as they got what they wanted."

"That's not fair, Tory."

"There's nothing you can say. It never occurred to me that you would mangle your integrity to get what you wanted."

It couldn't have stung more if she'd slapped him. "I told you I hadn't intended for today to happen."

"The old 'I love you' game—you must have detested yourself for pulling that stunt. So that's my retribution, letting you live with that...." Grabbing her purse, she turned and walked out of his life.

Dear Reader,

Happy New Year and welcome to another exciting month of romance from Silhouette Intimate Moments. We've got another irresistible lineup of books for you, as well as a future treat that I'll be mentioning in a moment. First, though, how about a new book from one of your favorite authors, Nora Roberts? *Night Shift* will enthrall you—and leave you eager to read *Night Shadow*, coming in March. Readers of historical romance may recognize the name Catherine Palmer. Whether you know her name or not, you will undoubtedly enjoy her debut for Silhouette Intimate Moments, *Land of Enchantment*. Round out the month with new books from Sibylle Garrett and Joyce McGill, two more of the authors who make this line so special.

Now for that future treat I mentioned. Next month we're presenting "February Frolics," an entire month made up of nothing but first novels written by authors whose futures look very bright indeed. Here at Silhouette Intimate Moments we're always trying to find fresh new voices in the romance field, and we think we've come up with four of the best. Next month you'll get a chance to see whether you agree with us—and I hope you do!

In coming months, look for new books from more of your favorites: Dallas Schulze, Heather Graham Pozzessere and Marilyn Pappano, to name just a few. And every month, enjoy some of the best books in romance today: Silhouette Intimate Moments.

Leslie J. Wainger
Senior Editor and Editorial Coordinator

JOYCE McGILL

A Loving Touch

SILHOUETTE·INTIMATE·MOMENTS®
Published by Silhouette Books New York
America's Publisher of Contemporary Romance

SILHOUETTE BOOKS
300 East 42nd St., New York, N.Y. 10017

A LOVING TOUCH

ISBN: 0-373-07368-2

First Silhouette Books printing January 1991

Printed in the U.S.A.

Books by Joyce McGill

Silhouette Intimate Moments

Through the Looking Glass #347
A Loving Touch #368

JOYCE McGILL

began her writing career by doing articles for her high school newspaper, but soon became more involved with the theater. After winning several state awards for Best Actress, she went on to college to earn her B.A. in drama and literature. For some years, she acted in professional and community theaters and made films and commercials before returning to writing. Ms. McGill previously published young-adult romances under the name Tracy West.

Chapter 1

The sign was obviously homemade, faded black letters on a board nailed to a tree. "Cedar Hollow." Michael Gallagher braked at the crest of the hill, gazed down on the cluster of ramshackle buildings huddled below, and groaned. This was what he'd driven an hour and a half to reach? *This* was Jake's alpine paradise?

"Nothing but mountains, cool breezes and an occasional bear to make things interesting," his partner, Jake Burnside, had said as he'd dropped the keys to his cabin on Michael's desk. "You've got vacation time coming, so why not use it now? And since you'll be in that vicinity, it wouldn't hurt to ask around. I'll bet any amount you want to name that somebody up there knows where she is."

Michael, city born and bred, glowered at his surroundings, feeling like an alien on an unfamiliar planet. It was so quiet! No rumble of D.C. traffic. No summer heat to scorch the soles and fry the brain. No headache from the glare of blazing sun on white marble monuments. What the hell am I doing here? he asked himself, slapping at a gnat.

The temptation to turn around and head back to Washington reared its head, as it had at least once every ten miles since he'd crossed the District line into Maryland. He had come on an almost impossible mission, hoping to locate a woman who had disappeared into these mountains a good ten years before. Yanking the gear shift into Park, he set the emergency brake and gazed morosely at the cluster of rough-hewn edifices below. He had expected a small town, but this made *Tobacco Road* resemble a thriving metropolis, and he had a sinking feeling that these mountains were probably replete with garden spots like this, which would make his quarry that much harder to find.

The tap tap on the window of the Mercedes brought him bolt upright in his seat, the shoulder harness snapping tight across his chest, and Michael turned to stare into the gaunt face of a rangy policeman peering in at him. Clearly a fan of *Smokey and the Bandit,* the officer wore the opaque aviator glasses, the broad-brimmed hat, the Sam Browne belt. But the finishing touch to his uniform—the no-nonsense revolver on his hip, holster unsnapped—was enough to remind Michael that he'd be wise to treat this country cop with the same respect due his counterpart in the city. The last thing he needed was to spend the night in Cedar Hollow's excuse for a jail because he'd said the wrong thing in the wrong tone of voice. Keep your cool, he warned himself, and touched the button to lower his window.

The plastic name tag above the officer's badge announced that he answered to the name of Dobbins. Michael set his features into an expression that he hoped reflected mild curiosity, unquestioning innocence and overt respect for the man's badge. "Good morning. Something wrong?"

The response was a scowl. "Mornin'. I was just about to ask you the same thing, seeing as how you've stopped in the middle of the roadway, obstructin' traffic."

Michael, knowing full well that he'd pulled over far enough for anyone to pass, glanced in his rearview mirror.

Other than the cruiser parked behind him on the shoulder, he hadn't seen a car, coming or going, in the last fifteen minutes, but pointing that out might be all Dobbins would need to give him a ticket.

"Sorry," he said with an apologetic smile. "I thought I had missed my turn. I stopped to check my map."

"Mind stepping out of the car and letting me see some identification?" Dobbins moved back from the door, his hand in kissing distance of the revolver.

I'm going to kill Jake Burnside, Michael promised himself as he got out and pried his license from his wallet.

The policeman scanned it quickly, watchful eyes darting from the laminated rectangle to its owner and back again. The photo was a good one, and what little information it contained confirmed the obvious: six-one, 172 pounds. Hair: black. Eyes: blue. Date of birth: 8/1/55.

A measuring gaze raked Michael's tautly muscled frame, ticking off relevant information the license did not supply—the designer tie loosened to free the unbuttoned neck of the silk shirt; the custom-made shoes; the Rolex watch glittering in the sun.

Dobbins bobbed his head and returned the license. "Well, next time pull farther off the road. Where you headed?"

"Somewhere over there, if I read my map right. I'm using a friend's cabin. Jake Burnside's."

The officer barked a laugh, and the wariness disappeared from his pale eyes. To Michael's relief, he snapped the holster shut. "You know Jake? He's a good ol' boy. Got big city wrote all over him, but he minds his business and that's all Hollow folk ask."

Message received, Michael thought. "I hope to do the same. I'm just here for some peace and quiet. And work." He tilted his head toward the attaché case in the front seat. Then, on a whim, he added, "By the way, Jake suggested I look up a woman named Ivy Sheldon. Does that mean anything to you?"

Dobbins snorted. "Sure. She's one of our own."

* * *

Tory Shelton coasted down the hill on her bike at a reckless speed, the breeze playing havoc with her short, sun-bronzed curls. Seeing Marty D. playing Big Bad Trooper for a stranger up on the next rise, she grinned and slowed her pace, grateful that Marty was too preoccupied to have seen her. She didn't have time for the Dobbins lecture on the dangers of taking this grade at full tilt. He'd been yelling at her about it since she was seven, and it cut no ice with him that she was now twenty-one years older.

Braking to a halt in front of her destination, Tory leaned the ten-speed against the bumper of an old pickup and trotted into the dim interior of Sam's General Emporium and Barber Shop, letting the screen door slap against her shapely rear so it wouldn't slam closed.

"Sam," she called, and headed for the last row of shelves. "It's just me. I need another box of raisins."

Sam, scissors in hand, appeared in the doorway separating Emporium from Barber Shop. "Okay. Leave the money on the counter; I got somebody in the chair. You making more oatmeal cookies?"

"Got to." Tory dug coins from the pocket of her cutoffs, and shot him an impish grin, laughter spilling from her large dark eyes. "I ate part of the batch I made last night. I promised Helen I'd bring six dozen for the cookie booth, and you know her, she'll count every last one."

Sam eyed her petite figure and shook his head. "It's a wonder you ain't big as a house, eating like that. How things going at the fairgrounds?"

"There's a lot left to be done, but I couldn't stay any longer. I might go back after I finish the cookies."

The storekeeper raised one grizzled brow. "You better wait till after the sun goes down. You're as brown as a berry already."

Tory laughed, the full-throated sound bringing a smile to Sam's wrinkled face. "I don't care," she said. "This is my time of year. Gotta run. See you tomorrow."

"Say, how about carrying a couple of receipt books for Helen to save me a trip? Won't take me but a minute to find them; they've been gathering dust since you talked me into computerizing."

Tory sighed—silently—but settled down to wait. There was no way she could refuse Sam Greenwood anything. He and Marty Dobbins had practically adopted her after Pop had died, despite the fact that at eighteen, she'd been perfectly capable of taking care of herself. In fact, the people of the Hollow had been surrogate aunts and uncles most of her life. And her old classmates from college kept wondering why she insisted on living up here! The residents of the Hollow weren't the primary reason, but neither were they that far behind. She knew when she was well off. If you were in hiding, which, for all intents and purposes, she was, what better place to hide than among friends?

It was a second before Michael recovered from shock at being answered in the affirmative about Ivy Sheldon. "One of your own," he echoed blankly, not quite certain what it meant, given the woman's reputation.

"Born and raised here," Dobbins amplified. "Lived here practically her whole life. What, you got some work for her?"

Some work for her? That was a quaint way of putting it. "Well, I might have. It depends."

"She's good," Dobbins bragged, his narrow chest swelling with proprietary pride. "Lots of folks go to her, specially the businessmen over in Chestin where she lives now. Head back the way you came about four miles, take a left onto Arbor Road and go another couple of miles to where it dead-ends. She's the last place on the right. You'll see her sign."

"That sounds easy enough. Thanks."

"You probably won't catch her at home until Monday, though. Everybody's getting ready for the big fair tomorrow. Come on by, why don't ya? They'll be selling the best home cooking you ever had. A couple of miles that-away past old Jake's place. You can't miss it."

"Perhaps I will," Michael said, surprised at the invitation. Jake had warned him not to expect an open-armed welcome.

"They take a while to warm up to outsiders," he had elaborated. "Those folks leave you about as alone as you can get until they know you, and that usually takes two or three years. But feel free to toss my name around. Who knows? Long as I've been going there, it might make them open up."

I owe you one, partner, Michael thought.

"Well, we both better move," Dobbins said, "before some fool comes tearing up behind us. The driveway to Jake's is just past that grove of trees yonder." He pointed at the top of the next rise. "Look for me at the fairgrounds tomorrow. I'll show you around, seeing you're a friend of ol' Jake's. Take care, hear?"

Michael slid back under the wheel and buckled his seat belt, unable to believe his luck. He hadn't gotten a ticket, and Dobbins had seemed like an okay guy, not that different from a few cop buddies he had back in D.C. Of far more importance was the information the officer had supplied. Michael had been too stubborn to admit it to Jake, but he'd come prepared to scour these mountains, to stay as long as it took to get a line on Ivy Sheldon's whereabouts. And here she was, just a few miles away. That was a good omen—not that he believed in that kind of thing, he reminded himself.

Putting the car in gear, he drifted slowly down the hill past the motley collection of small commercial establishments, his architect's eye noting that they were of sturdy construction, their dilapidated appearance a clever con, courtesy of artfully applied paint. Grinning at how thoroughly he'd been taken in, he accelerated to climb the next steep grade.

Beyond it, the mountains rose, stately and serene, the June foliage carpeting their heights in a mottled, lush green.

A hawk of some kind circled, riding a thermal updraft like a feather on the wind. The sky, scrubbed free of city pollutants, was a blue Michael couldn't even put a name to. And the mountains themselves were a surprise, far higher and more massive than he had expected. There was a certain rugged beauty about the place, he had to admit. Maybe Jake was right—if he gave it half a chance, he might like it. But he hadn't come up here to commune with nature—he'd come to ferret out Madame Ivy or whatever she called herself now.

"I hope I don't look as big a fool as I feel," he muttered, raising the window against invading insects. Still, if this Sheldon woman was as gifted as Jake remembered, and if he could quash his cynicism long enough to put the least amount of credence in her and what she was supposed to be... Hell, he'd grease her palm with silver—or gold, if that's what she wanted. It didn't matter how silly he felt, how much it cost him monetarily or emotionally. This was more important.

Okay. He'd dig in for the weekend, maybe work on a couple of design ideas to take to New York—if he ever got there—then hit Arbor Road first thing Monday morning. If he came away with a clue, a tidbit, anything that would help him find his old friend, he'd turn in his skeptic's badge in a minute. Even if all she did was confirm his gut instinct that Lee Varnum was still alive...

Michael shook his head, incredulous. Never in his wildest dreams would it have occurred to him that he, a summa cum laude graduate and a highly successful architect, would be desperate enough to pin his hopes of finding Lee Varnum on the mumbo-jumbo ravings of a backwoods psychic. But the operative word was desperate. He had to find Lee. And Ivy Sheldon was his last hope.

After champing at the bit for the quarter hour it took Sam to unearth the receipt books, Tory stashed them and the raisins in the basket on the rear of her bike, noting that

Marty D. and the poor outlander in the Mercedes were gone. The heat of the summer sun settled like a weight on her bare arms and back; her skimpy halter clung to her small, round breasts like plastic wrap. Wheeling the ten-speed around, she crossed the road toward Lil's Beauty Shop, stopped, then decided to take the long way home.

It made no sense at all, considering that directly behind Lil's was the well-worn path she invariably used, a shortcut that reduced the distance between the shops and home by at least a third. It was also cooler, as the bike path meandered through a mile-long stretch of century-old shade trees. This had always been her route to Sam's, so the sudden urge to bypass the shortcut and take the two-lane highway home was completely irrational. She *never* went back that way on her bike.

She looked up at the hill she'd have to climb, the steepest in the area. Heat devils writhed above the asphalt like dancing jellyfish, a shimmering chorus line which stretched up over the rise to merge with the horizon. What little energy she had seemed to ooze from her body with the perspiration, but all the logical arguments against taking the main road carried no weight today, even though the mere prospect of pedaling her way to the top was enervating.

Instead, she walked. Pushing the ten-speed along the bumpy shoulder, Tory started up the hill, letting the variety of wildflowers at the edges of the road take her mind off the heat. Despite the temperature, she loved summer. Cedar Hollow greeted spring by turning into a world of pastels, but from June to August the colors intensified until the countryside fairly glowed with glossy greens, iridescent yellows and reds every bit as breathtaking as the Hollow's autumn wardrobe. Tory was so engrossed in her perusal of the flora that she almost missed the miniature explosion of sun rays on gold, almost dead center of the blacktop.

What was it? Propping the bike against a dogwood tree, she stepped onto the macadam and crossed to the middle, gripped by a taut anticipation. A tie clasp shaped like a T-square twinkled in the sun. At the point where the longer leg abutted the crosspiece, a tiny letter G glittered in bas relief. There was a sturdiness about the piece, an aura of strength. Stooping like a child examining a fascinating new find, Tory stared at it. It wasn't until the heat began seeping through the soles of her sandals that she realized she'd been riveted to the spot far too long.

There were no architects, draftsmen or engineers in Chestin or the Hollow. More to the point, there was no one she knew who could afford gold of this quality. This had to belong to the driver of the car Marty Dobbins had stopped. Tory tried to remember the man she had glimpsed, but could recall only dark hair and a blazing white shirt that matched the blazing white car. As valuable as this hunk of gold must be, he'd miss it before long. He'd probably backtrack looking for it and guess that he might have lost it here. If she didn't move it, however, someone would come along and mash it into the heat-softened tarmac. The challenge was, how to rescue it without handling it unnecessarily.

Tory patted her pockets for her gloves, found them empty and slapped her forehead in frustration as she pictured them lying next to Helen's purse at the fairgrounds. She could count on one hand the number of times she'd forgotten a pair of gloves. Now she had nothing she could use to pick up the tie clasp. The contents of her pockets consisted of a dime, two pennies and a blob of lint. She'd left home with just enough money to get the raisins; her purse would have been a nuisance to keep tabs on at the fairgrounds.

A leaf. If she could find one broad enough to wrap around the tie clasp, she could pick it up that way. There was nothing suitable among the wildflowers, but a nearby red maple was rife with broad and very serviceable foliage, if she could jump high enough to reach a lower limb.

In the distance, the clatter of an engine in dire need of a tune-up—Dick Simpson in his '62 Caddy—put an end to her good intentions. If he didn't flatten the tie clasp into the mushy blacktop, the next vehicle would. She couldn't bear

to let that happen; this tiny T-square represented a great deal
of sentiment to its owner, though how she knew that was a
puzzler, since she hadn't touched it. She had to do something soon. Mr. Simpson, as usual, had the pedal to the
floor. He would take that last dip and shoot up over this rise
like a cart on a roller coaster. Tory raised her foot to give the
tie clasp one clean kick into the growth along the shoulder
and in that same instant changed her mind.

There couldn't be any harm if she handled the thing very,
very carefully, given the mental screen she'd learned to erect
for such occasions. It worked ninety percent of the time; the
gloves were insurance against the remaining ten. Why
shouldn't it work now? Picking it up with the tips of her
fingers, Tory stood, giddy with relief. The only images and
thoughts in her head were her own.

Mr. Simpson, however, was approaching far faster than
she'd anticipated, and she vaulted toward the shoulder as he
zipped by with a blast of his horn, pure reflex making her
clutch the tie clasp tightly as she made the leap. The tiny T-
square nestled into the creases of her palm, and she gasped,
letting it fall into the undergrowth. It was too late. She could
still feel its outline, its weight. The emanations of the owner
seared her hand as if pressed into it by a white-hot branding iron.

Tory plopped down in the tall grasses beyond the shoulder of the road, her back against the red maple, her eyes
tightly closed. She had crowed too soon. A decade of caution bordering on paranoia hadn't made any difference at
all. Ten years of being careful what she touched. Ten years
and dozens of pairs of gloves, and lying about the necessity
of using them. All the tricks, the imaginative ruses had
worked, and she had hoped, oh, how she had hoped. But
the curse was still with her. The screen hadn't worked this
time.

She had heard a host of names for it—sixth sense, ESP,
cognition, tele-this and psychic-that. Whatever, Tory hated
it. It had fouled her preteen years and adolescence, this

mental quirk she'd never asked for and had prayed ever since to have lost. It was still with her, in her. After all this time.

She shouldn't have chanced it, and knew too well why she had. The cocoon she'd spun for herself, her safe, predictable world up here in the mountains, had begun to smother her. She had avoided admitting it, and now that she had, she was worse off than before, because no matter how keenly she felt the need to spread her wings and fly, leaving the Hollow was out of the question. If she hadn't been sure before, this provided all the proof she needed. She was still a freak, and the best place for a freak was home where she was protected from the starers and whisperers, the name-callers, the users.

Wiping her eyes, Tory got to her feet with a sigh of resignation, pulled a broad leaf from the maple and used it to retrieve the tie clasp from the clump of buttercups in which it had landed. She would take it to its owner; he was quite nearby, much closer than she would have imagined. Using the fleshy pad of the middle finger of her right hand, she rubbed it lightly over the initial just long enough to ferret out what little she needed to know.

His first name was Michael. The tie clip was very special to him; he wore it often. He was troubled. She sensed sorrow, steely determination, guilt. The reasons weren't clear, and Tory refused to concentrate harder to learn more. That part was none of her business. All she had to do was find the man with hair the color of midnight. She would give him his tie clasp, walk away and close the door of her prison again.

Michael swore and gave up. He'd checked the car, he'd even shed his slacks, hoping it might have dropped down his front, but it wasn't there. He'd worn the thing practically every day since Lee had given it to him. He could still see those deep gray eyes shining with pleasure as he'd handed over the box.

"You did it, boy. You passed your boards. You are an architect. Nobody uses T-squares much anymore, but I still remember what my first one meant to me and I hope this little one will mean as much to you. Wear it with pride."

How could he have lost it? And why now? If he believed in omens...

"Damn!" Michael growled, knowing there wasn't a chance in a million of finding it, considering the number of places he'd been today. It was all he had left of Lee, a constant reminder of the role the marvelous old bastard had played in the man Michael had become. He simply had to find it, at least make the effort.

Jake's vacation home was a cabin in name only, affording every creature comfort imaginable. After putting the remnants of the microwavable pizza in the refrigerator, Michael grabbed his car keys, yanked open the front door and almost ran over the girl who stood outside, her fist raised to knock.

"Michael... Gallagher." There was no question mark in her soft voice, no doubt expressed.

"Yes."

"I believe this is yours." On her palm was a deep red leaf. Cradled in the middle of it was the tie clasp.

Stunned, Michael took it, stared at it in astonishment, then looked up at her, feeling her eyes on him. What he saw in them made his pulse flutter at the base of his throat, but before he could speak, she turned to hurry down the steps. "Wait! Where did you find it?"

"On the hill where Marty Dobbins stopped you." She was climbing onto a battered bike with a ridiculous pink-and-white basket clamped above its rear wheel.

"Thank you. I can't tell you how much I appreciate this." He trotted down the steps. "Please, let me give you something for your trouble."

Shaking her head, she began to pedal away. "No, thanks. I'm just glad you have it back. 'Bye." Then she was gone, the reflectors on the rim of the basket winking a saucy farewell.

Michael gazed after her, her image etched in his mind. Oval face, nose dappled with tiny ginger-colored freckles. Tousled curls, new-penny bright in the afternoon sun.

But her eyes were what had captured him, a clear, warm, bottomless brown, like aged Scotch. And the *way* she had looked at him... He searched for a description, found it and promptly rejected it, because it didn't make sense. Sense or not, it wouldn't go away. Inexplicably, he recalled the day he'd run into Gordon Peterson, the Channel 9 anchor he'd watched every weekday for the last ten years. He'd walked up to the newsman and, without introduction, had begun talking to him with the easy familiarity of one old friend to another. Not until Peterson asked his name had Michael remembered that he'd never actually met the man before.

The petite redhead had looked at him with that same familiarity, her eyes saying that she *knew* him, knew him well. But she couldn't. In spite of her age—she was probably jailbait, or damned near it—he would have remembered if they had met before, if only because of the color of her hair.

Michael's lips stretched in a wry smile. If mountain girls blossomed as early as that one had, it was no wonder Jake spent at least one weekend a month up here. Jake Burnside was a dedicated watcher of women, no matter what their age. And all this time I thought he was in love with the mountains, Michael mused, chuckling under his breath.

Stepping back into the cabin, he closed the door, fingering the tie clip. He would not wear it again until he could get back to the city and have his jeweler check the spring on it. To lose Lee and the tie clip as well...

Okay, he had it back, his second stroke of luck in one day. If, as the old saying went, things happened in threes, he was on a roll. Perhaps it was just as well the girl hadn't been ten years older. That would have been the third bit of luck and if he had a choice, he'd just as soon Number Three came in the guise of Ivy Sheldon telling him where the hell Lee was.

He'd never been particularly superstitious before, but he wasn't too old to change, if that's what it took.

Energized, he grabbed his briefcase and settled down to go over a set of blueprints of Lee's pet project. He could lose himself in these in no time; the weekend would be gone before he knew it. He could forget everything while he was working, even the caressing warmth in a pair of bottomless brown eyes. It had always worked before.

It wasn't long, however, before he had to admit that this time, it might not.

Tory stopped at the end of the long lane leading from the cabin. Straddling the bike, she bent over and pressed her head against the handlebars, pressed hard to punish herself for her impulsiveness. She could have left the tie clip on the porch railing or the edge of the step. But he'd opened the door, and from that point, she'd lost her head.

She had known, for the most part, what to expect, and once she had the tie clasp in her hand, Michael Gallagher had become familiar enough to her so that she could have picked him out in a crowd—tall, well-built, very dark hair, eyes of an unusual blue. The flaw in the picture was that the image in her head, courtesy of the tiny T-square, had been his image of himself, which in comparison to the reality was as different as a photo in black and white beside the identical photo in full color.

He could not see the keen intelligence that brightened his eyes, the humor betrayed by the set of his lips. Nor could he imagine the strength of character he emanated. As a result, Tory had been completely unprepared for Michael Gallagher in the flesh. He was so virile, so profoundly masculine, but with none of the posturing she had seen in other men; his ease with who he was came from some deep inner well. It was as natural to him as his hair and eyes and skin.

As for Tory, something had stirred the normally quiescent waters of her own inner well, sending ripples across its surface in perfect, concentric circles, spreading outward toward the edges of her soul. She had felt a need so primal in nature that it had left her shaken. This was a new demon, one with which she was unfamiliar. It had an intensity all its own, and she wasn't sure she had the strength to fend it off.

Tory lifted her head and stared up into the trees, fixing on the familiar—the sprays of needles on the evergreens, the sunlight as it filtered through the branches. Slowly she became grounded, in control again and thinking clearly. For the first time she began to worry about Michael Gallagher's quick mind.

He would wonder how she had known the tie clasp belonged to him, how she'd managed to track him down. She could only hope he'd assume that Marty Dobbins had pointed her in his direction. He had no reason to suspect the truth. Who in their right mind would?

"What am I worried about?" Tory asked a squirrel giving her a wary eye. "He's probably just here for the weekend."

Even if he became curious enough to ask someone about her, her secret was safe with her friends in the Hollow. They would never give her away. She was making a mountain out of a molehill.

Pushing off and turning onto the main road, Tory headed for home, her spirits slowly rebounding. She had cookies to bake, and tomorrow and Sunday she'd be at the fairgrounds all day. By Monday he would probably be gone. She would never forget him, might even daydream about him. But if her luck held, and she was determined to make it do just that, she need never see Michael Gallagher again.

Chapter 2

Michael tied the laces of his running shoes the next morning and ambled to the wall of sliding glass doors that opened onto the deck. The view was incredible, the distant mountains rising in green-shrouded majesty.

Just beyond the deck was Jake's own private forest. Small birds darted from tree to tree, moving with speeds which reduced them to mere flashes of color. They were singers, all of them, beginning their preludes at first light, trilling to the sun above the horizon. Lee would love this place, Michael mused. One of these days he'd bring the old man up here just to watch the sheer joy in his eyes when Lee saw the view.

"Damn it, Lee, where are you?" Michael whispered, a question he'd asked a hundred times since that balmy Saturday six weeks before when Lee had sailed off down the Chesapeake in the *Lady Leslie*. It was the last anyone had seen of him, and he had been searched for by the best—the Coast Guard, police departments from D.C. to Virginia Beach, plus a private investigator Michael himself had hired. Lee Varnum was nowhere to be found; it was as if he'd sailed to the edge of the earth and had dropped off into oblivion, leaving nothing—no boat, no debris to give them a clue what had happened to him. And they'd all given up. Lost At Sea, Case Closed stamped across a parade of missing persons reports.

Michael refused to accept it, at first out of guilt because he was to have gone with the old man but hadn't gotten back from New York in time, guilt that for a fraction of a second he'd entertained the notion that Lee had deliberately disappeared to throw a monkey wrench into his protégé's plans to move to New York, guilt that in spite of everything, whether he found Lee or not, he would eventually make the move anyway.

Only recently had Michael come to feel, perhaps to save his sanity, that if Lee were dead, he would know it. He would *feel* it. They were just that close. And it was only because he'd exhausted all orthodox means of finding him that he hadn't hung up on Jake when his partner had phoned with the preposterous idea that he employ a psychic.

"Hell, if police departments and the CIA use them, why shouldn't you?" Jake had asked.

Jake Burnside had convinced him to visit the Wayland Institute for Parapsychology Research in Washington, an entity Michael hadn't known existed and where, for the first time, he had begun to wonder. The documentation they'd shown him had been too solid to reject out of hand. Unfortunately, of the two people on their lists for such a task, neither was available. But Jake refused to let the matter die, falling back on his prodigious memory to dredge up the name of a mountain girl whose exploits he had followed back in the seventies.

"I wouldn't have paid much attention to the whole business," Jake had said when he'd called from his father's hospital room in Florida, "except that Dad had gone up to the cabin for the weekend and was there the first time she tracked someone down. Here, he'll tell you."

Michael had listened with mounting disbelief as Jacob
Burnside Sr. elaborated on how Ivy Sheldon—he was pretty
sure that was the name—had led searchers to the family
whose Piper Cub had crashed in the mountains.

"They'd have died of exposure if she hadn't found them.
That was the start of it, and she popped up in the news for
the next few years, finding missing persons. She came from
one of those two-bit towns up there somewhere. You ask
enough people, son, and you're bound to run into somebody who knows where she is now."

"Ivy Sheldon." Michael had written the name, had stared
at it, still resistant.

Jake took the phone from his father. "So track her down.
I would do it myself, since they know me, but I can't leave
here until this old goat is back on his feet. I'd like to see you
settle down in the Big Apple with a clear conscience, pal.
The office can do without you for a while. Go for it, Mike.
What harm can it do?"

Turning his back on the vista, Michael leaned against the
railing and wondered for the umpteenth time why he was
wasting time hanging around the cabin. The deadline for the
firm to submit the drawings for Woodland Rise would ex-
pire the end of July, and Lee's lifelong dream of building a
community for the disabled would be a dead issue. Lee was
the senior architect of Varnum and Associates. Without his
signature and seal on the drawings, as required by law, the
drawings were worthless. The acreage in question would be
up for grabs, and no one would blame Montgomery County
for signing it over to Cross and Crosby, who were just waiting to put up yet another stack of posh condominiums.

Six short weeks in which to save the project. That he was
here at all, Michael reflected, was ridiculous, but since he
was, he'd be damned if he'd fritter away a whole weekend.
He would check the lady's place on Arbor Road, and if she
wasn't there, he'd cover every inch of the fairgrounds until
he found her. More than likely, she'd be running a fortune-
teller's booth, reading palms or predicting the future for five

dollars a whop. Decision made, he retrieved his keys from the rosewood credenza.

Fifteen minutes later, Michael stared in confusion at the small ranch house at the end of Arbor Road in Chestin. Perched on a gently sloping lot, it was compact and neat under a deep green roof with matching shutters. Window boxes overflowed with flowers offering a riot of contrasting colors against the white siding. It made for a charming picture, but Michael was unable to appreciate it for the moment, his attention riveted on the neatly painted sign on a post at the curb: Wordsmiths. Mon.-Fri., 8-6. Sat. By Appointment Only.

"Wordsmiths?" Michael shook his head, the relationship between the name and the service she was alleged to perform eluding him. He pulled into the driveway, went to the door and rang the bell, but a certain quietude about the house had already convinced him that no one was home. Returning to the Mercedes, he retraced his route. A couple of miles past Jake's, Dobbins had said. With a growing suspicion that he'd been directed to the wrong woman, Michael drove toward the fairgrounds.

"Get with it, Bill! If that's the best you can pitch, they're gonna whip the socks off you when the softball game starts."

Tory, perched on a collapsible seat above a giant tank of water, laughed at the determined expression on the face of Chestin's only used car dealer. Sheltered by a three-sided enclosure of chicken wire, she pointed at the target. "That thing's as big as a house! I can't believe you've missed it twice! Come on, dunk me!"

"You asked for it, shorty," Bill Jablonski snarled with mock menace. Tucking his pudgy body into an exaggerated pitcher's windup, he held the pose for a second, then whipped his arm forward. The ball hit the target squarely, the cushioned seat dropped from under her and Tory landed in the tank, flailing her arms to send up a miniature tidal wave. The bigger the splash the better, she'd learned, and several shrieking onlookers found themselves drenched.

"That's more like it," Tory called, climbing the ladder to her perch. "Okay, who's next? Two tosses for a dollar for adults, three for a dollar for kids. Pay up, guys. This is for charity, remember?"

She'd been up and down the ladder for the last hour and a half, prodding the timid, goading the gleeful. It looked as if the dunking concession would be a money-maker again this year; she'd lost count after the eleventh hurler. Once her shift was up, the principal of the middle school would take her place, and a score of his students awaited his arrival with imps of Satan dancing in their eyes.

Tory checked the scene around her. It wasn't quite noon, yet the grounds were already crowded and a steady stream of fair-goers made their way from the parking area a block away. A gentle breeze wafted past, redolent of barbecuing chicken and ribs. The food concessions would open for business at noon, and Tory's stomach growled with impatience; she'd eaten breakfast at seven. Ignoring her discomfort, she shouted encouragement to little Chuckie Gant, then forgot him as her body stiffened; she'd been invaded by the same tension and sense of anticipation she'd experienced the day before as she'd stooped in the middle of the road to peer down at the tie clip.

Why was she suddenly breathless again, her bare arms pebbling with goose bumps? Why this feeling of waiting for something? What was there to wait for? The tension wouldn't go away, becoming more insistent, a phantom stealing up behind her.

Then she saw him, the tall, dark-haired man entering the fairgrounds from the parking lot. Michael Gallagher. Tory gasped just as Chuckie hit the bull's-eye and unprepared she plummeted into the tank, landing on her back, her mouth still open. Water flooded her nose and mouth, hit the back of her throat, teased her windpipe. Flailing in earnest this time and fighting panic, she emerged coughing and spluttering, to the screams of laughter from bystanders unaware how close she had come to drowning in three feet of water.

Somehow she managed to clear her lungs without betraying the extent of her distress. Her face frozen with a smile, she settled onto the cushion, praying her relief dunkee would come early so she could escape the booth and lose herself in the crowd. She felt exposed here, just high enough above everyone so it would be difficult for him to miss spotting her. And it hadn't mattered before, but she was now also conscious of how little her one-piece swimsuit covered, despite the fact that it was fairly modest compared to the bikini she'd decided it would not be politic to wear.

"How much longer?" she called to the high school student collecting the money and keeping track of everyone's shift.

"Ten minutes. You okay? Want me to fill in until Mr. Wanamaker comes?"

It was tempting, but Tory shook her head, having lost sight of Michael for the moment. She was worried for nothing. Considering the size of the crowd and the fairground, there was little chance they'd run into each other once she'd finished her stint here. "No, I'm fine. All right, guys," she called, her voice slightly hoarse from coughing, "where's the next Dwight Gooden? Let's get this show on the road!"

Michael cut across the grassy area, angling toward the fairway and the double row of stands housing shooting galleries, ring tosses, pay-your-money-and-try-your-luck. As he'd anticipated, there were several small tented enclosures among them, the perfect setting for a fortune-teller and her crystal ball. It was with grim satisfaction, however, that he found he wasn't far off the mark. There was indeed a fortune-teller's booth, but in this case the seer had opted for the convenience of modern technology. A middle-aged woman, properly swathed and veiled, stood watch beside a personal computer and a dot matrix printer.

The computer was programmed to display a series of questions and multiple choice answers. The customer typed in the letters corresponding to his or her chosen responses, red lights glowed and disk drives whirred, after which the printer whined out a page of text that was held for ransom until a dollar had changed hands.

"For cryin' out loud, Mrs. O'Donnell," one indignant teen protested, "I could have done this on my own computer for nothing. You showed us how last year in Programming Two." Grumbling under his breath, the young man forked over the bill, accepted the sheet and left.

Michael followed him, undeterred at having struck out his first time at bat. This fair was no two-bit operation squeezed onto a vacant corner lot. An event of this size could support more than one fortune-teller. All he had to do was poke his nose into the right tent.

The next one he broached housed a photographer's setup—a cardboard cutout of bodybuilders with holes for the heads of the patrons—and the final tent sheltered a caricaturist. His frustration rising, Michael marched past hawkers shouting invitations to bean the birdie or burst the balloons. He'd been so sure...

"Hey, Gallagher!"

Startled to hear his name, Michael looked back over his shoulder. Officer Dobbins, a giant panda under one arm, waved to him from the shooting gallery he'd just passed, and Michael doubled back, relieved at the sight of a familiar face.

Dobbins seemed delighted to see him. "You came! Glad ya found the time. Been on any rides yet?"

"No, I just got here."

"They're over on the back side—Ferris wheel, parachute jump and everything. There's one helluva neck-snapper called the Whiplash. Guaranteed to make you upchuck if you're dumb enough to chance it on a full stomach."

Michael laughed. "I think I'll skip that one. Before I forget it, I really appreciate you steering the young lady to me yesterday."

"Say what?"

"My tie clip came off when I got out of the car to show you my license. She—a teenager, really—found it. I assumed you told her to check with me."

"Wasn't me."

"Oh." She must have been in one of the stores; she could have seen Dobbins stop him from there. He dismissed it, intent on pinning the man down about Ivy Sheldon. "By the way—" he began, but was interrupted by a series of metallic squawks from the police radio clipped on the policeman's belt.

Dobbins snatched it to his mouth. "Unit Six. What's up?" The response was completely unintelligible to Michael. The officer sighed. "Ten-four. Duty calls," he said, replacing the radio. "The first lost kid of the day. You gonna be here for a while?"

"Yes. I thought I might try to find Ms. Sheldon."

"She's around somewhere," Dobbins assured him, backing away. "Try the food concessions. She'll be selling baked goods and helping out over there. Maybe I'll run across ya later." Hefting the giant panda over his head, he disappeared into the crowd.

Michael turned to gaze at the three remaining pandas on the top shelf of the shooting gallery and, for a moment, considered trying to win one for Leslie, Lee's daughter, a passionate collector of stuffed bears. The moment was short-lived; he wasn't in the mood and she probably had several pandas already. Besides, if he found the Sheldon woman, he'd feel that much more foolish approaching her with a three-foot bear under his arm.

There'd been no need to ask directions to the area where food would be served. Plumes of smoke from the barbecue pits drifted upward, marking the spot and scenting the air with enticing smells. Following his nose, he made his way through the crowd. He skirted a group of wide-eyed youngsters watching a man on stilts, and waded through a forest of balloons, dodging a toddler engrossed in the intricacies of eating an enormous cone of cotton candy. The clearing ahead was ringed with hawkers shouting invitations to have one's weight guessed or to test one's strength at a set of hand grips. Passing them by with a shake of his head, Michael slowed to get his bearings, when a peal of laughter from his right stopped him in his tracks.

Low-pitched and bubbling with hilarity, it rose and fell, musically, infectiously, and Michael made a detour around a Winnebago parked next to an enclosure of chicken wire, drawn toward the sound as if it were a magnet. He had almost reached the front when he looked up into the face of the wood nymph who had returned his tie clip, and was unsettled to realize that he'd known it would be, that it could have been no one else.

Head thrown back, her copper curls glistening with drops of water, she roared with laughter as a bean pole of a man stood frozen in a grotesque parody of a pitcher's windup, tongue between his teeth. His arm came forward in slow motion, and the ball dropped six inches in front of his feet. The young woman in the cage gripped the seat with both hands, laughing with such gusto that she was in danger of falling off.

Michael circled the group, stopping at the outer fringes of those in front of the cage. When she saw him, her laughter ceased for a split second, her dark eyes widening appreciably.

The pitcher was offering excuses for his failure. "I don't know what I'm doing wrong. One more time, Tory. Double or nothing."

"As many times as you like, Norris," she called down. "With you pitching, I'll be dry as a bone when I get down."

The man named Norris gave several repeat performances, his contortionist windups becoming more and more exaggerated and his audience growing larger with each toss.

Michael was far more interested in the young woman named Tory. He'd been wrong about her. She was indeed a woman, not the ripening teen he had thought.

The top of her swimsuit was less revealing than the halter she'd worn the day before. The memory of the damp triangle of fabric clinging to her small, high breasts had made mincemeat of his concentration as he'd labored over Lee's blueprints. A good deal more leg was exposed now, too, thanks to the French cut of the bottom of her suit, of which Michael heartily approved. Seeing her now, he wondered if his imagination had been working overtime. Her face was alive with amusement at Norris's performance, but whenever those marvelous eyes grazed his, there was little in them beside a friendly acknowledgement of his presence.

Norris, claiming fatigue, gave up. "Just isn't my day," he said, glaring at the ball in his hand.

The young woman chuckled and started down the ladder. "Told you my suit would be almost dry before you finished." She reached the ground and turned just in time to see Norris assume the position again and hurl the ball. It hit the target squarely, tripping the release. The empty seat collapsed with a clatter, and he grinned.

"You big faker!" she yelled, leaving the enclosure. She wrapped her arms around his waist and hugged him, her nose buried in the man's bony chest. "Thanks, Norris. The day-care center thanks you, too."

Norris hugged her back. "My pleasure, since one of the squawlers they keep an eye on is mine. Now, lemme go see how much damage Molly's done in the bingo tent." He strolled away, looking pleased with himself as he crammed his wallet back into his pocket.

Michael waited while she spoke to several bystanders and wished her replacement, a pudgy, balding man in a turn-of-the-century swimsuit, good luck. She took a towel from a stack beside the attendant's stand and a pair of gloves, which she pulled on before ambling over to Michael, an uncertain smile on her lips.

"Hello, Mr. Gallagher. Welcome to the Founder's Day fair. I'm surprised to see you here."

Her voice, a warm contralto, was huskier than he remembered. "Dobbins told me about it yesterday and suggested I come by."

"Marty? You passed muster in a big way," she said, towelling her hair briskly. "He's usually escorting strangers out of town, rather than inviting them to stay."

Michael chuckled. "He was about to do just that, at first. I guess I must have pushed the right buttons. It occurs to me, you know my name, but I'm not sure about yours. It's Tory?"

"Right. Short for Victoria."

"Makes sense. Well, thanks again for returning the tie clip, Tory. How did you know it was mine and where to find me?"

Her features tightened. "This is a very small community," she said, draping the towel around her neck. "Someone new sticks a toe over the township lines, and within seconds everybody knows what color his socks are and whether he needs his shoes resoled. Have you had lunch?"

Off balance at the abrupt change of subject, Michael took a second to shift gears. "No. Why?"

"We're selling tons of food over in the picnic area. We'll even pack it for you to take back to town. Be sure to sample the chili; it's so hot, it's served in fireproof containers. Well..." She extended a hand. "It was nice seeing you again, but I've got to change clothes and run. Hope you enjoy the fair."

Michael took her hand, vaguely surprised at the strength of her grip. Petite, she was, perhaps an inch or two over five feet, but she was far from fragile. Her sun-bronzed body was beautifully shaped, her breasts small but full, suiting her perfectly. Her legs were exquisite—long and smoothly muscled; either she frequented a spa regularly or had taken ballet all her life.

Almost immediately, Michael reversed his opinion. Somehow he couldn't imagine her performing endless repetitions on a Nautilus. There was something about her, a glow, that spoke of the outdoors, of fresh air and sun.

"Michael, I really do have to go."

"Pardon?"

She looked pointedly at her hand, still firmly enclosed in his grasp.

"Oh. Sorry." He released it, but the feel of her fingers around his palm lingered, as if they were still there. "Why the gloves?" he asked. "Or are you setting a new fashion statement?"

"Don't I wish. Sensitive skin, that's all. If I come in contact with the wrong thing, I break out."

"Oh. Sorry. You're giving up on the fair so soon? Dobbins gave me the impression people come and stay all day."

"They do. I'm not leaving, I'm just scheduled to take over a cookie booth in forty-five minutes."

Perhaps his luck had changed. She could point out his fortune-teller. "Have you eaten yet?"

She hesitated. "No. Why?"

"Any possibility of our having lunch together?" There was another silence and Michael sensed an odd tension. Hurrying to fill the void, he said, "I'm harmless and a perfect gentleman. I'm also hungry enough to eat a bear. So, would you join me for lunch, Ms.—"

"Shelton," she supplied absently.

Shelton? She couldn't be... Michael's thoughts took an erratic leap to the small white ranch house with the picket fence and the sign at the curb. It had not fit his impression of the kind of place he'd find his psychic, but it suited Tory Shelton to a tee. "Wordsmiths?" he asked.

He had surprised her. "Yes. You've seen our ad?"

"No, Dobbins told me about you, but..." How could he find out what he wanted to know without sounding like an idiot? "The name Wordsmiths threw me. What exactly do you do?"

An impish grin made her resemble the teenager she'd seemed the day before. "Well, I took a little license there. It's desktop publishing, word processing, some graphics, if it isn't too complicated. I have a plotter, but I'm still learning to use the software." She tilted her head to one side. "Why do I get the impression that wasn't what you wanted to hear?"

Michael blinked, unaware that he'd telegraphed his disappointment. "Sorry—again. I asked Dobbins if he could steer me to a woman named Ivy Sheldon and he went right into a commercial for your services. But the person I'm looking for is in a different line of business."

"Oh." Her expression changed, became remote, wary. "What does she do?"

A debate raged between Michael's first inclination to be honest with her and his concern over what she would think of him if she knew. Ego won. "She's a consultant of sorts. It's a bit difficult to explain."

When he made no further attempt to overcome the aforementioned difficulty, she shrugged, watching him closely. "Marty assumed you meant me. I've never heard of any Sheldons in this area, but a kid named Larry Sheldon helped Cumberland's basketball team mop up the floor with our high school kids last winter. As good as he was, anybody in that vicinity could tell you where he lives."

Cumberland, Michael thought, annoyed that he had relied so heavily on the policeman's word. Still, the trip to the fair needn't be a total loss. "The invitation for lunch still stands," he said, "unless you're meeting someone—your husband, or significant other, as the saying goes?" She wore no rings, but he'd just learned a bitter lesson about taking things at face value.

Tory Shelton looked up at him, her small chin raised, yet he had the distinct impression that there was something going on in the depths of those golden-brown eyes; he just wasn't sure what.

"I'm not meeting anyone," she said quietly. "Give me a second." Moving away quickly, she skirted the dunking booth, climbed into the Winnebago and closed the door.

Michael shoved his hands into his pockets and leaned back against the trunk of an old elm, frustration gnawing at his gut. For a man who'd cut across the parking lot hell-bent on finding his fortune-teller, he had certainly gotten the wind knocked out of his sails. He'd found the wrong woman, and was back to square one again.

Fighting despair, Michael watched the ebb and flow of traffic, but felt his gaze stray toward the nearby mountain. This was Michael's first foray this far west in the state. As often as Jake had tried to lure him into coming along, he'd always opted for resorts along the shore, where the ceaseless whisper of the ocean was like a caress, massaging the tension from his body and his soul. And if he needed energizing, he invariably headed for Manhattan, his hometown, to let the constant thrum of traffic and the fast pace set his pulse racing. But he was beginning to understand his partner's willingness to make the long drive from D.C. at least once a month. It was lovely up here, a banquet for the eyes, every shade and shadow on the soaring mount a testament to nature's versatility with colors.

She fit here, Michael thought, surprised to discover that Victoria Shelton had slipped into his mental meanderings. Her penny-bright hair, autumn-brown eyes, the marvelous tan of her skin were all a complement of her surroundings. It was no wonder he thought of her as a wood nymph. He was sorry she wasn't his Ivy Sheldon, but since she wasn't, finding his psychic could wait a while. He could spare an afternoon, if Tory was free to spend it with him.

Michael came erect with a guilty start, bewildered by the sudden, subtle shift in his priorities. For the last six weeks he had been consumed with the search for Lee Varnum. The urgency of his mission was still there, invading a part of every waking hour. Despite that, sometime within the last fifteen minutes something had changed. As important as finding Ivy Sheldon might be, it had become just as important to delve into the mystery behind a pair of probing eyes that had gazed at him yesterday and had as much as said, "Michael Gallagher, I know you."

Tory eased the door shut behind her and leaned against it, her body trembling, her pulse racing. Closing her eyes, she pulled in deep, calming breaths, laboring to defeat the panic to which she'd almost succumbed moments before. Ivy. No one had called her that in years, once people here realized that she was serious about putting that part of her life behind her and would not answer to the sobriquet.

Christened Ina after her mother, and Victoria after her grandmother, she had been dubbed I.V. by her father to avoid confusion. The mutation from I.V. to Ivy was a natural progression, given Lester Shelton's lazy tongue, resulting in his failure to give equal weight to each initial. Tory, in fact, had thought her name was Ivy until her kindergarten teacher, having lost the battle to disabuse her of the notion, had sent her home with a written request that Ina the Elder clear up the matter. For all the uproar, she was still addressed as Ivy until she'd graduated from high school in Washington, D.C.

She had left the name in the capital then, returning to the Hollow and letting it be known that Ivy Shelton, psychic phenomenon extraordinaire, no longer existed. Her friends and neighbors, well aware of what she'd endured "down in the city," had gone along. Ivy Shelton was dead, long live Tory—until today. Mistaken last name aside, there was no doubt. Michael Gallagher was looking for *her*.

The truth of the matter was that Marty Dobbins had slipped up. She was certain that Michael's use of her old nickname had yet to register with Marty; he had probably responded automatically and enthusiastically, considering Michael's reference to his commercial for Wordsmiths. But if Michael Gallagher was looking for Ivy Shelton, he was looking for a psychic.

Where could he have gotten her name? The last newspaper feature about her had appeared eleven years before. How had he traced her and wound up right in her own backyard? Tory dabbed halfheartedly at her hair, still damp from her dunking at Chuckie Gant's hand, and wondered why the fabric of the life she had woven for herself had begun to ravel.

Until recently, she'd been happy or, more accurately, content. Occasionally lonely, but she had learned to live with that, and with the utter predictability of her days and nights. The closest description of her malaise was cabin fever, a claustrophobia of the spirit she had never experienced before. Chestin and the Hollow, the sameness, the insularity of her life had begun to wear on her. Her cocoon had become a prison, her chances of parole little to none because of who and what she was. And into this arid life had come Michael Gallagher, looking for her precisely because of who and what she was.

She inched the curtain aside and looked out. Michael, under a nearby tree, seemed deep in thought, the back of his head against the rough bark. His broad shoulders slumped, reinforcing her memory of the emotions embedded in his tie clip: a mixture of grief and loss, some onerous burden weighing him down. Other than that, he appeared relaxed, with little of the tension and restiveness of people who spent their lives in the city. But that was where he belonged, she reminded herself. He oozed urban sophistication. Such a man would not stay long in the Hollow. She was in no danger of exposure. No one would tell him anything, and in a couple of days, if not before, he'd be gone.

Back on firm ground again, Tory opened the tote bag she'd left on the bed, fingered her underwear, then decided there wasn't time to change. She'd kept him waiting long enough. She'd make do by pulling on a peasant blouse and shorts over her swimsuit.

It couldn't do any harm to have lunch with him. He was a novelty, a new face. To a person starved for conversation about something other than how her next-door neighbor's garden was faring or who would be elected mayor of Chestin, Michael Gallagher represented a seven-course meal. She would enjoy his company today, savor every word and gesture, tuck them away to remember on eternally long nights.

"Get out there," she told herself, and grabbed her tote bag. She would have an hour, maybe two with Michael Gallagher before he drove away, returning to his world, leaving her to hers. She wasn't griping; it was more than she'd ever hoped to have. Opening the door, Tory arranged her features in a smile and stepped out into the sun.

Chapter 3

"Tory, please, I can't possibly eat any more."

"Just a sliver, then, enough so you'll know what you're missing."

Tory cut a slice of cake so thin she could see through it and slid it onto his plate. Michael had already proved himself an able trencherman, having dispensed with two dinners, the second entirely different from the first. He hadn't had much choice in the matter, having been introduced to a good many of the cooks, most of whom had insisted that he try a little of their barbecued ribs, ham, or whatever they had brought. Now it was Tory's turn. She was determined that he would remember her if for nothing else, the taste of her prizewinning rum cake.

Michael wedged his plastic fork under half the slice, took a deep breath and the sliver disappeared into his mouth. Tory inched forward on the picnic bench, watching for his reaction. She was not disappointed. He closed his eyes, an expression of pure ecstasy on his face.

"This is marvelous! Is the cook married? If she isn't, I'll marry her right here, right now. If she is, I'll shoot myself."

Tory smiled. "Told you you'd like it. The cook isn't married and is flattered by the proposal, but will have to decline. After all, I hardly know you, sir."

"You made this?" His blue eyes went round with surprise. "I've never tasted anything like it."

"Thank you. Can I cut you a respectable piece now?"

"Only if I can save it for later. You don't understand, Tory," he added quickly, perhaps detecting her disappointment. "I never eat like this."

"This much or this well?" Tory asked, angling for compliments and clues.

"Both. I usually have dinner in some restaurant or other. Cooking for one is a waste of effort."

Which answered the question she hadn't gotten up the nerve to pose. He lived alone. Now if she could only figure a way to find out whether he was a bachelor, separated or divorced.

He dispatched the other half of the slice and pushed his plate away. "That is world-class cake. What other talents are you hiding? You're certainly very good at not talking about yourself."

Tory was chagrined that he had noticed. So far she had managed to sabotage his attempts to find out more about her by introducing him to practically every adult they'd passed on the way, interspersed with a running commentary on this part of the state, since it was new to him. Once they had reached the food concessions and picnic area, it was simply a matter of leaving him to the mercy of friends selling the food they had prepared. Warming to his friendliness and no doubt to the ruggedly attractive face, they'd have spoon-fed him if they hadn't been stuck in their booths selling their wares. Now that the meal was over, however, she had run out of diversionary tactics.

"I am a good cook," she admitted, "but that's the only talent I can brag about. What about you?"

He shot her a knowing look. "I'm not falling for that. The subject under discussion is Victoria Shelton. Come on, tell me about yourself."

Tory deliberately took her time responding, wishing she could find something, anything she didn't like about him so it would be easier to resist the frank interest in his eyes, the impression they managed to convey that while they were fixed on her, she was all that mattered. She suspected he was the type of person who, when he asked, "How are you?" had the query taken literally and found out far more than he wanted to know. He was probably a walking file cabinet filled with people's ailments, misfortunes and seamy indiscretions. She had only one secret to protect, but if she wasn't careful she might find herself spilling the beans even before she realized they'd been shelled.

"Honestly, there's not much to tell," she began. "I was born and raised about ten miles from here, worked my way through a local college, came home and started a secretarial service, which eventually became Wordsmiths."

"You own the business?" he asked, a new respect in his regard.

"I am the business, with occasional part-time help— Helen. You met her."

"The baked potato lady."

Tory grinned. "Right. She's a whiz with computers and word processing programs, and I've got enough work to keep her busy. I'm trying to talk her into signing on full-time, perhaps even becoming a partner."

"In other words, you've made a success of it."

Tory gave that a few seconds of consideration before she nodded. "Yes, I have. I guess I should crow a little, shouldn't I? But thus ends the story of Victoria Shelton. Now you."

Michael's eyes narrowed. "You're cheating. I refuse to believe that's the sum total of who you are."

Tory tensed, wondering if he was fishing now, and why. Was she wrong about having fooled him? He hadn't mentioned his Ivy Sheldon again. Had she allowed that to lull her into a false sense of security? "What else do you want to know?" she asked.

"Oh, the kind of music and books you like, what you do in your spare time, things like that."

It seemed no more than anyone else just meeting her might ask. Relaxing a little, Tory said, "I'm an only child, which makes me a bit of a loner. I read a lot, novels mostly. And catalogs. I love catalogs. Music? I like all kinds, but my favorites are the old songs by Rodgers and Hammerstein, Jerome Kern, Gershwin, Cole Porter. As for spare time, well, I usually spend it quilting. Oh, and working with the physically challenged."

"No kidding? Doing what?"

"Teaching typing and computer basics. Enough about me. It's your turn, Michael Gallagher."

"Okay, okay." He captured a stray crumb from his plate. "I was born in New York, lived there until my mid-teens, then moved to D.C. I've been there ever since, except while I was in college. I'm thirty-six, an architect, and a workaholic, which is probably why I'm still single. That's it."

That was far from "it," Tory thought, remembering the nuances of character and personality still etched under the skin of her palm. And the question remained: Why was he here? Why was he looking for Ivy Shelton?

"So you're on vacation?"

The fact that he hesitated gave him away as nothing else could have, since Tory had divined that indecision was normally alien to him. "Let's call it a working vacation," he said. "My partner, Jake Burnside—I'm using his cabin— isn't human unless he gets up here at least once a month, so I decided to see what the attraction is. Jake's rabid about this place."

Certain now that he would not divulge the real purpose of his visit, Tory said, "You must have come expecting a lot. I hope you aren't disappointed."

"Disappointed?" His gaze homed in on her, the deep blue of his eyes intensifying as they grazed her features, causing a seismic disturbance in the pit of her stomach. "How could I be disappointed? So far it has exceeded my expectations by a mile."

"How?"

"Well, it's every bit as beautiful as Jake said. I've met a lot of friendly people, and have eaten the best food I've had in years in the company of a lovely, enigmatic young woman."

Tory tried not to blush and failed, feeling warmth rising into her cheeks. "Thanks for the compliment. And I'm glad you like it here."

"Tory?"

She turned around, seeing Helen Stiles approaching, her normally placid smile absent. Tall, rangy, and as unpretentious as the gingham dress she wore, Helen was twenty years Tory's senior, approaching her fiftieth birthday with unconcern. She'd been a widow as long as Tory could remember, and if anyone served as a model of contentment with herself and her single status, it was Helen. At the moment, however, she was clearly discontent about something.

"Uh-oh, what's wrong?" Tory asked her.

"Becky, that's what. She's finked out on us, so you'll be handling the cookie booth by yourself. Think you can manage?"

"Can I help?"

Michael's question jerked Tory, nonplussed, back around to stare at him. Before she could respond, Helen asked bluntly, "Can you make change?"

"Helen!" Tory yelped, taken aback.

"Don't 'Helen' me," her friend said. "I taught a lot of supposedly bright kids who couldn't subtract forty-seven from a hundred without a calculator in their hands. Most of them couldn't even tell time by an analog clock. Well?'' she demanded, scowling down at Michael.

"Forty-seven from a hundred is fifty-three." His lips twitched with a smile he couldn't control. "And my watch isn't a digital."

"Then consider yourself pressed into service. Five minutes, you two." Turning, she marched off.

Michael waited until she was out of earshot before asking, "*She* works for *you*?"

Tory went off in peals of laughter. "Isn't she marvelous? She taught high school for twenty-five years and resigned in protest when our school board decided that only kids on the academic track needed to take math."

Briefly pain flickered in his eyes. "She reminds me of a friend. Any sacrifice for a principle. Well," he said, coming back to her, "shall we?"

"It was nice of you to offer, Michael, but I really can manage the booth alone. Why don't you go enjoy yourself? There are a hundred other things you could do."

"Are you firing me before I even get the chance to prove myself?"

Tory wondered if she imagined the hurt expression in his eyes, and relented. "I didn't hire you, so I guess I can't fire you. If you're serious, we'd better get moving."

She stacked his plate on hers and dumped them in the trash container as they headed for the cookie booth. She had decidedly mixed feelings about having his help. On one hand the extension of the deadline was a windfall, more fodder to chew on later, especially during nights when the vastness of a cloudless, star-strewn sky made her feel that much more alone. Now at least she could look back on an hour or two during which she had felt more alive than she had in years. Michael radiated energy like a force field, one which enveloped anyone in the focus of the camera of his eyes. He also exuded an animal magnetism to which she found herself responding, her first experience with lust at first sight. Her body tingled, every fiber humming like the string of a violin massaged by a bow. Yes, she'd have a great deal to remember, and she'd been filing away each detail to call up at will.

On the other hand, until Helen's arrival, her time in Michael's company had had finite boundaries. There had been a certain comfort in knowing that after they had eaten he would be gone. As much as she enjoyed being with him, his stint with her behind trays of cookies was simply prolonging the inevitable. It was also pushing her luck. The longer he stayed, the more chance there was, no matter how remote, that something would go wrong. According to Murphy's Law, she could count on it.

Uneasiness gnawing at the marrow of her bones, Tory briefed him on the varieties of merchandise and their costs. A line had formed during the changing of the guard, and once the indoctrination was over, they found themselves too busy to do anything other than wrap, bag and make change.

Michael was an instant hit, taking to the job as if he depended on it to pay the mortgage. He was patient with the children, refusing to rush them, letting them take their time in deciding not only the kind they wanted but which particular cookie. Adults he cajoled into buying more than they'd asked for by making them feel they were getting a bargain. "Let me tell you something—in D.C. cookies like these go for fifty cents apiece and they're not nearly as good."

During a rare lull in activity, Tory asked, "Is that true? Do cookies like these really cost fifty cents apiece?"

His raffish grin set butterflies aswarm in her middle. "I have no idea," he said sotto voce, with a wink for good measure before he turned to the next customer. "What'll it be, sir? Chocolate chip? How about oatmeal raisin or these gingersnaps, crisp as a winter morning? Why not all three?"

After he had sent the customer away with two dozen cookies, Michael gazed off into the distance at a group huddled under a shade tree. "What's going on over there?"

"Chess. They're playing Leland Quarles, the regional junior champion. The loser has to donate five dollars to the pot. Are you interested? All the money goes to charity."

"I'll pass. I'm good, but I'm not sure I could face being beaten by a kid. Am I nuts or do I hear singing?"

Tory listened to the assorted activities surrounding her. "Oh, that. The madrigal singers are rehearsing. There's a talent show tonight."

"Madrigal singers? Up here?"

Tory glanced up at him and laughed, guessing his thoughts. "For your information, Mr. Gallagher, we're into books and education and cultural activities just like city folks. Ever heard of Maria Casner?"

"The mezzo-soprano? Of course."

"Homegrown talent. We like country-western and bluegrass, but we also like classical music, and have our own symphony orchestra and a ballet company."

Michael tipped his head to one side in thought, a bemused expression in his eyes. "You read me right, and I apologize. I came up here with very definite ideas about the kind of people I'd meet."

"Hillbillies," Tory supplied. "Moonshiners like Snuffy Smith in the comics."

"Not quite that extreme, but I was certainly off-base. If you're insulted, I don't blame you. Again, I apologize."

"Both apologies accepted. Here comes the clan McDonald," she warned, as one of the Hollow's larger families approached. "Let's see you talk Ian into buying one cookie more than he needs. By the way," she added, lowering her voice, "the cookies with the jam in the center are called Scottish almond shorties."

"Got ya."

Tory watched, almost choking on laughter as Michael used the information to call up images of the Highlands. When Ian walked away, the tray of almond shorties was empty.

"You are dangerous," she told him. "How'd you manage to become such a consummate con artist?"

"I learned at the knee of a master." His gaze turned inward for a moment, reflecting a deep sorrow. After a second, he shrugged it off. "What do we have to fill that empty tray?"

Tory refilled it with Janie Woodyard's lemon bars and put out the first of the hazelnut spritz wafers. She was on her knees, rooting under a table for a pack of napkins when Marty Dobbins's voice cut through the babble surrounding the booth.

"No! I'm telling you, Sal, forget it. Just give us a little more time, will ya?"

Tory's antennae began to vibrate. Backing out from under the table, she stood up. Several yards away, Marty Dobbins was engaged in an animated exchange with Sally Baggett, whose face, lines of strain around her wide mouth, kept turning in Tory's direction. She and Sally went back to the days when they'd been members of the same Brownie troop, both of them too poor to be able to afford uniforms. Years later, Sal had waddled across the stage to receive her high school diploma looking as if she might go into labor any second. Gabe Jr. had been born two days later, minutes after Rev. Packer had pronounced Sal Wardner and Gabriel Baggett man and wife.

At the moment, Gabe Jr., now ten years old, was keeping his distance, watching the discussion between his mother and the policeman with poorly disguised anxiety. Sal, a baseball cap clutched to her chest, stood with her shoulders hunched, her chin raised. Tory recognized the signs. Sal had made up her mind. This was one argument Marty D. would lose.

It was not until Sal turned around and looked her squarely in the eye that Tory realized that she was the topic under discussion. She was staring the trouble she'd anticipated in the face. After a quick glance at Michael, who was engrossed in a five-year-old's life and death decision over a choice between chocolate chip and pecan sandie, Tory slipped out of the booth. "Be right back," she tossed over her shoulder, knowing full well that was wishful thinking.

"Pecan sandie it is," Michael announced, and wrapped a napkin around the little boy's choice. "Now, the way this works, you eat it slowly, biting off just a little at a time. Makes it last that much longer, okay?"

"Okay." The child stared at him in wonder, as if he'd been offered a whole new philosophy of life. "Thanks, mister." Prize in hand, he strolled away.

Michael had served the teenaged flirt next in line, surprised at how much he was enjoying himself, before he became aware that Tory had left the booth. She hadn't gone far, just far enough so that he could catch nothing of the conversation she was having with Dobbins and a third person, a wispy brunette with a thin, haggard face. It wasn't, in fact, so much a conversation as a very tense monologue directed at Tory by the agitated young woman. Tory caught his eye and gave him a strained smile, then ever so casually turned so that her back was to him, shaking her head in response to whatever the woman was saying. Dobbins glanced his way, moved a step nearer to the brunette and took her arm, interrupting what appeared to be an impassioned harangue.

"I don't care!" the woman shouted, her voice shrill enough to cut a swath across the noise of crowds, the fluting notes of madrigal singers and the distant wheeze of a calliope from a carousel on the far side of the grounds. Shaking him off, she shoved something at Tory, who retreated, but the brunette bore down on her.

Suddenly the women in the nearest booths hurried from behind them to join the three, surrounding them, blocking Michael's view. What the hell's going on? Michael wondered, distracted as he shoveled a half dozen cookies into a bag for an impatient mother with an infant straddling her hip.

The group separated, stepping back, and he saw Tory speaking to a towheaded youngster Michael hadn't noticed before. The boy stared at her, wide-eyed, shaking his head stubbornly at first. Then he nodded tightly, his chin quivering as Tory shook a baseball cap under his nose.

"Oh, God!" the brunette wailed, her hands flying to cover her mouth. "My baby!"

Without warning, Tory headed across the fairgrounds, running flat out. The brunette began to collapse, folding in on herself like a balloon leaking air.

Dobbins caught her and lowered her gently to the ground. "Somebody see to her," he snapped at the gawkers milling around her, and several women moved forward. Yelling into his radio, the policeman took off in the direction Tory had gone, nightstick and cuffs slapping against his thin hips.

Michael wasn't sure what was going on, only that something was wrong. Grabbing the cash box, he vaulted over the tables, dashed to Helen's booth and handed her the till.

"Hold onto that," he said, and whirled around to catch a glimpse of Dobbins's brown uniform disappearing over the rise beyond the barbecue grills.

"Michael! No!" Helen shouted, and reached for him, but he slipped from her grasp. Darting past a toddler oblivious to everything but the hot dog he was cramming into his mouth, Michael spotted one of Tory's gloves and snatched it up before sprinting toward the smoking grills.

Any remaining illusions he had harbored about this being a two-bit version of a county fair were dispelled once he hopped the rope setting the boundaries of the refreshment section. The grounds were enormous, about a mile squared, he guessed, and for the first time he realized how providential it was that he had stumbled onto Tory at all. Had he entered from this end, he might never have run into her.

He stopped to get his bearings, and suffered a moment of anxiety when he thought he might have lost them. Tory seemed to have disappeared, but the policeman's brown cap set him apart from the mob. Michael pursued it, pulling the hem of his shirt free of his slacks as the chase took him around the perimeter of the entertainment area, past Ferris wheels, carousels and bumper cars.

Dobbins was well beyond the fairgrounds, having crossed the street, stopping traffic with an authoritarian lift of his hand. He began threading his way through a grove of pines, and gradually Michael narrowed the distance between them. It was not as easy as he'd thought; he was running steadily uphill, and his calves began to burn. It must have been torture for Dobbins; he had slowed to a walk. Michael's moment of triumph at having caught him was fleeting as he drew abreast of the panting policeman. There was little accomplishment in having overtaken a middle-aged man clearly unused to such a prolonged sprint. The same could not be said for Tory; she was nowhere in sight.

"What gives?" he asked, running in place. "Where's Tory?"

Dobbins bent over, hands on his knees, and struggled to catch his breath. "She's all right," he panted. "Go on back. We'll be along directly."

"Look, man, perhaps I can help. Now, what's going on?"

"We'll . . . handle it," Dobbins said firmly, straightening with an effort. "Nothing for you to be concerned about." His I-mean-business inflection was sabotaged when his legs gave out and he plopped down like a marionette, strings suddenly cut. "Too old for this," he wheezed, reaching for the radio clipped to his belt. He pressed the button and hesitated, eyeing Michael warily. "Looka here, who's minding the cookie booth? You'd best be getting on back."

Michael, ignoring the hint, left him and trotted in the general direction the policeman had been heading, keeping to a well-worn footpath that snaked through the trees. It was only logical that this was the way Tory had gone, and he dared not wander far from it. The grove thickened immediately, the evergreens so close to one another that the branches meshed overhead to block out the sun, bathing the woods in a dusklike gloom. Shortly, the sounds of the carnival rides were muted, then silenced altogether, replaced by the nervous twitter of birds, the scurry of hidden animals and the crunch of his running shoes. Fallen trees blocked the path in several places, casualties, he guessed, of a recent windstorm that had raised havoc with trees in the District of Columbia.

Michael glanced back over his shoulder, feeling more and more uneasy. Perhaps he should have waited for Dobbins or, at the least, have found out where this led. Common sense dictated that he should go back; the footpath was becoming more and more indistinct, as if people seldom wandered this far. Only the memory of Tory's sudden flight egged him on. She had taken off like a woman running for her life, and he could not ignore his gut instinct that she might need help.

Just about the time logic and caution had about convinced him to turn back, Michael realized the trees were thinning. The eerie gloom was lifting, and an occasional sunbeam pierced the heavy growth overhead, brushing his shoulders with light and warmth. In an instant the thick grove was behind him, and he skidded to a halt, his heart racing double-time. Less than a car length ahead, the ground disappeared in a sheer drop to the surface of a lake at least fifty or sixty feet below. Rattled at how close he had come to running over the edge, Michael dropped to his knees on the rough grass and inched toward the lip of the escarpment.

A survey of the features of the scene around him convinced him this was the site of a long-abandoned quarry. Directly opposite, jagged walls of stone, a rock climber's dream, offered a semblance of giant stairs from the woods down to the surface of the water. There was no such access on Michael's side; the ledge on which he stood was an overhang, the granite wall beneath curving inwards, as if gouged out by a massive spoon. Without lying prone with one's head protruding off the edge, it was almost impossible to see where the water lapped gently against the bank below him. As accustomed as he was to traipsing across steel girders hundreds of feet above the ground, the overhang unnerved him.

At its highest point, he judged the escarpment to soar perhaps seventy feet above the lake. The lowest, toward the narrow end of the paramecium-shaped body of water, was littered with the corpses of fallen trees. One near the edge hung upside down from its roots, refusing to release its grip on the soil from which it had been torn. The scene was heartrending and desolate. But where was Tory? There was no sign of her along the rim of the cliffs.

Shading his eyes against the glare of sun off the water, Michael started around to his right, hoping that a check from the highest point would aid in spotting her, if she was indeed here somewhere. All it gave him, however, was an unobstructed view of the dark green of pines and balsams standing tall against a cloudless, azure sky. He had run all this way for nothing.

He headed back around the rim and stopped. Thanks to the remarkable acoustics of the setting, he heard, rather than saw, the signals that betrayed the presence of a swimmer—a splash, followed by a gasp for breath. Dropping to his knees as close to the edge as he dared, Michael looked down. The sun had transformed the surface into a sheet of liquid gold, against which the blur of copper curls near the bank toward the narrow end of the lake was barely detectable. Had she fallen in? Overshot the rim, as he almost had? Of course not. These were her stamping grounds. She would know there was barely five feet between the trees bordering the lake and the edge. If she was in the water, it was where she meant to be.

"Tory!" he called, his voice carrying easily, even above the rise and fall of sirens in the distance. They seemed to be coming from beyond the other side of the quarry, but he couldn't be absolutely sure.

Tory looked up, dashing water from her eyes. "Michael! Get Marty!"

"Okay, but are you in trouble?"

"Just get him! Hurry!" She jackknifed, her rear bobbing to the surface, shapely calves and small feet sending water flying as she submerged.

Michael glanced back in the direction he had come. There was no sign of Dobbins, no sound of anyone coming through the woods. The undertone of urgency in her voice suggested that even though she seemed to be in no danger, she needed help immediately. But for what? What the hell was she doing down there?

He emptied his pockets and unlaced his shoes, his mind racing. He'd be stupid to jump from this height; he was an able swimmer, but his one experience at trying a gainer from a ten-meter board twenty years before had taught him a hard lesson when he'd almost killed himself. He was willing to make the dive to help Tory, but from an elevation lower than the forty-plus feet above the water he judged himself to be.

Leaving his shoes, he ran to his left down the slope toward the narrower end of the lake, stopping opposite the point where he thought she had emerged from the water's surface. There was perhaps twenty or so feet down to the water, higher than was comfortable for him, but the best he'd get. Besides, Tory had to have gone in from up here. He couldn't have arrived any later than five minutes after she had. Even if she had run to the far side of the lake, it would have taken her longer than that five-minute period to climb down the giant boulders across the way. She must have jumped in from this side, which meant he needn't worry about the water being too shallow for a leap from this height. Moving to the edge, he pulled in a deep breath, leaned forward and allowed gravity to take care of the rest.

It was then he saw the pale flash of her white peasant blouse near a tangle of branches at the edge of the water. With one hand she supported the head of a small boy whose body was submerged up to his chin. Her left hand and arm were underwater, tugging at something he couldn't see. She looked up, saw him on his way down, and her eyes widened with horror.

"Michael, no!"

With barely a yard to go before impact, he had little time to wonder at the reason for her protest. He hit the water cleanly, slipping beneath the surface in a dive worthy of Greg Louganis and learning the answer to the question almost immediately. The lake bed was littered with the debris of fallen trees, whole branches piled across each other like giant Pick-Up Sticks.

There was no way for him to avoid them altogether. He felt a stinging sensation as his right shoulder scraped against rough bark. Twigs tugged at his shirt like gnarled fingers as he neared the bottom. Twisting, he slowed his momentum and began an ascent, straining to spot any obstruction that might impede his progress to the surface. He slithered between two branches, jackknifed around a third, and smiled grimly. He would make it with no more than a scratched shoulder.

Suddenly his left temple exploded with pain, and the water around him became a haze of pink. He felt heavy, as if his arms and legs had taken on incredible weight. A gray mist rose before his eyes and became a whirlpool, its gaping mouth widening, drawing him in, pulling him down. From some other dimension, Tory called his name and he struggled toward the surface. Sunlight bathed his cheeks, his chin, summer-sweet air rushing into his nostrils. She grabbed him and eased him onto his back, one hand pushing him upwards so he wouldn't sink again. He opened his eyes. Her face, inches from his, was a deep pink blur.

"Oh, Michael! Your head!" Her voice was shrill with alarm. "You're bleeding!"

The pain was back with such intensity that nausea rose into the back of his throat. "Hit something," he managed, closing his eyes. It didn't help; the sun, directly overhead, burrowed through the pores of his lids and scored his pupils, escalating the pain toward the limits of his tolerance.

Tory shook him roughly. "Michael, don't you black out on me! Come on, you've got to stay afloat!"

"Not sure I can," he mumbled.

He felt the collar of his shirt bite into his neck and opened his eyes to find her twisting it viciously.

"You listen to me, Michael Gallagher," she said, the cold steel in her tone cutting through his lethargy. "I can't help you and Danny, too. He's trapped under a tree trunk, and the water's up to his ears. God knows how long he's been there. His strength's about gone and I have to hold him up until someone comes."

"Tory?" a small, strangled voice called from somewhere behind him. A vague memory of a child's face straining toward the sun drifted through the miasma of pain in Michael's head.

"Hold on, Danny, I'm coming! I don't have any choice, Michael," she said, lowering her voice. "It's him or you, and you lose. Either you float on your back or you drown because you didn't try. If Danny drowns, it'll be because *I* didn't try hard enough. It's up to you. You're on your own." Releasing her hold on his collar, she swam away.

Michael took a deep breath and felt his body gain buoyancy. Fine. If breathing was all that was required of him, he might be able to manage. Anything else was out of the question. The pain in his head was a dragon spitting fire, scorching the hidden corners of his brain. As long as he didn't have to move...

"Can't see," a child's voice complained. "Somebody's here?"

"Yes, but he's hurt, so we'll have to keep working alone. I'm going to try one more time." Tory was all gentle reassurance. "You've done so well, Danny. Do you think you can hold on a little longer?"

"Dunno." The response was part wail, part gasp. "Awful... tired. Can't feel my legs anymore."

"I know, honey. It's been rough, hasn't it? The rescue workers will be coming any minute—hear the sirens? In the meantime, we'll keep at it. I'm going to let you go and scoot under again to see if I can't get that thing to budge just another inch. Okay?"

"'Kay. Hurry, all right?"

Perhaps it was the plea in the brave little voice that got to him. Or the waver. Whichever, Michael sensed that time was running out for Danny. Tory was right; what was a throbbing head and a little blood—okay, a lot of blood—up against the life of a child? Rolling onto his stomach, he closed his eyes tightly and fought against the nausea that threatened to overwhelm him. He lifted one arm, extended it, pulled against the water. Then the other. It was like swimming through syrup, each stroke sapping precious strength he'd need once he reached them. Slowly he closed the gap. Tory was still underwater. God, the lungs that woman must have!

Danny, his back against the bank, his head tilted up as far as it would go, rolled his eyes toward him. "Who's that?" he croaked, water swirling around his mouth.

"Hi, Danny. Don't try to talk. My name's Michael. I'm here to help."

Tory came up, spluttering, and saw him. "Michael! I'm not sure you should be moving around."

"Never mind that. Any luck down there?"

She shook her head, and just watching the action made his throb that much more. "It's so heavy. Even if I brace my feet against the bank, I can't get it to move. Look, the rescue workers are here." She waved an arm, her face brightening. "Your Mom, too, Danny."

Michael turned and saw a cluster of people swarming along the top of the boulder-studded wall across the lake, among them the thin brunette being comforted by a second young woman in uniform. Two men were unloading a bulky yellow package Michael recognized as an inflatable boat, and Dobbins's bean-pole frame wrestled an outboard motor from the rear of the rescue vehicle. It was clear that the men would have to climb down from that side carrying the boat and the outboard motor, no easy task, considering the size of the huge rocks. Once they reached the water, the motor would have to be attached. All that would take time, time Danny's flagging strength could not afford. He'd shown no reaction to the news of his mother's arrival.

Michael swallowed, gathering courage and what little stamina he had left. "Listen, Tory, we can't wait for them. You hold Danny's head while I see what I can do."

"Are you sure?" She reached over to touch his cheek-bone and withdrew a hand stained with fresh blood.

Michael saw no point in responding. Taking a deep breath, he submerged and after a moment could see the extent of the problem. The tree pinning the child was wedged across his chest at an angle, one end of it embedded deep into the base of the bank like a fat arrow. Working his way to the free end, Michael grabbed it and tugged. There was no give at all; it was firmly fixed.

Abandoning that tack, he tested the method Tory had used, planting his feet against the bank and trying again. He sensed movement, an inch, maybe two, not nearly enough. To pull it the distance needed to lift Danny from behind it would take more strength than he had. Think, Gallagher, he told himself as he shot to the surface. And make it fast.

Tory's eyes sent the message that she knew he'd had no luck. "It's all right, Michael," she said gently. "They're coming as fast as they can."

Michael glanced over his shoulder. The rescue workers were securing ropes to nearby trees and dropping them over the edge. He turned back to look at Danny. Tory's hand was anchored firmly under his chin, which was just as well. The boy's eyes were closed, his face pale.

"Danny?" he said.

He didn't respond. Color drained from Tory's face.

"Don't let go of him," Michael ordered. Unmindful of the excruciating pain in his head and of the steady flow of blood from his temple, he struck out toward the site where he had entered the water. Searching under the surface, he selected the stoutest branch of the lot with which he had tangled, and towed it back toward the bank.

"He answered me, but he's groggy," Tory said, her expression clouded with alarm.

"Switch sides with me," Michael said, moving around to Danny's left. Raising the branch until it paralleled the line of the child's body, he lowered it, wincing as the rough bark scraped the skin from the boy's arm, but there was no way to avoid causing the injury; the branch had to be positioned against the side of the tree trunk that faced the bank. Slipping below the surface, he braced himself, seated the lower end of the branch at the sloping juncture of the bank and the lake bottom. He pulled it toward his body, leaning backward until he was almost horizontal, using his weight and the last of his strength. The muscles in his lower back screamed in protest, tightening, fighting him.

At first nothing happened. When it did, it happened suddenly, catching him off-guard. The trunk came away, sending him to the bottom and almost pinning him. Scrambling out of its way, he shot up to the surface to find Tory easing the boy into position to tow him across to the other side.

"You did it!" she said.

He managed a weak smile, in no condition for celebrating. "Let's get going."

Together they ferried their quarry to the safety of the rocks. He climbed out first, a feat which seemed even harder than anything he'd done so far, and with her help from below, lifted Danny out of the water onto a hard, flat spot a couple of feet above the lake.

Tory levered herself onto the ledge, her eyes brimming with gratitude. "Oh, Michael, thank you!"

"Any time," he responded hoarsely, wondering why his right leg felt as if it were on fire and why the lake appeared to be tilting up toward him. His last conscious thought was "Oh, hell," as he landed in the water with a giant splash and passed out cold.

Chapter 4

Tory nudged the door of 324 ajar and peeked in. Even though it was after eight, the room was still dark, the curtains and blinds closed tightly, casting an aura of gloom that made her want to yank the covers from the window and let in the morning sunshine. But according to Philly—Dr. Ransom, she corrected, chiding herself for calling him by the name by which he'd been known as a child—the bright light might bother Michael. His eyes would be sensitive.

Concussion. Dangerous loss of blood from a severely lacerated scalp. Prolapsed disk. Bruised shoulder. The litany of injuries had shaken her, especially after Dr. Ransom—the heck with it; Phil was the best she could do—after Phil's incredulous reaction to her recitation of Michael's heroic efforts to help Danny.

"Are you kidding me?" he'd demanded. "Hell, Tory, considering how much blood he'd lost, it's a wonder he didn't black out long before he finally did. All the exertion made the bleeding that much worse. He was shocky when you got him in here, mild, but shock's nothing to play with. I hope you know this man risked his life out there.''

Tory crossed quietly to the closet to deposit the clothes she had laundered for him the night before. She lined up his shoes and placed the contents of his pockets, rescued from the bank of the quarry by Marty Dobbins, in a dresser drawer, making no attempt to block the emanations from his personal belongings. The inner man was firmly embedded in each item she touched, his keys and key ring, his money clip, his billfold, and the inner man was one to whom she found herself strongly attracted.

Not that he was perfect. In a contest for obstinacy, he would beat a mule hands down. He also had a temper, but here the saving grace was that it had a slow-burning wick, and once he'd exploded, that was the end of it; he held no grudges. He was too hard on himself, pushed himself unmercifully and strived for a perfection he couldn't possibly attain. His list of positive assets, however, far outweighed the negatives. And if she was drawn to the inner man, Tory had to admit that the outer one was giving her a fit, too.

She moved to the bed and gazed down at the dozing figure, the patch of white gauze above his temple in stark contrast to the gleaming ebony of his hair. A sudden tremor shook her as she recalled the solid feel of him, the firm, healthy musculature of his torso as she had lifted his unconscious form from the bottom of the lake. Once she'd pulled him over to the rocks, she'd had to wait for help; there was no way she could have gotten him up onto the ledge alone.

But as terrified as she'd been until he'd begun breathing normally, a part of her had relished the opportunity to cradle his body in her arms, his broad back against her chest. Had he been conscious, she was sure he'd have felt her heart tap-dancing at top speed. She would never have dared press her lips to his earlobe either, but she hadn't been able to help herself. As it was, that had been the least of the things she'd wanted to do. What was it about him that made her feel as if her veins flowed with champagne, fizzy and sparkling, leaving her heady and not quite in control? All she had counted on was an hour or two of memories for her mental scrapbook, not the special effects that would now accompany them. Michael Gallagher was too vital and virile for her own good. The sooner he was able to go back to Washington, the better.

He frowned and turned his head to one side, his nose twitching. Slowly he came awake, the pained expression deepening, then subsiding as his eyes focused on her.

"You're still here," he said groggily, his lips bowing into a smile that reached Tory's heart and squeezed. "I thought I was dreaming. Go home and get a good night's rest, Tory. No sense in your staying here all night."

"I didn't. It's—" she glanced at her watch "—eight-ten a.m. Time for breakfast."

"You're kidding." He started to sit up and winced. His teeth clenched and he eased down onto the pillow again. "I thought the one hangover I've had in my life would be the worst I'd ever feel. I was wrong. Am I dying or what?"

"Or what." Tory shoved a chair to the foot of the bed so he wouldn't have to move his head to see her. "You don't remember what the doctor said?"

His brow furrowed in concentration. "I'm not sure. The day's in pieces. I know we freed Danny and— How is he?"

"Fine. Scratched and bruised, but that's about it. And you freed him, not 'we.'"

"But you kept him from drowning. I remember pulling him onto the flat place on the rocks, and that's about all. The next thing I remember is some kid talking about taking X rays and ordering me to lie still."

Chuckling, Tory tucked her feet under her. "The kid is a doctor who's as old as you are. All the Ransoms are baby-faced. That's it? That's all you remember?"

"The rest is fuzzy around the edges. What's the verdict? Will I live?"

"To a ripe old age," the aforementioned baby-face announced, stepping into the room. He was a mocha-colored Dennis the Menace—minus the forelock—all grown up, a stethoscope around his neck. He scowled at her. "Tory, what the hell are you doing in here? You know what time visiting hours start."

"Don't pull the head-M.D.-in-charge with me, Philly Ransom," Tory shot back. "You and I know people wander in and out of here whenever they please."

"Yeah, well, do me a favor and wander out. I've got to examine my patient and the proprieties must be observed. Scram."

"Tell you what." Michael inched up gingerly in the bed, paling with the effort. "Give me my clothes and we'll both get out of your hair."

Phil snorted. "Don't I wish. You are not the most cooperative patient I've ever had, Mr. Gallagher."

Tory rose and pushed the chair out of the way. "Michael, this is Phillip Ransom, M.D., your doctor. Take whatever he says with a grain of salt, since the word is he got his medical degree from a mail-order house in Sheboygan."

"Just wait until it's time for your flu shot," Phil growled, hustling her out of the door. "You'll pay for that—in the hip. Go amuse yourself, shorty. There are some brand-new coloring books in the children's ward."

Tory swung at him, but Phil, long accustomed to jousting with her, ducked and closed the door.

Her playful mood dissipated immediately. She took a seat at the end of the hall to wait, sitting on her hands in order to squelch the temptation to nibble at her nails, an urge she hadn't experienced in years. Michael had upset her equilibrium to such an extent that her teeth itched to gnaw on a cuticle. Quite aside from the physical and emotional upheaval he caused, she now had the additional worry over his reading of her actions of the day before.

"So how's he feeling?"

Tory jumped. She hadn't heard Marty's approach, an indication of how preoccupied she'd been. His uniform was so crisply starched, he fairly crackled when he walked.

"Better, I think. Philly's in with him now."

"Did he say anything? Ask any questions?" Marty sat down, his eyes bright and clear. It was obvious that of the two of them, he was the only one who'd managed to get a good night's sleep.

"Philly showed up before he had time to ask any questions."

"Well, we're ready for him when he does," Marty said, his lips set in a grim line. "I hope Sal realizes the trouble she may have caused."

Tory rushed to her defense. "You can't blame her, Marty. If I'd been looking for my kid for over an hour, I'd have been frantic, too."

"I'm not knocking her for that, but the least she could have done was let me take you toward the woods where Gallagher wouldn't see what was going on. Helen says she's pretty sure the ladies managed to block his view of what was happening, and he couldn't hear anything. She was the same distance away and she couldn't."

"In which case we're home free," Tory said, getting up to pace from one corner to the other. "And we've come up with a logical reason for why I knew where to look for Danny. Everyone's passed the word, so that's taken care of."

She moved over into the sunshine, shivering at the black chasm she had felt looming at her feet when she'd realized what Sal was asking of her. Michael or no Michael, what else could she have done? She already lived with the memory of the little boy—a stranger—who'd died years before because she hadn't found him in time. There was no way she could turn her back on a friend she'd known all her life and on a child she'd known all of his.

"The thing that worries me is that he saw you with Danny's cap," Marty said. "The question is what he'll make of it."

Uncertainty gripped Tory's midsection. Under other circumstances, it was doubtful Michael would recognize the significance of the exchange. Since he'd arrived in the Hollow in search of a psychic, however, he might. If he'd made the connection between what he'd witnessed the day before and the person for whom he was looking, he would realize she had intentionally misled him. And they would part as enemies, because nothing he said would make her reopen that chapter of her life.

Tory pulled herself out of her brown study, seeing for the first time the misery in Marty's eyes. He had finally remembered the evening before that Michael had specifically asked for "Ivy," and now blamed himself for possibly having blown her cover. Sitting down beside him, she slipped her hand through a thin arm. "Marty, stop looking like that. We can ride this out."

"If it wasn't for me, there wouldn't be anything to ride out." He removed his cap and scratched at his thinning salt-and-pepper hair. "I screwed up. I swear, Tory, I didn't realize he asked for you by your old name."

"Oh, stop it," she said. "If he'd asked Sam or half the people in the Hollow, for that matter, they'd have probably reacted the same way."

"Maybe so, but it was me, not them. There's something else I might as well get off my chest while I'm at it. I'm the one called the newspapers when you found that family whose plane crashed. I blew the whistle on you. You gotta understand, Tory, times were so tough. You were something good to crow about."

"Marty, I've always known it was you." She smiled at the astonishment in his weather-worn face. "You and Sam. I never blamed you."

"If I'd known things would get out of hand the way they did, reporters swarming like flies, and then your daddy up and dragging you off to the city that way... He's in his grave, but I'll never forgive him for that. Renting you out like some damned bloodhound." Anger flared in his eyes. "The way you looked when you finally came home, all burnt out and used up. If that starts again because I slipped up with Gallagher—"

"That's enough," Tory said, squeezing his hand. "I'm an adult now. If Michael wasn't fooled, I'll handle it."

The door of 324 came open, and Phil stepped out, the picture of exasperation. "Tory, will you please talk to Mr. Gallagher? I'm late for rounds and he won't listen to me."

Tory bounced off the sofa, pulling Marty with her. "What's the problem?" she asked, following Phil back into the room.

"He insists on leaving, and I'm strongly advising against it. We're only talking about his staying a few days."

"I don't have a few days to waste," Michael said. His jaw was set, his expression one of grim determination. "I have to go. I'm telling you, I'll be fine."

"By the end of the week, yes. Today, tomorrow? Not by a long shot. You suffered a mild concussion, but that was peanuts. I sutured a flap of scalp the size of my palm, Mr. Gallagher. Scalp wounds tend to bleed profusely, and you did, enough so that you were close to needing replacement."

Michael's eyes were wide and startled. "As in transfusion?"

Phil sighed. "The fact that you don't even remember our discussing it should show you the shape you were in. Oh, don't worry, I'd have vouched for the donor. Of course, you might have found yourself sprouting bright red curls but other than that..."

Michael turned his head carefully in Tory's direction, his brows elevated in a silent query.

"No big deal," she assured him hurriedly. "I have some on deposit in a 'Just in Case' account. We're both Type O, and I figured I owed you, pardon the pun. I didn't want you to worry about . . . anything."

His expression softened, gratitude emanating from the depths of eyes the color of the sky just before dark. "Thank you, Tory, very much."

"You have been through a lot, Michael," she said, to cover the discomfiture the warmth in his voice had caused. "You really should stay. If you're on vacation, it's not as if you have to be back on the job tomorrow morning."

"It's not that kind of vacation," he responded, his tone inviting no argument. "I'm here for a purpose. I've got to be free to move around."

"And what I'm trying to tell you," Phil said, sounding much put-upon, "is that you not only shouldn't be moving around, you may not be able to, comfortably, anyhow, for several days."

"The headache's not that bad," Michael protested, the tightness around his eyes and mouth putting the lie to each word.

"For the last time, Mr. Gallagher," Phil said, stuffing his stethoscope into his pocket. "You can recover from the concussion—it wasn't that severe. The bumps and bruises will heal. The prolapsed disk is another matter. The back of your thigh hurts like blazes, doesn't it?"

"Hell, yes. So?"

"The disk is pressing on your sciatic nerve. Both your back and leg need a rest. You can stay off it now until the pressure's relieved and stand a good chance of it never bothering you again. Or you can ignore my advice, play the stoic and guarantee recurrence, or worse, a chronic condition for life."

Michael gave a grudging nod. "I need rest and quiet, fine. As long as I have access to a telephone to conduct business, there's no reason I can't rest back at the cabin."

"There's no reason you couldn't use the telephone right there at your elbow. And if I remember correctly, the bedrooms of the cabin you're staying in are on the upper level. No stairs on that leg. You'll regret it.''

"So I'll sleep downstairs on the couch."

"Burnside doesn't have a couch," Marty announced. "I've been there, so I know. There's just one of those love-seat things that sits two. A kid could fit on it, but not you."

Michael glared at him. "Thanks a lot, Dobbins."

"When I say rest, I mean bed rest," Phil insisted. "I mean having your meals brought to you, and not fixing them yourself. Getting up to relieve yourself and for no other reason. Look, Mr. Gallagher, if you want a second opinion, I'll be happy to call in another doctor, but I warn you, he's going to say the same thing I have."

Michael eased himself to a sitting position and swung his legs to the floor. "Look, Dr. Ransom, I don't need a second opinion. The only thing I need is to get out of here. I appreciate your concern, but I have a deadline to meet. Now, if there's some sort of waiver you need me to sign, I'll sign it. And I'll be okay. I'm stronger than you think."

Out of patience, Tory lost her temper. "Stop wasting your breath, Philly. He's not going to listen." She marched to the closet, snatched his clothes from the hangers and hurled them across the room at him. Michael watched, clearly nonplussed as she opened the dresser drawer, grabbed his underwear and socks and sent them flying toward the bed, his briefs catching him across the face. "If he wants to be stupid and leave, sign the damned release form and let him."

"Why do I get the impression this isn't a vote of confidence?" Michael asked.

"Oh, yes it is—in me." Scooping up his wallet and keys, she strode to his side and slammed them down on his night-stand. "He needs a place with no stairs— I live in a ranch house. He needs a bedroom— I've got an extra. He needs someone to fix his meals—my office is in the basement and I'll come up and cook for him. And he *will* stay in bed and get the rest he needs *or else!*"

Marty stared at her incredulously. "Uh, Tory, I'm not sure that's a good idea."

Phil's eyes danced with devilish glee. "Oh, revenge is sweet. I'll go take care of the paperwork, write your prescriptions and see that your breakfast is served immediately. You're going to need all the energy you can get. Ring for a nurse when you're ready to leave and she'll wheel you out."

"I can walk."

"Hospital regulations. Either you go through the front doors in a wheelchair or you don't go at all. I'll stop by and check on him in a few days, Tory. Mr. Gallagher, I think you're going to be okay, whether you like it or not. Take care." He left quickly, looking quite pleased at the turn of events.

"Tory..." Marty began.

Phil came right back in as if the door had revolved. "By the way, I was too preoccupied to say it yesterday, but thanks for what you two did for Danny. I hate to think what might have happened if you hadn't seen those little guys sneaking off to the quarry, Tory. Maybe now someone will do something about fencing off that place. And this time I'm gone for good." He winked at her and went out again, his rubber-soled shoes squishing against the tiles.

"Tory, we gotta talk," Marty said.

"Will you need help getting dressed?" she asked, ignoring the policeman.

Blue eyes bored into hers. "Are you volunteering for that, too?"

"Be glad to." Tory shot him a venomous smile, and bent to extract a plastic basin from beneath his bedside table. "I'm sure you'll want to get washed up first. It's been a while since I gave anyone a sponge bath, but I think I still remember how it's done."

"Uh, that's okay." Michael beat a hasty retreat, pulling the sheet up over his lap. "I'd rather take a shower and if I need help dressing, I'll ask Dobbins to do it."

''Fine. Take your time. I'm going to the cafeteria for a cup of coffee.''

Tory darted from the room before Marty could shanghai her for the sermon she saw formulating behind his pale gray eyes. It was the last thing she needed to hear, because anything he said would be right. She took the stairs to the first floor, hoping to avoid running into anyone she knew, since she wasn't in the mood to talk. What she needed was solitude, and a few moments to think and pull herself together. After leaving the cafeteria line with a large coffee, she settled at a corner table with her back to the room and tried to figure out how she would get through the next few days.

Offering to take Michael home with her was probably the most impulsive thing she'd ever done, and completely out of character. The only reason she'd survived the years since her return to the Hollow was because she'd planned her life every step of the way, not veering from that blueprint by so much as an inch, yet in the last three days she seemed to have tossed everything she'd worked toward out of the window. And now the one person who had come to the Hollow hoping to get in touch with her, most likely to use her as others had years before, was to be a guest in her home for a week—because she had volunteered to take him in!

She'd had no intention of offering, hadn't even realized the thought was there, even though staying with her was the most practical solution to his problem. There were no motels or rooming houses in the Hollow, nowhere else he could stay. It was as if fate was setting her up, boiling a pot of stew in which she and Michael were the main ingredients.

Tory had never given serious consideration to the concept of fate ruling one's life and was not at all comfortable with it now, especially since it implied a person had no say about anything that happened. And she would not, could not accept that. She had to be the manager of every moment of her life, if only to ride herd on the psychic glitch in her makeup, gloves or no gloves. With Michael Gallagher on the scene, that control was vital. He must never know who and what she really was. The only asset to having him under her roof was that she could insure he would return to the city without the slightest notion that he had found the woman he'd hoped to see.

Nursing him back to health would be the easy part, however; to contain her feelings for him was another matter. There was grave danger ahead unless she could wall in her physical and emotional reactions to him. It took no psychic prognostication to know that to avoid falling in love with Michael Gallagher would be the hardest thing she would ever have to do.

Michael, the lone occupant of the rear of the police cruiser, opened his eyes to look at the passing scenery, trying to guess how much farther they had to go. For all his insistence that he felt well enough to leave, his five minutes in the shower had forced him to admit to himself that Dr. Ransom was right about his physical condition. He'd had to dry off sitting down, too exhausted to do otherwise. The pain in his buttock and thigh was tiring. As a person to whom fatigue was anathema, his complete lack of energy came as a very unpleasant surprise.

By the time he'd managed to dress—with Dobbins's help, to his embarrassment—he was grateful for the hospital regulations requiring that he leave in the wheelchair. He couldn't have walked from his room to the parking lot under his own steam. He had none. His boiler was empty, cold.

"How ya doing back there?" Dobbins asked, eyeing him in the rearview mirror.

"Fine. How much farther?"

Tory turned around. "We're almost there. You look terrible. Sure you don't want to go back to the hospital?"

"Positive. I really appreciate your offer, Tory, but if you're having second thoughts, believe me, I'll understand. If you work at home, the last thing you need is an unexpected guest to upset your routine."

"You won't. The guest room is ready and you'll have a private bathroom, so there won't be any traffic jams in the mornings. And I'd have to cook for myself anyway, so fixing a little more is no problem."

The thought of food nearly had disastrous results on his stomach, so Michael rushed to change the subject. "Well, we can try it for a day or two. That's probably all I'll need. Dobbins, if I give you the keys, would you mind going to Jake's and bringing me a few things? I was living out of a weekender, so it's just a matter of collecting it and what little I left in Jake's bathroom."

"Be glad to. I'll do it after I drop you two off." Suddenly, he leaned forward. "Uh-oh. You've got company, Tory."

"Oh, Lord," Tory said under her breath.

Michael squinted out the window, relieved to see that they had arrived at Tory's trim white rancher where a woman waited in the open door, gazing anxiously at the squad car. It was a second before he recognized her: Danny's mother, in Sunday raiment, a frilly pink dress and wide white hat.

Dobbins scowled. "Tory, how many times I got to tell you to stop leaving your place unlocked? Anybody could just walk in and cart off every piece of equipment you own. Then where would you be?"

"Free to take a vacation for the first time in seven years. I hope you're up to this, Michael. Sal's bound to have a speech prepared, and she won't rest until she gets it said. I'll do what I can to see that she keeps it short."

"You and whose army?" Dobbins quipped, and turned into the driveway. "Nobody ever shut her up yet."

He hopped out and hurried around to open the doors. Michael ignored the hand the policeman extended to help him out and managed on his own, gritting his teeth with the effort. Once on his feet, he swayed, the muscle in the back of his thigh cramping as if in the grip of a giant fist. He stood without moving for a moment, fighting for equilibrium and masking it by patting his pockets as if he might have left something in the car.

A glance in Tory's direction, however, demolished any hopes he had of fooling her. She met his gaze squarely, and Michael had the strong feeling that she saw right through him, knew that pride alone held him upright, and would therefore make no move to touch him or offer her support, as Dobbins had. The fact that she cared enough to go along with his meaningless show of bravado touched him. He smiled his appreciation and, without warning, found himself staring at a blank mask. Her face had become a closed book, her thoughts concealed behind shuttered lids. She was marble, cold, unyielding.

Then the moment was over. Dobbins came around to his right, and Tory fell in on his left, letting him set the pace. Michael focused on putting one foot before the other without limping, averting his gaze from the three steps to her front door, which loomed like the Alps. Fortunately, Danny's mother moved down to the walk, effectively blocking their progress and giving him a breathing spell. A spray of marigolds spilled over her hands, and she extended them with a tremulous smile.

"Mr. Gallagher, it was my boy you helped yesterday." Tears glinted on her lashes. "I just want to thank you. It ain't much, but I don't know what else to say."

Michael took the flowers. "Thanks is enough. How is he feeling?"

"He's done worse to himself just romping around on the playground. He'll be by to see you when you're feeling better. I'm real sorry you got hurt."

"It's not as bad as it looks," Michael said, and touched the bandage. "I've got a pretty hard head. That saved my bacon."

"Well, you saved my Danny's, you and Tory. If she hadn't seen those boys of mine and their friends sneaking off toward the quarry, he might be there still. And Gabe Jr. wasn't about to admit he'd been there—he knew it would be curtains once me and his daddy found out. It'll be a spell before he sits easy again."

"Sal," Dobbins said, "can't you see the man is—"

"Oh, hush up, Marty." She turned her back on him. "I'll let you go, Mr. Gallagher. Tory, Philly called his mama to say that you might need help, so she's lining folks up. Me and the Ladies' Auxiliary will take care of all the cooking while Mr. Gallagher's here. Lunch is on the table, and dinner's in the refrigerator. Helen'll be over later to see if you need anything. Now, I got to run or I'll miss eleven o'clock service. I'll say a prayer for y'all."

"Uh...thank you," Michael said as she edged past them and climbed into a well-worn station wagon parked on the street.

Dobbins breathed an audible sigh of relief. "That's over. Let's get you inside before somebody else shows up."

"Here, I'll take the marigolds," Tory murmured, removing them from his hand. She hurried into the house, leaving Dobbins to grip Michael's elbow with a steadying hand. Michael took the steps on wobbly legs, his forehead beaded with perspiration. It occurred to him that Tory might have left because she knew he'd need help and would not want her to witness it.

The cool air and fresh wildflower scent that was Tory's signature met him at the door, which opened directly into the living room. Dobbins released him, and he moved toward the nearest chair, a plump, no-nonsense recliner, collapsing into its welcoming comfort.

"You okay?" Dobbins asked, hovering above him.

"Fine. Just need to catch my breath."

"Take your time. I'll go see what Tory's doing."

Michael looked around, charmed by what he saw. No smothering country kitsch here, which is what he'd expected. Evidently Victoria Shelton preferred eclectic simplicity, light and color in her small, L-shaped house.

The walls and carpet of her living room and formal dining room were white, her furnishings a mixture of Scandinavian and Shaker, the uncluttered lines a neutral background for brightly colored upholstery and cushions. Vases of fresh flowers contributed a soft, feminine touch, contrasting with the healthy dark green of strategically placed palms, ferns and jade plants.

The whole setting gleamed softly in the filtered sunlight streaming through windows draped with snow-white sheers. He wasn't certain what he'd expected, but this was a pleasant, tasteful surprise, a perfect place to recuperate.

Reminded of his condition, Michael closed his eyes. For the first time he considered taking Dr. Ransom's advice to heart and doing precisely what he'd been advised to do. Initially he had balked, with the search for Ivy Sheldon in mind. He had to track her down soon. All right, he could call Information from here to see if she was listed in Cumberland. If necessary, he would find the family of the high school basketball player Tory had mentioned and hope they could help. But unless Tory had more than one line, her home phone was also her business phone and would be in use during the day. He'd have to wait until her office hours were over, hope for a few minutes alone....

"No, don't shake him! Just let him sleep."

The sound of Tory's voice yanked him awake. Michael opened his eyes to see Dobbins stooping to peer into his face, the remains of a ham sandwich in one hand, and mustard decorating one corner of his mouth. How long had he been asleep?

He sat up, trying to clear the fog from his brain. "Just resting my eyes," he said, unable to squelch a sheepish smile.

Tory stood in the doorway of the dining room, drying her hands on a kitchen towel. "Would you like something to eat? There's enough food out here to feed a football team."

"Maybe later, thanks. I'm still digesting breakfast."

"Come on, let's get you to bed," Dobbins said, popping the last of the sandwich into his mouth. "Then I'm on my way to get your gear."

"Now, Marty. He'll need his night things first."

"Oh. Yeah. Better let me have the keys. Be back before you know it."

Michael wondered if he was overly sensitive or whether Dobbins was as uncomfortable at leaving them alone together as he seemed. "Would you mind bringing my briefcase, too? Perhaps I can get some work done while I'm here."

"Sure." Dobbins took the keys and started out, but hesitated at the front door. He looked at Tory, then Michael, then Tory again, his mouth pinched with disapproval. "Be right back, fifteen minutes at the most," he said, his words laden with unusually heavy emphasis. "Don't you move, Gallagher." Then he was gone.

Michael stared at the closed door, a frown marking the onset of an afterthought he had failed to take into account. "It occurs to me that this might not be such a good idea after all," he said.

"Why?" Draping the dish towel over her shoulder, she came into the room and perched on the arm of the sofa.

"I forgot this isn't D.C. where no one would think twice about an arrangement like this. This is your hometown, and my staying here puts you in an awfully compromising position. You have your reputation to consider."

Her smile began as a mere twitch of the lips and escalated rapidly into delighted laughter. Michael watched her, enchanted by the sound. The women he knew indulged in tinkly, ladylike imitations of amusement, too sophisticated to throw back their heads and roar as Tory had.

"I'm sorry," she said. "It's sweet of you to even think of it, but as you said, this is my hometown. These people know me. If they are concerned at all, it'll be because they don't know you."

"Well, if they'd seen me get out of the squad car, they'd know how harmless I am. Damn it, even sitting hurts." He pushed himself to his feet and moved behind the recliner to lean over the back, his forearms supporting his weight. "All kidding aside, Tory, I really am grateful. I promise I'll follow Dr. Ransom's orders to the letter, and stay out of your hair."

"I'm glad to hear it, but I'll be downstairs all day, so we won't even see each other until after five, and if I luck out on a big job, not even then."

Michael had some difficulty masking his disappointment. "I still think I could have managed alone at the cabin, but not easily. I'm in your debt, as the saying goes."

"You're in my... Michael, you jumped into the lake because you thought I was in trouble. You couldn't possibly have seen Danny from where you were standing. This is how I thank you. Sit down, please, because if you fall down, wherever you land is where you'll stay until Marty gets back."

He grimaced. "I'm afraid I might not be able to get out of a chair again either. If you don't mind, I think I'd better get horizontal."

"Of course." Tory hopped up, eyeing him uncertainly. "Can you make it alone?"

"I think so." He stood up straight, waiting out a second or two of vertigo and took a deep breath. "Lead the way."

She moved quickly to the hallway off the living room, and he followed her into a short passageway that ran along one side of the ell. Two doors opened on his left, a third faced him at the end of the hall.

"This is your bathroom," she said, rapping her knuckles against the first door. She opened the second. "And here's the guest room. Let me turn down the bed."

He leaned in the doorway, waiting while she whisked the chenille spread to the foot of the bed. It was a pleasant room, walls painted a medium blue with white trim and molding, and contained an old-fashioned brass bed, a mahogany dresser probably twice as old as either of them, and a gingham-covered easy chair. A footlocker served as the nightstand. Beyond a pair of French doors in the rear wall,

Michael could see a deck, which appeared to run the length of the wing.

"It's all yours." She plumped the pillows and stepped back. "I hope you'll be comfortable. Oh, one more thing." She went through the connecting door to the bathroom and returned with a glass of water. Opening her palm, she extended the small yellow pill she held and waited until he'd swallowed it. "Good. I'll leave so you can relax until Marty gets back." She started for the door.

"Tory?"

"Yes?" She stopped and looked back over her shoulder at him.

Michael's mind went blank, the words he'd planned to speak wiped from his memory as if they had never existed. Perhaps it was the way her eyes reflected the soft light streaming through the French doors. Or it may have been the enigmatic expression on her face. Whatever the cause, Michael flashed back to the first time he'd seen her and the impression he'd gotten that somehow she knew him very, very well.

"Tory, have we ever met before?"

Wariness altered her features ever so slightly. "You mean before Friday? I don't see how we could have. I haven't been more than twenty miles from home in the last ten years. Why?"

"I . . . just wondered."

"I'll be in to check on you later." She went out and closed the door gently.

Michael dozed off almost immediately, trying to guess how much later "later" would be. He wished she had stayed a little longer, wished he'd been in condition to hold a decent conversation with her. But he was too wiped out, too tired to . . .

He pried his lids ajar with difficulty. That the sun's rays no longer penetrated the panes of glass in the French doors was the only clue he had that hours had passed since he'd closed his eyes. The sky had slipped into early evening colors. He lifted his head from the pillow, saw his pajamas folded neatly across the foot of the bed, his toilet articles lined up on the dresser and knew it was time to throw in the towel. For him to have slept through Dobbins's return and the unpacking of his possessions, he, normally a very light sleeper, must be in really bad shape—or that little yellow pill was dynamite. The sooner he no longer had to take it and could walk upright instead of bowlegged like a chimp, the sooner he could get on with beating the bushes for Ivy Sheldon.

After changing into pajamas, he started for the bathroom to brush his teeth, then remembered he'd forgotten to pack toothpaste before he'd left D.C. He checked the medicine cabinet, but found it empty, as was the hallway, and when he peered around the corner, the living room. He was about to close the bathroom door when he heard voices. It was a moment before he could put a name to the speaker: Helen something, the woman who worked for Tory.

"... all taken care of. Everyone knows their lines."

"God, Helen, it's bad enough I have to lie about all this, but to ask everyone else to..."

"We'd do it whether you asked or not. We look out for our own. But why put yourself at risk by inviting him to stay with you?"

"Payback, pure and simple. He won't be here that long, and once he's gone, there'll be no reason for him to mention me to anyone. Things go back to the way they were. Free again."

"How you call not daring to go beyond these mountains being free is the strangest line of reasoning I've ever heard. You're living in a jail without bars, that's all."

"Which is better than the alternative, and a hundred times better than the prison I escaped from in the city. There are jails and jails, Helen, and I'll take this one any day. I'd better check the oven before Michael's dinner turns to charcoal. Will you see if he's awake?"

Michael used the connecting door to the bedroom to get back, belly-flopping painfully across the bed a second before Helen opened the bedroom door.

"Michael?"

He faked rousing groggily. "Yes?"

"Sorry to wake you, but dinner'll be coming in five minutes."

"Is it that late already? Thanks. I'll be ready for you."

She backed out, and he pushed himself into a sitting position, trying to make sense of what he'd heard.

Tory, a fugitive? The notion was too outlandish to consider seriously. He prided himself on being a good judge of character, and Victoria Shelton appeared to have more character than any woman he'd met in years. Still, she was the one who'd spoken of prison, of Cedar Hollow being her jail of preference.

And if people were lying to protect her, that would include Dobbins. Whatever she'd done, he'd have to know. Obviously the code of the mountains, the kind of inbred isolationism he had expected to find, ran deeper than the rule of law. "She's one of our own," Dobbins had said, speaking of Tory. Helen had just used the very same words. Whatever her crime, they would keep her secret. And if there was a warrant out on her, it would also explain her comment that she hadn't been twenty miles from the Hollow in years, and her reticence to talk about herself.

She was in no danger from him. If she hadn't lifted him off the bottom of that lake yesterday, he'd have drowned. He would keep her secret out of pure gratitude.

He snorted. Gratitude had nothing to do with it. Tory Shelton hadn't been far from his thoughts since their first meeting. The smoldering embers in her eyes intrigued him, betraying a side of her she had yet to reveal. It was a shame he'd never see it, but also just as well. The first woman he'd met in years that he failed to forget as soon as she was out of sight, the only woman he'd allowed to deter his search for Lee. A fugitive. His luck was running true to form.

Chapter 5

The next few days were vague passages of time for Michael, thanks, he assumed, to a succession of lethal yellow pills. Except for rousing himself to eat, he slept the days away. The whispers that eventually woke him late Thursday afternoon were initially woven into the script of a dream, even though they had nothing to do with the scene playing itself out in his head. They persisted until sleep lost its grip on him, and he lay still, trying to separate dream from reality.

"We wake him up and Tory's gonna skin us."

"Well, how the Sam Hill are we supposed to say what we're supposed to say if he's asleep? 'Sides, Ma said we wasn't to come home until you thanked him, and damn if I'm taking another whippin' on account of you."

Michael rolled over and opened his eyes. "You're off the hook. I'm awake. Hi, Danny. You look a lot better than the last time I saw you."

They might have been twins, were it not for the difference in their ages—both blond, blue-eyed, freckled, gap-toothed.

Danny moved a step closer to the bed. "Hey, Mr. Gallagher. You feelin' better?"

"Lots. What's your name?" he asked the older one.

"Gabe Jr. We just wanted to thank you for what you did Saturday, and we're real sorry you got hurt."

"It was worth it." Moving carefully, Michael sat up and shoved the pillows into a backrest. "Tell me something, Danny. How'd you manage to get yourself trapped that way?"

"I was swinging from the tree, had it bouncin' up and down real good, only it started coming up out of the ground and I got scared and let go and it fell on top of me."

"It was his own dumb fault," Gabe Jr. sneered in disgust. "Everybody else knew to leave that one alone. It was hanging too far over the water. He had no business going back by himself after we left, anyway."

"I'd guess he knows that now," Michael said, hoping he didn't sound judgmental. He'd pulled a few stupid stunts himself as a kid. "How long had you been in the water before Tory came?"

"I don't know. Hours."

Gabe Jr. snorted. "Couldn't have been more than forty-five minutes. I know 'cause I got me a new watch for my birthday. We got there 'bout eleven-thirty and only stayed till twelve 'cause we wanted to be the first in line at the fried chicken booth. We left Danny outside the rides, and it'd have taken him ten minutes to get back to the quarry."

"Well, it felt like hours," Danny said grumpily.

"Well, it weren't. Anyhow, we just come to thank you and we got to go now."

"You're welcome. Thank you for coming."

"Yes, sir. Come on, pinhead." Gabe Jr. grabbed Danny by the back of the shirt and yanked him toward the door, but stopped so abruptly that the younger collided with him.

"Oh. Uh . . . it's a lucky thing Tory saw us heading for the quarry, ain't it, Danny?" he said a shade louder than was necessary.

Danny's head bobbed up and down, eyes wide as he looked back at Michael. "It's a lucky thing she saw us, it sure is. 'Bye." They scooted backward out of the room, almost falling over themselves.

Michael chuckled. He knew their appearance had been a command performance, but he'd appreciated it nevertheless. He had enjoyed watching the interplay, the squabbling and name-calling, all unaffected boyishness. There'd been something odd about their exit lines, however. If he hadn't known better he'd think they'd been coached. Something else about their conversation gnawed at him, but he couldn't put his finger on what the problem was.

"Soup's on!"

Helen Stiles swooped in carrying a tray, a bright smile lighting her homely angular face. "You look better," she pronounced, unfolding the legs under the tray. "How's the head?"

"Still on. This smells great, whatever it is."

"Roast beef, wild rice, broccoli, biscuits and iced tea." She placed the tray across his lap and unfolded an enormous linen napkin for him. "Now, you dig in. If you want more, there's plenty."

The prospect of eating alone wasn't particularly appealing. "Where's Tory?"

"Still at work. Doesn't know when to quit. I'll be right back. I promised Sal I'd send her some ham by the boys. Aren't they a pair?"

Michael nodded, buttering a biscuit. "They seem like nice kids."

"They are. If Tory hadn't seen those rascals on their way to the quarry, Sal would be planning a funeral today. Back in a minute."

Michael hesitated, the biscuit en route to his mouth. There it was again, the feeling that he was missing something,

something that didn't compute. Too many painkillers, he decided. Too much sleep. It was time to begin weaning himself from the prescription and the bed. His headache was gone, and now he'd become aware of the bruised muscles of his shoulder, a minor inconvenience, all things considered. He felt better, stronger.

The leg no longer burned, and the threat of cramping had lessened. Tomorrow he'd get up, maybe try out the deck while the day was still fairly cool. He was dying to read a newspaper. Once his gray matter had something to chew on and he was back in a thinking mode, he could figure out what was bothering him about the boys' conversation. He bit into the biscuit. Yes, today would be his last day on his back.

When he awoke again, the tray was gone, and the light reflected off the ceiling, tinting it with the colors of sunset. The house was still, the air conditioner whispering quietly, its white sound so soothing that in a matter of seconds his lids began to droop. They stopped at half-mast, the hair on the back of his neck standing at attention. Someone was in the room. He lay still, in no mood for perky chitchat. The ladies who'd served his meals were either cheerful to a fault or so solicitous they made him wonder if Ransom had lied to him and he was in worse shape than he'd been led to believe.

The longer he faked sleep, however, the more inquisitive he became about the identity of his visitor. The members of the Ladies' Auxiliary were all bustlers, even Helen who, though she appeared to like him, seemed so edgy around him that she, too, fidgeted in his presence. Whoever was in the room had not moved, the sound of breathing the only clue that someone was there. Unable to contain his curiosity any longer, he opened his eyes just enough to see. Tory was curled up in the chair beside the bed, a closed book in her lap. She wore her leisure uniform, an abbreviated tank top and white shorts. Her feet were bare.

"You are awake. I wondered. How do you feel?"

His spirits lifting, he rolled over and sat up. "Not bad. I was beginning to wonder if you'd moved out. I haven't seen you since Sunday."

"But I've seen you," she said, putting her book aside. "I've looked in on you several times. Phil will be glad to hear that you've been a model patient. He'll be by tomorrow to check your stitches and change your dressing."

"It must be healing—it itches."

"Good. Well, I'm going out and just wanted to see if you needed anything."

"A date?" Michael asked, hoping he'd managed to sound only casually interested.

"Not the way you mean. Thursday evenings are reserved for seniors at the local pool. I'm on my way over to the retirement complex to pick up five of them. I don't usually stay, because someone else is assigned to take them home. But the pool staff is short a lifeguard, so I'm substituting."

Michael crossed his arms, which caused a twinge in the bruised shoulder. He massaged it absently. "You're really into community work, aren't you, teaching disabled kids to type and chauffeuring senior citizens around. Do you work with the Cedar Hollow welcoming committee, too?"

"There isn't one." She shot him a wry smile. "People move out of the Hollow, not in. Is your shoulder bothering you?"

"A bit. It's more annoying than anything else."

"Uh-huh. Let me see it."

"Certainly, Dr. Shelton." Michael unbuttoned his pajama top and exposed his left shoulder. It resembled an artist's palette, shades of blue, purple and yellow mottling the skin.

Tory whistled. "I hope it feels better than it looks. I may have something that will help. Be right back."

Michael shrugged out of the top and lifted his arm above his head, encouraged that despite the discomfort, he could still move it freely.

Tory returned, a small white jar in her hand. "Scoot over and turn your back to me," she said, perching on the edge of the bed.

"What is it?"

"You don't want to know." She scooped some dark brown glop into her palm. "It's an old home remedy that works. I should have thought of it before. It'll make you smell like a polecat for a few minutes, but since there's just the two of us here, who cares?"

"I don't smell anything."

"You will. And this will burn for a second or two, but the results are worth it. Ready?"

"Uh...I'm not sure. I—"

She didn't wait for him to finish, the flat of her hand smearing the concoction along his upper back and shoulder. The odor registered first, every bit as potent as she had predicted. "Good Lord, Tory, forget it. I've passed landfills that smelled better than that gunk. Ow!" Heat traced the path of her palm, burning with an intensity that startled him. "Hold it! Does that stuff have acid in it or something?"

"No. Be still. It won't last long. Turn around so I can get your front."

"Not on your—"

"Never mind." She vaulted over his legs to the other side of the bed and had spread the salve from the hollow of his neck to his upper arm before he'd had time to finish his protest. Having been bested, he sat still, his teeth clenched as the fire blazed across his skin.

"Now." She placed the jar on the floor. "Face down, please."

"Why?" he asked, aware of a pleasant tingle where the heat had begun to cool.

"Time for phase two. The worst is over, I promise."

Reluctantly, Michael settled onto his stomach. "If I believed in past lives, I'd swear you were head torturer during the Inquisition."

"Men are such babies. Shhh, now."

He turned his head toward her and saw her kneel beside him, her lean, smooth thighs at his waist. Bending over him, she placed her hands at the base of his neck and began to knead, her palms pressing hard and firm against the muscles of his back. In a matter of seconds, he realized that not only did she know what she was doing, she was good at it.

His eyes closed as she worked her way across both shoulders, gentler on the bruised side but with a touch that seemed to take the soreness away. Her hands, surprisingly strong, worked a magic that left him free of tension he hadn't known was there. Before long, the odor of the salve seemed to have dissipated, replaced by the soft scent that was Tory's alone. He breathed it in, letting it fill his lungs, heady and refreshing as mountain air. To his dismay, the combination of the cologne and the warmth of her thigh against his was becoming a problem.

It began as a familiar stirring in the vicinity of his navel, a tiny spark in danger of igniting into an embarrassing situation. Michael was tempted to ask her to stop. Calling on all his powers of concentration, he emptied his mind instead, centered himself in hopes that the ploy would prevent the spark from becoming flame. Her hands, however, working their way slowly, methodically down his torso, made mincemeat of his attempts. She stopped at his waist, and after a second, he felt her soft fingertips on each side of his neck behind his ears. The flame leapt, became a flash fire searing a path from navel to groin. He froze and ground his forehead into the pillow.

She must have felt his muscles lock. "Sorry. Did I hit a sore spot? I don't see a bruise or anything."

"It's okay. In fact, I feel great. Thanks."

"I'm not finished. Time for the flip side. Over," she directed, patting his uninjured shoulder.

"No, that's enough. Your hands must be tired."

"You're talking to someone who works with her hands all day. I've just gotten started. Come on, belly up."

He shook his head, his face still pressed into the pillow. "I can't, Tory. If I turn over, my belly won't be the only thing that's up, and that's about as delicately as I can put it."

Her first reaction was silence, and he lay unmoving, certain that he'd offended her. Then the bed began to shake. Michael looked back over his shoulder to find Tory still on her knees but bent over double, her shoulders jerking. He sat up quickly, momentarily forgetting his condition, and snatched the covers into his lap just in time, lumping them together into a concealing mound. Tory peeked between her fingers, saw him struggling with the spread and exploded, laughing full throttle, the same contagious sound that had lured him toward her at the fairgrounds.

"Oh, God, I'm sorry," she began, but was beyond the ability to say any more, overcome with hilarity. Arms wrapped around her head, she laughed, her body convulsing, until she was short of breath and gasping. She pressed her fists into her sides and fought for control, lost, and began the battle anew.

Michael leaned on one elbow, fascinated at the way she seemed to embrace laughter, giving in to it, enjoying it. It didn't matter to him that his discomfort served as the source of her jocularity; in fact, he liked making her laugh, enjoyed watching the crinkle at the corners of her eyes, the way her nostrils flared.

He waited until the impish smile on her lips was the only remnant of her outburst. "And here I thought I might have offended you."

"Oh, Michael, how precious." She regarded him thoughtfully, her head tilted at an engaging angle. "There's a courtly side of you that surprises me."

He wasn't sure how to interpret that. "Should I be insulted or not?"

"I meant it as a compliment. Only a gentleman, in the old sense, would be concerned about what my neighbors would think of your staying here with me. And the guys I know would have been embarrassed by having an erection—either that or they'd have intentionally flaunted it. You were more worried about how I'd react to it. I'm . . . touched by that."

Uncomfortable at being painted in such genteel colors, especially since he had more than a passing interest in the distinct possibility that she wasn't wearing a bra, Michael changed the subject. "You're in the wrong business. Seriously, Tory, a good masseuse can write her own ticket. If you got certified, you could make a mint with those hands."

Her face became very still. She spread her fingers and looked at them. "Thanks, but I'll stick to pounding a keyboard."

He leaned back, deciding to indulge in some gentle probing. "Have you ever considered moving your business closer to Washington or Baltimore? Granted, you have a built-in clientele here, but there can't be that many of them."

"There are enough. No, I wouldn't consider moving. This is home, and I'm meeting a need. That means a lot to me."

He spent a futile half second trying to talk himself out of pushing any further before asking, "What about your needs, Tory? I'm not just talking about a roof over your head and food on the table. Except for Dobbins, I haven't seen another adult male come into this house. If you had a going relationship with someone, he'd have been here by now, especially with me invading his territory, so I assume you aren't dating. Don't you get lonely?"

She didn't answer, her eyes fixed on his chin. "Sometimes," she said, finally, softly. "It passes."

There was such honesty and quiet dignity in her response that it ripped into Michael's heart. Armed with what he'd heard Sunday evening, he saw her more clearly than she imagined. Whatever she'd done, she was paying for it dearly, sacrificing far more than mere freedom of movement.

Testing his conclusion, he asked, "Tory, if I invited you out to dinner, would you go?"

"Tonight? You can't—"

"No, not tonight. After I get back to town. I'd like to take you to one of my favorite haunts. Being the gentleman I am, I'd come pick you up and bring you back. What do you say?"

She hesitated, a tiny frown pulling her brows together. "That would make for an awfully late return. There's a couple of nice restaurants around here, one in Chestin and—"

"How about the symphony? Or a play at the Kennedy Center?"

She stirred, obviously uncomfortable with the direction the conversation was taking. "I'm not sure, Michael. I stay so busy."

"A Friday or Saturday night then."

"I'd really rather not go into Washington."

"Oh, you know the city?" Michael watched her closely.

"I lived there for several years. They aren't pleasant memories."

This was news, since he'd had the impression she had always lived in Cedar Hollow. Something told him he'd be pushing his luck to ask the reason for her unpleasant memories. "Baltimore then."

"No!"

He had struck a nerve. "Why not? Great ethnic restaurants. Or we could hit the Inner Harbor, take a cruise to Fort Henry and back."

"A cruise." It was a whisper filled with longing. Her eyes lost focus as if she could picture it, the yearning so obvious that it was painful to hear. He reached for her and pulled her into his arms, wanting to protect her, to offer rescue, anything that would pierce the hard shell of loneliness in which she seemed encased.

Tory was very still, her small body against his, her breath warming the hollow of his neck, triggering the release of an iridescent bubble of déjà vu, so tiny and fragile that it was a second before he recognized it for what it was. He could swear he had lived this moment—or one very much like it—

in some other place, some other time. Eyes closed, he could almost reconstruct the sensations—arms holding him tightly, warm breath bathing his neck, soft lips brushing against his earlobe, a butterfly's kiss. False memory or not, its effect was real, fanning the sparks that Tory's hands had ignited. He had to end this before—

Tory moved back a little and looked at him, her eyes alive with questioning. His gaze was pulled to her lips, to the corners which turned up on the end to lend the impression that a smile hovered a second away. It was a mouth that begged to be kissed, and he felt himself being drawn toward it as if he had no will of his own. Her lips parted, seeming ready for his kiss, just as a sudden rumble of distant thunder echoed in the stillness. She blinked. The spell was broken, and she swiveled out of his arms and stood up, her face pale.

"I'd better go. I'll try not to wake you when I come in." She backed toward the door, reaching for her purse and the ubiquitous gloves on the dresser. "Thanks for the hug. Everyone needs one once in a while."

Michael followed her lead. If a simple hug was all it had seemed to her, he was not about to reveal how close it had come to being something else entirely. "A great prescription for practically any ailment. But you didn't answer my question about the cruise."

"We'll talk about it later. Get some rest. Don't forget, Phil will be here tomorrow."

"I'll be ready for him," he said, deciding it would be wiser not to push. She looked as if she was running scared, and he was in no condition to chase her. "Do you mind if I use your phone while you're gone? I need to check in with a couple of people in D.C. I'll use my phone card."

"Help yourself. If Sal calls, tell her I'm on my way. Good night." She started out, and reached behind her, about to pull the door closed.

Michael stopped her. Now that his head was clearer, the mention of Danny's mother drew some conclusions he had not been able to make earlier. "Tory, if the quarry's so dangerous, why didn't you stop the kids when you saw that's where they were headed?"

She became a statue, her hand hovering above the doorknob. After a second she took a step back in. "I did. I gave them the usual spiel, the same one I heard when I was growing up. If I'd stopped to think about it, I'd have tried another tack, because nothing anyone said ever stopped me from swimming in the quarry. They were probably halfway through the woods before I'd gone twenty yards. Anything else?"

"No. I just wondered."

"Good night then." She stepped out, closed the door and was gone.

Michael had plenty to keep him occupied until he was certain the coast was clear. He kept repeating her response to his question about stopping Danny and his brother, with the same result after each run-through. Something still wasn't right. Something didn't jibe.

His train of thought jumped to another track, thinking of the way Tory had dodged his attempts to get her into town. Helen had been right: Tory would not venture very far from the Hollow. And if she seemed determined to steer clear of Washington, her reaction to his suggestion that they go into Baltimore had been visceral. Was that where she'd run afoul of the law?

Michael did nothing for a good fifteen minutes, making only halfhearted attempts to talk himself out of pursuing the idea that her response to Baltimore had sparked. If he did, his sole purpose would be to satisfy his curiosity; he had no intentions of making use of the information. But the more he saw of Tory, the more the possibility that she had committed a crime of any kind seemed incongruous. Granted, people changed, but one of the things about her that appealed to him was the conviction that her foundation was solid. She knew who she was and appeared to live by the tenets she'd learned as a child. Therefore the picture of her as wily fugitive, evader of justice, did not sit easily in his mind—or his heart.

It was time to stop waffling. He went into the living room, barely limping, he noticed, and sat down by the phone, his decision made. If anyone could get the information for him, Ed Chavous could. He'd been a police reporter for years and had a memory for Washington and Baltimore area trivia that never ceased to amaze his friends. He also had access to countless computer memory banks, a few of which would land him in jail should anyone ever find out.

"Victoria Shelton, huh?" Ed's nasal voice twanged with anticipation at the challenge. "Rings a bell, only the first name doesn't seem right. And I don't associate it with a police case either, so it may not be your bail jumper after all. I'll start working on it tonight and call you."

"You can't. I'm at Jake's place in the mountains, so—"

"Cedar Hollow? You lucky dog. I've been up there with him a time or two—in the old days. The best fishing in the world. Okay, I'll phone you there. I've still got the number somewhere."

"I might be hard to catch," Michael said quickly. "Just drop it in the mail to me at Jake's. 42 Wood Road. I really appreciate this, Ed."

"So buy me a beer when you get back. Lee's body turn up yet?"

Michael winced. Tact wasn't one of Ed's strong suits. "Not as far as I know."

"A damned shame. How's his kid doing?"

That, however, brought a smile. Leslie was far from being a kid. "Pretty well. I'm calling her next. Thanks again, Ed. And keep whatever you come up with to yourself, okay?"

"Make it two beers, then."

The dial tone purred in his ear. Ed was notorious for hanging up without warning, and Michael didn't begrudge him this bit of one-upmanship. Ed had been confined to a wheelchair for the last three years, thanks to a drunken driver. If being the first to end a phone conversation contributed to his sense of wielding some control over his life, so be it.

With a good deal of reluctance, Michael called Leslie Varnum, praying that she was in better spirits than the last time he'd seen her; she was Lee's only child and they had enjoyed a unique relationship. To his relief, her sunny personality seemed to have resurfaced for the first time in weeks, the proof in the return of the lighthearted banter they had enjoyed for years. She also piqued his curiosity. She had, in her words, fantastic news to tell him, but not on the phone.

His pulse jumped. "About Lee? You've heard something?"

He knew immediately he'd jumped to the wrong conclusion. It took her too long to answer.

"No, something else. Daddy's gone, Michael. We have to get on with our lives. When will you be back? I can't wait to tell you."

Of necessity, he'd had to explain that he wasn't sure how soon he'd be returning, and why.

"It's not serious, but I won't be driving for a few days yet. I might be able to get back by the weekend, but don't count on it." He didn't want Leslie or anyone else looking to see him in the near future. Once he left Jake's he'd be heading farther west.

It took another ten minutes to assure her that he was in good hands and lacked for nothing. He found himself envying Ed's tactics for ending calls, but could not bring himself to hang up too abruptly. She was as close to a younger sister as he'd ever have, and once she'd gotten over her crush on him, had come to terms with her place in his life.

It had helped them get through the early days of Lee's disappearance. Now, it appeared, she was back on her feet, for which Michael was both grateful and resentful, especially as it appeared she had given up on her father. The last time he'd talked to her she'd been weakening, but still hopeful. Now he was truly alone in his belief that somehow, somewhere Lee Varnum was still alive.

When he'd finally managed to break the connection with Leslie, he used the impetus the conversation with her had given him and dialed Information. There was no listing for an Ivy Sheldon, but with the help of a cooperative operator, he was given numbers for several Sheldons who lived in the western part of the state. Of those calls, five claimed no knowledge of his party, and two didn't answer. With a sense of having made a start on his delayed search, he went to bed.

But the summer moon had long since disappeared before he could relax, his thoughts resolutely returning to the memory of the magnetic pull of Tory's mouth, and how small she'd felt in his arms. He began to hope that, for once, Ed might come up empty. The less he knew, the better. He had to work around the protective streak she brought out in him; he could not let it interfere with what he had to do for Lee. It would be hard enough to walk away from her as it was, but walk away he would and, as Leslie had put it, get on with his life. And that meant finding Lee Varnum.

Chapter 6

Tory flipped the switch on the power strip that controlled the word processor and printer, rubbed eyes gritty with fatigue and indulged in a head-to-toe, muscle-relieving stretch. Seven-ten p.m. She had worked eleven hours straight purposely remaining in the office late, to avoid Michael as along as possible. He'd been up and around all day, probably waiting for Philly; she'd heard his footsteps pacing back and forth, and during a quiet period when her stomach's demand for sustenance had driven her upstairs, she'd spotted him napping out on the deck in the sun. She'd been tempted to wake him before he was broiled alive, but was too embarrassed about the night before to face him.

She'd set herself up for losing control by giving him the massage. Smoothing the salve on his shoulder, feeling the resistance in taut, firm muscles had been the trigger, whetting her appetite. From that point, the raw, pulsing need with which she had lived from the moment she'd faced him on the porch of the cabin had moved into her hands, her fingers and palms demanding more contact with the sinew and strength of this man. The massage had fed that hunger, but rather than being sated, it had become that much more intense and diffuse, spreading through her body like a fever.

She'd almost kissed him. Thank God for Mother Nature; the approaching thunderstorm had, in effect, caused a delay in what was stacking up to be a very dangerous game. Michael would never know how close she'd come to making an idiot of herself. His embrace had been meant to comfort, to offer solace. It had succeeded in doing neither. There was no comfort in learning that the lonely nights to come would be far worse than those to which she'd become accustomed, and no solace in knowing that as much as she hungered for his arms, his touch, his lips, this was all she would have of him. Her imagination had gone haywire, making her read desire in eyes filled only with caring and concern. From there, things had gone from bad to worse.

His invitations to dinner and the theater had completely thrown her, and she hadn't thought fast enough to accept now, knowing she could turn him down later. If he asked again, she would take that route, might even manage an evening out with him before he returned to the city. On the day he left the Hollow, however, she'd say goodbye and mean it. There would be plenty of time—a lifetime—to get over feeling guilty and deceitful at sending him away without admitting who she was. Now that she knew him as well as she did, she had no doubt that entertaining the notion of using a psychic had probably cost him a great deal. That could not matter. She would not take on anyone else's pain again, neither his nor the person he wanted her to find.

Footsteps sounded on the steps to her basement office. The door at the bottom of the steps opened, and the boyish brown face of Dr. Phil Ransom peered in at her.

"Damn, Tory, you keep worse hours than I do."

"Hi, Philly. I was just shutting down for the night. How's the patient?"

"Lookin' good. His scalp is healing nicely, and the bed rest has relieved most of the sciatica."

"Can he use stairs yet? And drive?"

Phil hesitated. "I'd rest easier if he had a day or two out of bed before he starts living dangerously. By the way, did he buy the party line about how you knew where to find Danny?"

Tory shrugged, still uncomfortable with the subject. "Helen seems to think he has. They've become great friends. So you think it's all right for him to go back to the cabin in a couple of days."

Phil's brows inched toward his hairline. "Do I detect a bit of disappointment in your voice?"

"You do not." She faked enough indignation to be convincing. "I'm bushed, that's all. Anything else?"

"I don't think so. I'd better hit the road. I'm on call tonight." He unlocked the door that opened onto the driveway, then turned around, fixing her with an assessing gaze. "On second thought, there is something else—a personal opinion."

"About what?" Tory pulled the dust cover over the printer and neatened her desk.

"Today was the first chance I've had to really talk to Gallagher for any length of time. He's okay. I like him. I assume you do, too, or he wouldn't be here."

Tory stopped what she was doing, uncertain where he was headed. "What's your point, Philly?"

"Well, since you ask . . ." He jerked a thumb toward the ceiling. "You could do a lot worse than Gallagher, but you damn sure couldn't do any better."

She gaped at him. "What?"

"I'm taken, so who's left in spittin' distance worth giving the time of day?"

Tory laughed. "You don't think much of yourself, do you, Phillip Ransom?"

"I'm serious, short stuff. You can't stay locked up in the Hollow forever. Stop cheating yourself out of a normal life.

There are some dynamite people you'll never meet if you don't cut the cord and leave this place pronto. One of them is upstairs in your living room. Don't let him get away, Tory. You'll never find another one like him, not here, maybe not out there either. In other words, get your cute little fanny upstairs before he decides to leave with the competition, who, by the way, is some kind of gorgeous.''

"Someone's up there with him?"

"A Leslie something." His eyes gleamed with mischief. "I get the impression she and Michael are very close. Their greeting was warm, to say the least. And she's... Never mind. Go see for yourself. Good luck." He made a hasty exit before she could respond.

Tory crossed to the door and slammed the dead bolt home. A sleek black Jaguar sat in the driveway. Gorgeous and rich, Tory thought. I should have known. A knot of anxiety twisted under her waistband. After last night her ego was too fragile to face any woman who had a claim on Michael, especially one who could afford a Jag.

And Philly Ransom blatantly pushing her into Michael's arms had been a shock. Helen seemed to be leaning in the direction as well, much more tactfully, but her intent was clear. What was it about Michael Gallagher that made instant friends and allies of people who were usually reserved and suspicious of outsiders—*her* friends, *her* allies? Was there nothing she could count on anymore?

She opened the door upstairs and startled Michael, who was dropping ice into three jelly glasses. He seemed very much at home; he even complemented the butter-bright kitchen, wearing a pale yellow knit shirt, brown slacks and loafers. His hands became still, and he scrutinized her as if he'd never seen her before, his eyes raking her from pate to pumps.

A quick downward glance to see what was unbuttoned, untucked, or hanging, assured her that nothing was awry. "Hi," she said brightly. "Need some help?"

''Well, it's about time you punched the clock.'' He removed a fourth glass from the rack on the counter. ''Another ten minutes and I was coming down to unplug your word processor. There's someone in the living room I'd like you to meet. I thought I'd play host and offer them something cool.''

''Them? How many are here?''

''Just two.''

The knot of anxiety tightened. One woman to face wasn't enough? ''You're using jelly glasses, Michael? Those are for kids who stop by. Shoo. I'll take care of the refreshments.''

''All right, but only because I don't know where things are.'' He started out, then swiveled around to her. ''You look . . . very nice, Tory.''

Pleased, Tory busied herself reaching for her best crystal. ''Thank you. Be out in a minute.''

It was in fact, four and a half minutes, during which Tory transferred ice from the jelly glasses, poured lemonade, garnished it with sprigs of mint, and arranged the goblets on a tray with napkins, coasters and a bowl of seedless grapes. She retied the bow of her blouse, tugged at the front of her navy bolero jacket and smoothed her form-fitting skirt over her hips. Balancing the tray, she took a deep breath, started through the dining room and felt her heart plummet to her knees. The visitor, in plain view on the sofa beside Michael, her long elegant legs crossed at the ankle, was a vision in white and gold. Gleaming blond hair cascaded around evenly tanned shoulders and the spaghetti straps of her white sundress. Her features were cameo classic, patrician, her complexion flawless. Adding insult to Tory's injury, she was tall, with the kind of poise that Tory associated with a life lived without want or need. And Phil had the nerve to call this woman competition? She was in a class by herself.

Tory swallowed, pasted on her brightest smile, and made her entrance, her lips forming a greeting that evaporated at the sight of the second visitor standing just inside the front door. If the woman next to Michael was gorgeous, the man in the corner defied description. He would make Adonis look like Quasimodo, Tory thought. He, too, was in white, tall, tanned, blond, with eyes the color of a storm cloud, and the clean-cut features of a model in a Ralph Lauren ad. Tory could imagine him at the helm of a yacht, the wind whipping his sun-bleached hair. He was, in a word, stunning.

Michael rose, took the tray from her and placed it on the cocktail table. "Tory, this is Leslie Varnum and Yale Farraday. Leslie and I go back almost twenty years. So does Yale, come to think of it. Leslie, Yale, my hostess, Victoria Shelton."

"Hi, there." Yale crossed and shook her hand, his palm swallowing hers. His dark gray eyes measured her with frank interest. "So you're the one Mike cracked open his skull to help. I see why."

"If that was a compliment, thank you," Tory said.

"Oh, it was. About half your size, Les, but other than that, she meets Mike's exacting standards and then some." He moved back to his post beside the door, and appeared content to remain there.

"Don't you just hate it when they talk about you as if you were a side of beef? Even an attractive one?" Leslie leaned forward and extended her hand, her lovely blue eyes wavering several inches above Tory's head. Tory's lips parted with surprise. Leslie Varnum was blind.

Recovering quickly, Tory removed her glove before taking the woman's hand. "Welcome to Chestin, Leslie."

"Thank you. And thanks so much for taking care of Michael. He said the little boy you two rescued is all right?"

"He's fine. We grow them tough up here." She picked up a glass and napkin and placed both in Leslie's hand, making certain Michael's guest had a secure grip on it before releasing it. "I'll put a coaster on the cocktail table, at twelve o'clock, directly in front of your right knee."

Leslie's smile was dazzling. "You've dealt with the blind before."

"Twice a week during the school year. I teach typing and word processing to a class of visually impaired kids."

"Do you? It's been so long since I've used my typewriter. I've been thinking I should try to bring myself back up to speed, but . . ." Her sentence went unfinished, accompanied by a gesture that bore a hint of impatience.

"Why bother, Leslie?" The expression of amused tolerance on Yale's handsome face set Tory's teeth on edge. "Dictate anything you want on a tape recorder and our secretaries will type it up for you."

"Stick to your guns, Leslie," Tory said firmly. "I know how much satisfaction you'd get doing it yourself. In fact, I'll send you a copy of the tape my kids use for typing exercises."

Her chin came up. "I will, and thank you. I hope you don't mind our popping in out of the blue. Michael called last night, and when I found out he'd been hurt, I had to see for myself that he was all right."

"I told her I was in good hands," Michael said, with a shrug and a grin for effect, "but she didn't believe me."

"Yes, I did." She leaned in Tory's direction, her tone conspiratorial. "The truth is, I had something I couldn't wait to tell him, so I used the bump on his head as an excuse to check on him. He didn't know I was coming."

There was an ingenuous quality about her, but Tory also detected a streak of stubbornness. Good for her, she thought, and resigned herself to the realization that she liked Leslie Varnum.

"How did you manage to find Michael?" she asked. "I have yet to see Chestin on a map."

Yale made a contribution to the conversation for the first time. "It wouldn't matter if it was on a map or not. I have no sense of direction, so I just stopped at several places to ask the way. Still got lost, and wound up with a police escort right to your door."

"They ran into Dobbins," Michael elaborated. "He was headed here anyway, so they followed him."

"Marty? What did he want?" Tory felt a vague sense of betrayal. He hadn't even come downstairs to see her.

"He intercepted a courier about to drop off a package for me at the cabin." He jerked his head toward the large brown envelope at his elbow. "Some work I forgot to bring. I got the impression he'll be by again later."

"Then you are feeling better if you're thinking about work," Tory said, with only a casual glance at the envelope. "Your attaché case hasn't been moved since Sunday."

"Don't remind me. I have a lot to catch up on."

Something stirred restively in Tory's consciousness. Michael had just lied. She had no idea why she knew, but she hadn't the slightest doubt. To cover the awkward silence, she took refuge in her role as hostess, retrieving a goblet and taking it to Yale. "Forgive my manners. This will cool you off. It must have been a long, hot drive from Washington."

"I doubt that seriously." An enigmatic smile played around Michael's mouth. "Nobody sweats in a Jaguar."

Tory's face flushed red, stung at the patronizing implications of his remark. But a hint of pink had also risen under Yale's devastatingly square jaw.

"It's a good car," he said stiffly, and Tory realized that Yale, not she, had been the target of the barb. She watched as the two engaged in a staring contest and decided she'd had enough.

"You two enjoy your visit with Michael, but I'll have to ask you to excuse me. If I don't change clothes, I'll suffocate."

Leslie located the coaster and placed her glass on it. "I will see you before I go, won't I? I'd like to get your advice on a word processing system."

"We really shouldn't stay long, Leslie." Yale moved to the recliner, but remained standing. "It'll be late when we get back, and tomorrow's a workday for me."

"How are things at Cross and Crosby?" Michael asked, elbows on his knees. Despite his casual air, his body emanated tension.

"Oh, terrific and getting better every day." Yale's offhand manner was as false as imitation leather. Smugness was written all over his face.

Fed up with interplay she didn't understand, Tory rescued her lemonade. "I'll see you before you leave, and you're welcome to come back anytime."

"Or Michael could drive you down to see me. I'd love to have you."

Tory felt Michael's eyes watching her. "Thank you. I'll remember that. Is there anything else I can get before I disappear?"

Yale shook his head with a brief, tight smile.

"I'm fine." Leslie settled back and reached to find Michael's hand. "*We're* fine."

"Then I'll go get comfortable and join you later." It wasn't the most graceful exit, but it was the best she could do.

Closing her door on the sanctuary of her bedroom, Tory stepped out of her shoes, frowning. What was going on out there? Were Michael and Yale in competition for Leslie? Plopping down on the bed, she stared across into the mirror. If they were both trying to win Leslie's hand, she could understand why. Tory gazed down at her trim blue suit, wondering why she'd been so concerned about how she looked. With Leslie Varnum in the room, there was no contest, another reason, as if she needed one, to see that she kept her head about Michael Gallagher.

Leslie's blindness had shocked her, but other than that, she was precisely the type of woman she would expect Michael to date. They were perfect for one another, both urbane, poised, comfortable with wealth. And if Leslie had been concerned enough to come all the way to the Hollow to check on him, she was more than just a casual friend. The proprietary manner in which she had stroked his arm was further proof. Even from the short time she had spent with them, it seemed obvious to her that Michael was winning and Yale was losing. So stick to dreaming, Tory, she told herself, and began to undress. The sound of Michael's laughter, oddly harsh, reminded her of the other question to which she had no answer: why had Michael lied?

Michael stood in the doorway and watched as the sleek black car pulled out of the driveway. Tory, at the foot of the steps, waved until they were out of sight, then turned to come back into the house, a peculiar attentiveness in her eyes making him all the more conscious of the envelope he'd left on the end table.

He had known Ed would make fast work of his request, but to have sent what he'd found by courier rather than through the mail meant that the contents had to be dynamite. Leslie and Yale arriving on Dobbins's heels had been rotten timing, making it awkward to excuse himself and open the package. Waiting for them to leave had taught him a new meaning of frustration. Now that they were gone, he was still in a bind. There was Tory to deal with. The subtle change in her face at his explanation about the envelope worried him. The gaze she turned on him now was more watchful than usual. Hell, he'd waited this long, he could wait a little longer.

"Thanks for being so gracious to them," he said, holding the storm door open for her. "If I'd had any idea Leslie was thinking of coming, I'd have talked her out of it."

"Why?" She passed him, turning sideways as if to avoid any contact with him, and began collecting glasses.

He stopped her, his hand on her arm. "It was an imposition, especially after the kind of hours you worked today."

She met his eyes for only a second, then broke the contact, both visual and physical, moving away. "I didn't mind. Besides," she said, picking up the tray and starting toward the kitchen, "they're your friends. Was Leslie born blind?"

"Yes. Some sort of congenital condition."

Michael settled in a chair, watching as she emptied the
goblets and washed them by hand, moving around the
kitchen with no wasted motion. She seemed more at ease
now, the Tory he'd become accustomed to, in T-shirt, cutoffs and thong sandals, an entirely different person from the
one who'd come up from downstairs earlier.

That person had startled him. The glossy auburn curls
had been the same, yet different, as if they'd been tamed in
some expensive salon, and his pulse had jumped at seeing
the way her plain blue pumps emphasized her smoothly
muscled calves. The short jacket, exposing her small waist
and rounded hips to best advantage had, along with increasing the rate of his circulation, combined to transform
her into the prototype of a smooth, confident professional
who knew her worth and held her own in the business
world—his world. He'd found this alternate personae no less
appealing and wondered how many other sides there were to
her.

"How old is she?" Tory asked.

The question brought him out of his musing. "Leslie?
Twenty-six. I know she seems a lot younger."

"I take it she doesn't work."

"No, but one of the things she came to tell me is that
she'll be starting a new job week after next."

Stretching to put the goblets on a top shelf of an overhead cabinet, Tory glanced back over her shoulder at him.
"You don't approve?"

He moved to her side and replaced the crystal for her.
"Let's just say I have mixed feelings. Give me your impression of her."

"Mine? Why?" Her gaze was a mixture of caution and
curiosity.

"I'm interested."

She turned away brusquely. "I thought she was beautiful
and charming, with a great deal of poise."

"That's it?" Michael was disappointed.

His voice must have given him away. She swung around to face him, making no attempt to hide her annoyance. "Michael, I just met her, so what else could you expect me to say?"

"The truth about what you thought of her."

"All right," she snapped. "She's beautiful, charming, poised, but has obviously allowed herself to be talked out of doing things she's capable of doing. She's a lot tougher than she appears, but she's taken the easy way out by not bucking whoever's been sitting on her."

Michael smiled. "Right. If only Lee could see it."

"Who's Lee?" Tory's irritation appeared to have passed.

"Her father, the greatest guy in the world. He's a widower and has raised her alone. She fought special treatment when she was a kid, insisting on going to her neighborhood school. She went to an out-of-state college over his objections, majored in accounting and graduated near the top of her class."

"Then I was wrong. I figured she'd probably had tutors all her life."

"Leslie? She *was* a tutor, in high school. She had a dynamite job waiting for her when she got her degree. Unfortunately it was in the midwest and Lee pulled some strings and, suddenly, they didn't need her anymore."

"Did she know he was responsible?"

"I didn't think so. Now I'm not so sure."

"Because she's found another job?"

"She'll be working at Cross and Crosby, Yale's company."

"Ah."

"They're competitors of our firm—Lee's firm, in case I didn't make that clear. Varnum and Associates."

Tory whistled in amazement. "She's really putting a strain on the apron strings, isn't she? Her father must be livid."

"That's the problem," Michael said, approaching the subject from an oblique angle. "Lee's . . . out of town and doesn't know."

"And she isn't about to call and tell him." There was a second or two of silence, during which he got the impression she had something on her mind. Finally she asked, "Where does Yale fit into the picture?"

Yale. He should have known. Tory wouldn't be the first woman to fall for that face. "That was the other thing she came to tell me. She and Yale are engaged."

Tory swiveled slowly around to look at him. "How do you feel about that?"

Michael sighed. "I really don't know. Yale's an old friend, from junior high, to be precise. We came up in the same kind of environment, single-parent home with not a lot of money coming in."

Astonishment flared in Tory's eyes. "You? Poor?"

"Probably not by today's standards. I was never hungry, and I had a roof over my head, but it was a no-frills existence. College would have fallen into that category for both Yale and me. Without Lee, I'm not sure what I'd be doing today. We met him when we were about fourteen—but that's another story."

"Would you like to sit out on the deck?" Tory suggested, almost shyly.

Michael's fingers itched to open Ed's envelope, especially since there had been a change in her the last few minutes, a loosening up. She no longer seemed as watchful of him, and he was tempted to beg off, take Ed's report and retreat to the guest room.

"But you must be tired," Tory said. "Go on to bed, Michael. I just thought that since it's cooled off..."

She had handed him the perfect excuse. He didn't take it. It occurred to him that they had spent little time together, all things considered. Then, too, opening that envelope might sound the death knell to their fragile relationship. Depending on Ed's discovery, his feelings might change, so he'd be wise to make the best of her offer. "That sounds terrific. I think I can last a while longer," he said with wry appreciation for the dual meaning of his response.

Dusk lay gently on the mountain that hovered above the house, the shadows cloaking its peak in velvet green against the mauve-streaked sky. Birds twittered in the woods beyond, sounding fretful that the day was ending. It was, as Tory had predicted, refreshingly cool.

Tory collapsed on a redwood lounger and slipped her small feet out of her sandals. Arms lifted high above her head, she stretched and emitted a deep sigh, the combined activity pulling her T-shirt taut across her small round breasts. She closed her eyes, her sun-bronzed face raised to the late evening sky.

Michael took a chair at right angles and settled back to watch her. Seeing her smooth, tanned legs reminded him of their warmth as she'd knelt beside him on the bed the night before, her fingers kneading tension from his shoulders and raising havoc lower down. Her laughter rang in his memory, the sound like the pure tones of good crystal. What a damned shame he'd never get to know her better. If only...

Michael stopped himself with a mental kick in the shins. If only nothing. She'd already caused him almost a week's delay. Yale was right. He doubted he'd have jumped off a cliff into unfamiliar waters for any other woman. How could this one have made such an impact on him in so short a time?

She was the complete opposite of everything that usually attracted him. He had never dated anyone under five-seven or five-eight, had always been drawn toward height, very long hair, narrow hips and cleavage, reminders of the rich women who paraded in and out of Park Avenue hotels dripping furs and exuding boredom.

And here was Tory Shelton, mountain girl, five-two at the most, freckle-faced, a mop of curly reddish-brown hair, rounded hips, the breasts of a teen, whose laughter made him smile inside and out, whose touch caused utter turmoil. She sighed with pure pleasure, opened her eyes and turned her head to him. He might see many emotions in those marvelously luminous eyes, but never boredom. Tory drank life in, reveled in it. If she approached love—physically and emotionally—with anywhere near the same intensity, some lucky man would be her slave for life. It would not be him. He had to leave. She had to stay.

"Sorry," she said, and smiled. "I was just leeching the workday out of my bones. You were telling me about Yale. Will he be a good husband for Leslie?"

"If he really loves her. God, I hope he does, and is not playing a game of one-upmanship. Yale is ambitious and has a competitive streak that I seem to trigger, though I don't know why. It's been going on since our college days."

"But we're talking about marriage. How has Leslie become the grand prize in this competition?"

"Because we're very close and that bugs the hell out of him. My God, she's practically a sister. He's been dancing attendance since he moved here two years ago, and it looks like he's finally waltzed his way into her heart. My concern is with the timing. Les has been through a good deal of emotional turmoil recently, and I hope Yale hasn't taken advantage of that."

He said it knowing Tory would be too polite to ask for details. What she did say, however, surprised him.

"Whether he's taking advantage of it or not, there's nothing you can do. Interfere and it may ruin your relationship. Give her the benefit of the doubt, Michael. She has eyes that see a dimension sighted people can't. I read that somewhere. If Yale doesn't really love her, she'll detect it."

"If he's just using her for his own ends—whatever the hell that might be—I'll kill him," Michael growled.

Tory reached over to place a hand on his knee. "Leslie is not a child. Yale can use her only if she allows herself to be used. That's her choice to make."

Her tone was as gentle as her touch, but there was no missing the ring of steel underscoring her words. "That sounds like the voice of experience speaking," he said, blatantly fishing.

"There are many different ways of being used. It happened to me a long time ago, but I was too young to see it at first. When I did and was in a position to put an end to it, I swore I wouldn't let it happen again. I mean to keep that promise. That's my choice." After a second, she removed her hand. "Leslie will make hers."

Michael knew that Tory had left a great deal unsaid. Could he chance a little more digging without crossing the line? "It occurs to me that I've never heard you mention your parents, and I haven't seen any photographs anywhere."

"Lordy, you're as transparent as plastic wrap. The pictures of my parents are in my bedroom," she said. "My mother died when I was three, my Dad when I was eighteen. If you're trying to ask if he abused me, the answer is yes, but not in the way you mean. Lester Shelton was just a very greedy man and a rotten father."

"I'm sorry," Michael said, backing off. "The subject must be painful for you."

She shrugged. "I'm probably a stronger person for having experienced it. It taught me a lot about love."

Michael leaned forward, elbows on his knees. "Like what?"

"How much it can hurt, no matter which end you're on, the one who loves or the one who is loved."

"But Tory, it doesn't have to hurt. Most of the time it probably doesn't, the blues aside."

"I know that—theoretically. But all I've ever seen is the negative side of it, so to me, moonlight and roses are nothing but great lyrics in a golden oldie."

"You've never been in love? Never wanted to be?"

She chuckled, a hard, dry sound. "Fortunately—as my Dad would say—I'm old enough not to let my wants hurt me. A Cinderella waiting for her Prince Charming I'm not."

"Tory." Michael hitched his chair closer. "Tory, don't do that to yourself. At least leave yourself open."

She smiled, a symbolic stretch of the lips, no more. "I haven't shut myself off, which is just as well. If you stop to think about it, glass slippers have got to be damned uncomfortable."

Her attempt at comic relief fell flat. Whatever had gone wrong in her life had not only imprisoned her here, it had left a toxic residue in her soul.

"Come on, Tory. Love can be wonderful. It's the only emotion capable of making you care about someone else more than you care about yourself."

She turned her head to meet his eyes squarely. "Tit for tat, Michael. Is that the voice of experience speaking?"

Michael was mute, the images of the three women who'd been more than passing fancies parading through his mind. All cut from the same cloth, so much alike that it was difficult to remember which face went with which body, which one he'd taken to which ball, which concert, which bed.

He'd been fond of them; they'd been fun and easy to be with, beautiful tokens of his eligible bachelorhood, his success. And each time he'd tried to convince himself that there was no reason not to get married and settle down, he had failed. All three times. None had reached him, touched him deeply enough. So where did he get off preaching to Tory about love?

"You're a very sweet man, Michael Gallagher," she said, "and I'm sure you mean well, but this is my life and I have to live it my way."

Michael decided it was time to make a diplomatic retreat. "All right, I give up," he said. "If you aren't waiting for a prince, how do you feel about new friends?"

"They're always welcome. Are you putting in an application?"

"Are you accepting them?"

"All the time." Her smile was warm and genuine this time, with only a hint of underlying sadness.

"In that case, I'm filling one out right now." He pushed himself to his feet and leaned down to plant a platonic peck on her forehead. His intentions were good, but something went wrong when she looked at him, her eyes a deeper color than usual, a rich dark brown like fertile earth. Before he knew it, he was paving a four-lane highway leading directly to hell with not an exit ramp in sight.

He moved from her forehead to her nose, then to her mouth. He felt her stiffen with surprise, her lips at first quiescent, then slowly, seductively parting, her tongue sliding along the juncture of his lips. Michael lifted her legs and sat down, lowering them across his lap, then pulled her closer, his arms circling her tiny waist, the tip of his tongue meeting hers in gentle greeting. He nibbled at the soft tissue of her lower lip, probed the inner recesses, his senses becoming more acute at the pressure of her small breasts against his chest and her fingers on his nape, then traveling down his back, her touch like tiny jolts of electricity.

He slipped his hand under her T-shirt to the warm, bare skin of her exposed midriff and traveled up under the knit fabric of her tank top, his pulse racing at the discovery that she wore no bra. His palm cupped her breasts, his fingers grazing her flirtatious nipples. Everything was happening too fast. He was a patient and practiced lover, secure from years of experience at pleasing a woman, but the prospect of kneeling between Tory's firm, shapely thighs, of easing into her brought an immediate return of the tumescence that had sent Tory into peals of laughter, and an agony of longing began to build in his gut.

Her tongue teased the corner of his mouth and her hand stole to his face, her fingers moving along the line of his jaw to his ear, launching a grenade that fragmented deep inside him with a force new to him. This was more than his usual reaction to a woman's kiss, the uncomfortable rigidity only one manifestation of what he was experiencing. As much as he yearned for the sweet imprisonment of her body, another part of him acknowledged, with no little surprise, that he wanted much, much more than physical intimacy. Before he could fully comprehend the implications of this rev-

elation, she stood up and backed away from him, breathing
rapidly.

"God!" she said, hands raised. "If that's your idea of an
application for friendship, I shudder to think what you'd do
if you were applying for anything more serious."

He shook his head, clearing it. What the hell had happened to him? He usually had more control than that. "I'm
sorry, Tory. I don't know what else to say."

She turned away. "I'm sorry, too," she said softly, her
back to him. "I'm not a tease, Michael, and I'm not such a
lonely, sex-starved woman that I'd let things go any further. Let's say I kissed you back to thank you for caring.
Believe me, that's all there was to it."

Michael wasn't sure whether or not to accept her explanation at face value. It would never have occurred to him
that that was a kiss of gratitude, but he had to admit that his
opinion might be colored by his emotional reaction to the
embrace, with which he would have to come to terms. He
had to ignore the link being forged between them. Lee had
to come first, and to find him he had to find the elusive Ivy
Sheldon. That was number one on his list of priorities.

Whether he was successful or not, his next move would be
to his hometown, New York City, a dream he'd had from
the morning he had left it as a teenager in the back seat of
Lee's limo, only this time he'd be riding in a limo of his own,
figuratively speaking. But he couldn't deny what he felt for
Tory. Perhaps he wouldn't feel so badly about leaving her
to such an arid life if he could at least help her with her le-
gal problem. It was time to find out exactly what she'd done.

"I'd better turn in," he said, getting to his feet. "And,
again, I'm sorry for coming on like Don Juan. See you tomorrow."

"Tomorrow," she echoed, her back still turned.

Michael left the deck via the French doors to the guest
room, closed the drapery, then hurried to the living room to
get the envelope. He opened it carefully, sitting on the side
of the bed, extracting a file folder, a note from Ed clipped

to it. "Under the circumstances, thought you might want this a.s.a.p. It ain't as crazy as it seems. Hope it works. Ed."

He opened the folder and the contents, more than a dozen copies of microfiched articles, fluttered out, spilling across the spread. "Foxwall Student Leads Trackers to Downed Plane," one headline read. Michael frowned. How had Ed stumbled onto this? And how had he known this information might be useful? Jake must be back from Florida. Ed was probably still pumping friends or searching computer banks for the scoop on Tory.

Picking up the article, Michael scanned the first few lines.

Ina Shelton, a third-grader at Foxwall Township Elementary, is small for her age, but her large brown eyes see into another dimension.

"What?" He read the last phrase again. Tory had used the same words about Leslie.

Ina, who answers more readily to her nickname, I.V., has a unique psychic ability, as she and her father, Lester Shelton, just recently discovered.

The hairs on the back of Michael's neck began to twitch. He didn't want to believe this. He really didn't.

It was I.V. who led searchers to the Hyatt family, whose small private plane had been missing for two days. "Led us right to them," Deputy Sheriff James Cottan confirmed. "Just in time, too, with the weather clouding up for more snow. She..."

A red haze formed before Michael's eyes. The name was I.V., not Ivy. And *Shelton,* not Sheldon. He shuffled through the other papers hurriedly, his hand freezing above a two-column article topped by a grainy photograph. Enormous dark eyes peered at him from a picture-perfect oval, a child's face haloed by a mop of unruly, shoulder-length curls.

"Ina (I.V.) Shelton, the nine-year-old psychic who found the missing Zeller baby," the caption read.

Ina Victoria Shelton. Tory.

Rage gripped him, paralyzed him. She had lied to him. The enticing little witch had *lied* to him with a straight face. Springing from the bed, Michael paced the small room, his mouth taut with anger, his leg protesting the impact of heel against floor. Adrenaline pumping, he felt more clear-headed than he had since he'd damned near killed himself jumping into the lake to help her. All the tumblers fell into place, unlocking all the answers to all the nagging questions—for starters, how she'd known it was his tie clip and where to find him. *How she'd known where to find Danny!* Suddenly the curious scene he'd witnessed, the peculiar confrontation between Tory and Sal at the fairgrounds made sense. How could he have been so stupid?

Gabe Jr. with his new watch had given it away without knowing it. At the point he and Danny had started toward the quarry, Tory was just leaving the dunking booth. She *couldn't* have seen them. That had been the second lie, a whopper, and a community effort. How many times had he heard it: wasn't it fortunate Tory saw them heading that way? Even Ransom had said it. All this time the person he'd been looking for had been right under his nose. Precious days wasted with her watching his every move.

Michael hesitated, frowning. This was the "crime" that held her hostage? Or was anonymity what she was after? He went back to the bed, sat down and read the articles one by one. Jake had remembered accurately. Little I. V. Shelton had found over two dozen lost and wandering souls in a nine-year span. Obviously some had not appreciated her efforts; they had disappeared of their own volition. Balancing those were the children she'd located, a few genuinely lost, a few abducted by a parent, one uprooted by a total stranger, and one who had died. But he had the most important answer: she could do it. She could find Lee Varnum.

His anger more controlled, Michael turned out the bedside lamp and opened the drapery onto the darkness and an empty deck. Given the elaborate ruse she and everyone else had pulled on him to hide her identity, he'd be blind not to see that Tory had not wanted to be found, and the people of the Hollow were willing to lie to see that she was left alone. She ran a successful, self-supporting business, and considering the effort Sal had been forced to make to gain her cooperation, it was likely that Tory had put the other business—finding people—behind her.

And the gloves! That's why she wore them. He reran the tape of the scene he had witnessed at the fairground. He'd missed the most important part, again, thanks to her friends and neighbors literally covering for her, but he'd seen enough to piece it together now. Tory had resisted up to the moment Sal had ripped the glove from her hand and had replaced it with the baseball cap. Tory had intuited that Danny was in danger, and had been left with no choice; she'd had to act. It had almost blown her cover, but it had also done something else. It had shown Michael firsthand that she was genuine. He'd witnessed it himself.

His time was precious, but Michael was sure that to take the direct route—confronting her and asking her help with Lee—would get him nowhere. He was now, however, even more determined to benefit from her ability. To use her, he thought grimly, the phrase taking on new meaning. But to do it he would have to change her mind. She had to want to help him.

Say what she would, that kiss a few minutes before had been no mere thank you. She wasn't starved for affection? For love? The hell she wasn't! He had never deliberately set out to seduce a woman—he'd never had to—but he'd do it, do whatever it took. Ina Victoria I. V. Tory Shelton would help him find Lee. She'd do it for him, because he intended to see that she'd do *anything* for him.

Chapter 7

It was a little past seven when Tory walked past the open door of the guest room and stopped short. The bed had been made, the spread neatly folded across the foot of it. The top of the dresser was empty, and the aroma of freshly brewed coffee scented the air. It hadn't occurred to her she'd have to face Michael this early. She wasn't ready and had counted on having several hours of work under her belt first.

Downstairs, at least, she was in control of her life. And control was precisely what she would need to look Michael in the eye as if her lapse of the evening before had meant nothing. To do it without benefit of a restful night seemed more than she could bear. She had slept little, her only consolation that she wasn't alone. She had heard Michael using the phone, moving around as if pacing until well after three.

There was no point in putting this off any longer. It's my house, she reminded herself, marching purposefully toward the kitchen, with a surprised stutter-step at the sight of his attaché case and weekender sitting beside the front door.

He stood at the gas range, pouring coffee, presumably for her, since a half-empty mug sat on the table. He was in forest green today, his hair still slightly damp. The bandage was gone, the shaved area barely visible under the mantle of thick, black hair. For someone who'd been up almost all night, he looked none the worse for wear. In fact, there was more animation in his features than she'd seen since she'd met him.

"Good morning," he said, putting the pot back on the stove. "Sugar and cream, or black?"

"Good morning. Black, thank you. I saw your bags. Are you leaving?"

He placed her cup on the table and pulled out a chair for her. "I wanted to talk to you before someone showed up to start breakfast. We can do it over coffee."

Tory sat down, eyeing him surreptitiously as he moved around to take the chair opposite. There was, she confirmed, a definite difference about him this morning, reflected in the new liveliness in his face but running far deeper than its surface manifestation. He seemed more centered, as if he'd thrown off some immobilizing burden. Had one of the after-midnight calls he'd made brought good news?

"I've decided to go back to Jake's," he said, getting right to the point. "After last night, I figure I've worn out my welcome."

A wave of sadness washed over her. "You haven't worn out anything, but if that's your decision, I'll respect it. What about the stairs at the cabin? Think you'll be able to manage them?"

"I'll have to. I'm grateful for everything you've done, Tory, but you and your friends have spoiled me rotten long enough. You've made me feel very much at home, perhaps too much at home."

Tory folded her hands around her mug, hoping its heat would relieve the chill around her heart. She focused on the coffee, avoiding his eyes in case the desolation she felt was visible in hers. "I enjoyed having you. When will you be going back to Washington?"

"Not for a while yet."

"Oh." Her head came up, a puzzled expression in her eyes. "I just assumed..."

"I'm on vacation, but as it turns out, it'll be more of a working vacation than I'd thought. Something's come up, a deadline I hadn't anticipated. I might need your help, Tory."

Immediately on guard, she took her first sip of coffee. "How?"

"I have to complete a narrative—a bid proposal for a housing complex my firm is planning. Under normal circumstances, our office staff would handle it, but the schedule's been pushed up and it's caught us with one secretary too many on vacation."

"I see." Tory began to relax, on home ground now. "What precisely is a narrative?"

"A rationale explaining what we plan to do and why we selected a particular approach. We have to submit it to an ad hoc committee that selects which design best suits a choice tract of land in Montgomery County. A polished narrative carries a lot of weight. At the least, it reflects the professionalism of the firm submitting it. Think you can take care of it?"

"Of course, but perhaps you should take a look at my work before you commit yourself."

His smile had a guilty edge to it. "I already have. I went downstairs last night and saw what a fantastic job you did with that god-awful manuscript that reads like a textbook. I know I should have asked permission first, but it was after midnight when I came up with the idea and I didn't want to wake you."

"But you haven't even asked my rates."

"I don't care. We're in a bind. Name your price and we'll pay it."

Tory felt uneasy. On the face of it, it was typical of the kind of job she normally did, but something about this didn't feel quite right. "How long is this narrative and how soon will you need it?"

"I'm not sure about the length—it's in bits and pieces. I'll need a draft just so I can edit it. While you're working on that, I'll be writing the summary."

"And the deadline?"

"Monday after next—which means it'll eat up a good deal of your time. If you have other commitments that have first priority, say so, Tory. I can always farm it out to a place in D.C. I was just trying to avoid going back any sooner than I had to. This is probably the closest to a vacation I'll have for a year or two."

Tory decided not to ask why. "I do have other commitments, but Helen can take care of them."

"Good. The catch is—and this may change your mind about saying yes—we'll have to work together very closely for the next ten days," he said, seeming to choose his words carefully, "which is another reason I think it's better that I leave. I can deal with a professional relationship with you, but if I stay here, I can't guarantee that what happened last night won't happen again."

"It won't." Tory got up and took her cup, still full, to the sink. She had to get away from him. "It takes two. You're an attractive man, Michael, and I like you a great deal," she said, her back to him, "but I don't become intimate with a man just because I like him. Whatever impression you might have gotten last night, nothing more would have happened. But perhaps it's better this way. It leaves the air a lot clearer. So from this point, we're co-workers—"

"And friends, Tory?"

She wasn't really sure even that was possible. "We'll see. One thing at a time." Ready to face him again, she turned around. "When do you want me to start? I need to talk to Helen and revamp my schedule."

"Some time this afternoon. The office manager's sending it up by messenger. It should be here by one."

"Oh. I guess I thought that's what Marty brought you yesterday."

"No, that was a copy of the revised schedule for the bid, my assistant's subtle method of finding out if I'd bite." He rose and came to stand in front of her. "I hope I haven't ruined things between us, Tory. I really would like us to be friends. I'm counting on you to show me around. Jake was right. He said these mountains have a way of getting into your blood. I'd like to see more of the area."

"If there's time, I'll be glad to." Tory moved away. He was too close, too solid a presence, and like her mountains, hard to ignore. "You'll need a ride to the cabin. Helen can take you after breakfast."

He emptied the last of his coffee into the sink. "I'd just as soon skip breakfast today. I'm not used to the kind of blue plate specials I've been eating, and I might as well get accustomed to my old routine—coffee for breakfast, lunch if I happen to think about it, and something quick and easy for dinner. Jake's freezer is full and he has a microwave, so I should be in pretty good shape."

"In other words, TV dinners. Helen will die. Speaking of which—or whom—I'd better write a note for her." She tore a sheet from the pad under the telephone, and rummaged through the junk drawer for a pencil. Her normally organized kitchen had suffered in the hands of visiting cooks, and nothing was where it was supposed to be. It was a little thing, but it threw her off balance, planting a seed of frustration she knew had nothing to do with the missing pencil.

Michael went to the door of the deck and looked out, his expression almost wistful. "I'm going to miss this. You have a nice house, Tory."

She found a ballpoint pen and tore a hole in the paper, trying to coax dried ink to flow. Scowling, she tossed it into the trash and attacked the drawer again. "I like it—now. It's just been the last couple of years that I've felt comfortable in it."

He looked back over his shoulder. "Why? Was it in bad shape when you bought it?"

Tory realized she'd spoken without thinking, and considered evading the question, but there was no valid reason not to answer him. "Actually, it was almost new. My father bought the house with money he shouldn't have had to begin with, and I didn't find out how he'd pulled it off until after he died. It took me seven years to pay back the money. Then the house seemed mine."

"Were you legally obligated to assume his debts?"

"Not really. They weren't exactly debts, more like..." She searched for a way to phrase it. "Like overcharges. It wasn't illegal, but it wasn't right, either."

"What line of work was he in?" Michael asked.

Tory, digging in the drawer as if searching for gold, could feel his eyes on her. She'd talked herself into a corner. Nothing was going right this morning. "He was an agent. I have to give him credit. He was good at it—too good." She slammed the drawer closed, putting an end to the discussion. "I'll have to call Helen instead of trying to explain everything in a note. This won't take long. You can wait in the car if you like. It's unlocked."

"No hurry." He turned back to the scene outside, as if delaying the moment he would have to leave. Tory watched him as she talked to Helen, detecting still more indications of the difference in him this morning. It seemed to be a change in outlook, as if a weighty problem had been solved. A secret excitement hovered in his eyes. If she handled his tie clip today, would the grief and guilt she'd detected be gone? Had the person he'd wanted her to find returned? She almost hoped she had. Her own guilt would be easier to live with. And when, she asked herself, had she begun to think the missing person was a woman?

She replaced the phone. "I'm ready." When he didn't respond, she crossed to him, and saw that she needn't have been nearly as circumspect in her conversation with Helen; Michael, his hands shoved into his pockets, was in another world, his gaze glued to the panorama beyond her deck, his dark blue eyes filled with a strange longing. "Michael?" she said softly, and discovered that she'd been wrong. He was very much grounded in the reality of the moment.

"Have you ever noticed the way the mists evaporate up there? When I first came in to start the coffee, the top third was completely invisible, and the mountain's been doing a striptease ever since, as if she's slowly pulling her nightgown over her head. In a minute or two, she'll have stripped to the buff, nature in the raw. It's one hell of a sexy act."

Tory had to smile. "You're the only person I've ever met who thought of that mountain as female."

"Of course it is. Serene, mysterious, a titanic maternal presence watching over her brood. And she changes her wardrobe several times a day. Lying on the right side of the bed, I could see her reflection in the mirror. I'd wake up every couple of hours, and she'd be wearing a different color from the last time I looked."

Tory stared up at him, pleasantly surprised. This was a facet of his personality she hadn't picked up in anything of his she had touched. "Do you usually see things in such poetic terms?"

He turned, a quiet solemnity in his eyes. "That's what you and your mountain have done to me."

Aware of approaching danger, she sidestepped it with a lighthearted response. "So now I'm a muse. I'll have to add that to my résumé. By the way," she said, as if it was of no importance whatever, "I can get the name of the Sheldon boy, the one who plays basketball, if you want to call him about the woman you wanted to get in touch with."

He didn't respond immediately. Tory held her breath. After several seconds of silence, he shook his head briskly. "Thanks, but don't bother. I'm going to be too busy. Perhaps the next time I come this direction. And if we don't get going, I'll have wasted the whole morning." Turning, he walked through the dining room to the living room and, with his bags tucked under his arm, out the front door without looking back.

Tory finally exhaled, releasing tension and carbon dioxide on the same breath. If he'd changed his mind, it must not have been that important to him to begin with. It lessened her sense of guilt—not a lot, but some. She turned off the flame under the coffeepot, then went through the house, checking the locks on the deck doors.

On her way through the living room, she stopped. She could sense a difference already. The air-conditioning clicked on, and she jumped. It sounded louder than it used to. The rooms seemed larger, emptier. Disgusted with herself, she left the house, slamming the door closed. You're acting like a deserted wife in a soap opera, she decided, and rushed to the car.

She climbed behind the wheel and secured her seat belt, unsettled by Michael's presence at her elbow. The front seats had never seemed so close together before. She tried to think of something to talk about on the way to the cabin, but the words wouldn't come. He seemed content with the silence, so after a while she stopped worrying about it and gave herself a stern talking to. This was the first phase of his departure from the Hollow, and the sangfroid she had counted on was sorely lacking. Get it together, Tory, she told herself. There would be life after Michael. It wouldn't have the same sparkle, but it was better than no life at all. Wasn't it?

At the Burnside cabin, Tory set the emergency brake and released the hatch so Michael could retrieve his cases. His white Mercedes, which Marty had driven back from the fairgrounds, was parked around the side, covered with a thin coat of dust.

When she didn't move, he came around to her side of the car and leaned down to ask, "Aren't you coming in?"

"Oh." She hadn't anticipated an invitation, and her emotions began a tug-of-war, pulling her in opposite directions. On one hand she wanted to say goodbye, leave, and get this prelude to his eventual departure over with; on the other, she wanted to prolong the moments she spent with him. He settled the matter by opening the door and waiting, until she finally unbuckled her seat belt and got out.

The cabin was a delight, an A-frame, the redwood exterior perfectly at home among the thick grove of firs and pines surrounding it. The interior was simply furnished but rich in feeling, leather and gleaming rosewood, a braided rag rug the sole floor covering. An old-fashioned rolltop desk stood in a corner, not far from an inexpensive dinette table and vinyl-clad chairs. Beyond the balcony overhead were two doors, which Tory assumed were the bedrooms.

The centerpiece of the first floor was the massive stone fireplace, its hearth so deep that there was more than enough room for the large floor pillows tossed casually along its edge. That, and a deck every bit as large as the great room, caused Tory to sigh with envy. It seemed almost criminal that these two marvelous features graced a house so seldom used.

Michael deposited his cases on an island counter which set off the Pullman kitchen from the remaining space. "Would you like something? Orange juice? Or I could make coffee." He stooped to open the diminutive refrigerator, removed a half-eaten pizza from the Friday before, and dropped it into the tiny sink.

"This is the kind of thing you plan to survive on?" Tory asked. "God forbid." Just as she was about to chide him about his diet, her attention was captured by a series of drawings spread out on the dinette table. "What are those?"

Michael straightened. "That's what the narrative you'll be working on is about. It's the housing complex we've designed."

All thoughts of fleeing were buried under her fascination with the illustrations. They were rendered in soft pastels with a sure hand, depicting clusters of four single-story attached homes ingeniously arranged in a square, each with a fenced rear patio that opened onto a center courtyard. There were several different views showing how the complex fit the landscape, seeming a natural part of the environment. At the bottom left of each drawing were the words: Woodland Rise. Independent Living with Dignity.

"Independent Living?" Tory asked, sliding into a chair and pulling the drawings to her. "This complex is for the disabled?"

"I thought I'd mentioned that. These sections on the east side are for the blind and the deaf, this corner for people in wheelchairs, this for the ambulatory with impaired motor facilities, this one for those confined to bed. Here, let me show you the interiors." He reached into a portfolio leaning against a table leg, withdrawing yet another set of illustrations. Removing the first set, he spread his new find in front of her. "Most units have built-in furniture. It simplifies traffic patterns and leaves more room for residents in wheelchairs."

"And those with vision problems will know that nothing will be moved. No bumping into furniture that's out of position. Michael, that's marvelous! And the rooms are so airy and full of light. Who designed the homes? Mr. Varnum?"

"The concept is his—the designs are Jake's and mine. Lee's the heart of the firm, and this is something he's wanted to do all his life. If you work with him very long, you find his goals becoming your own, as if it was what you always wanted to do, too. We take on the more traditional jobs to pay the bills, but we specialize in redesigning existing residences for the use of the disabled."

"Michael, that's wonderful. I knew you were an architect, but this . . ."

"It's the chance of a lifetime if we can submit the package in time. The name of the development should be 'Lee's Dream' instead of Woodland Rise."

"This is the same man who sabotaged his daughter's first opportunity for independent living?"

Michael turned a thoughtful gaze on her. "I'll be damned. This design concept began as a house for Leslie, and somehow exploded into a complete development. It's been in the works for a couple of years, what with local red tape and zoning board meetings. But he wanted this for her. Maybe that's why he was trying to keep her close to home."

"Why didn't he tell her that?"

"Superstitious. He never talked about a project with anyone outside the firm until it was a certainty. Didn't want to jinx it. He's an original, and the most generous man I've ever met. If it weren't for him, I'm not sure where I'd be now. He helped make me what I am."

Tory felt her eyes widen. "How?"

"I was a kid on the borderline of everything. The neighborhood I grew up in was in transition, as the saying goes—on a downhill slide. My dad died in a construction accident when I was ten, and even though Mom and I weren't really poor, we weren't middle-class either. I probably never consciously thought about it, but down deep I'm sure I knew that high school was about as far as I'd be able to go. Who could afford college? That didn't leave much to look forward to, so I had a pretty lackadaisical attitude about grades."

"And Lee changed that."

"He was the speaker at the graduation ceremony for my eighth-grade class. Turns out he'd gone to my junior high when he was a kid. He said he would foot the bill for the college education of any of us who stayed in school, stayed out of trouble and kept a B average. He'd come up to see us once a month, and if we needed help, no matter what kind—tutors, counseling, a dentist—he'd see that we got it. We couldn't believe it. A lot of us began to think positively about our futures for the first time."

"I take it he kept his word."

"That, and more, for me. Mom died over semester break my first year of college. I called Lee. I didn't know what else to do. He came, paid for the funeral, packed my things and took them back to Washington with him. From that time on, his house was home base during summers, holidays, semester breaks."

"No wonder you and Leslie are so close. And Lee sounds like a terrific guy."

"He could also be tough. He demanded excellence and discipline and he got it. He paid for grad school on the condition that I'd work for him for five years once I finished. He said my college education would make me as good an architect as he was, and working with him would make me twice as good. I went for it."

"You've been with him ever since?"

"And haven't regretted a minute. He's been father, mentor, taskmaster, but most of all, friend. I'd do anything for him. I owe him everything."

"If you designed this," she said, eyeing the drawings again, "he owes you a lot, too. What's this dotted line in the middle of the living room?"

"A loft, the only concession to guest room space we could make and keep costs reasonable."

"Where's storage space?"

"All over the place. Lee's a sailor, so he knows a lot about making the most of every inch."

"Show me."

Tory was fascinated, and peppered Michael with questions, switching from floor plans to pastel sketches of finished interiors and back again. A heated discussion began when she discovered that there was no linen closet. Michael challenged her to find somewhere to put one.

"What's wrong with the bathroom? That's where you use towels, right? Let's see. Shelves. What about something overhead that could be lowered mechanically so that someone in a wheelchair could reach it."

"Draw it." He swept everything off the table. "Right here." He shoved a mechanical pencil into her hand, and Tory began to doodle on the tabletop. After a second, he did, too. When she next glanced at her watch, an hour and a half had passed.

"Michael, it's almost ten! I've got to go!"

"But we're practically there. You've got sound ideas. Just a little longer?" he pleaded.

"I can't. I have to meet a client." She stood up, hating to leave with their project so close to completion. It was also not lost on her that she'd just spent the most mentally invigorating ninety minutes of her life. "Maybe we can finish when I come back to pick up the narrative."

"What time will that be? I'd like to hear more of your ideas."

"After three, since I blew the time I should have been dropping off finished work and picking up from a couple of regulars." She glanced at the table. "Are you going to erase that?"

His eyes widened in mock horror. "Kill a whole morning's brilliance? Not on your life." Getting up, he walked her to the door, his limp barely detectable. "I enjoyed this. We make a good team."

"Don't count your chickens," Tory quipped. "The towel rack's not finished yet. See you later." She ran to the car.

Playing havoc with the speed limit, Tory took a deep breath, loving the morning smells, the breeze through her hair, the sun on the arm propped atop the open window. She felt energized. This kind of collaboration was new to her, and to be initiated into it by Michael had made it that much more exciting. She would enjoy working with him. He listened to her, made her feel as if what she thought mattered.

All that aside, being a part of something of this nature, helping to create a customized environment for people whose difficulties she'd come to know so well, meant a great deal to her. It also meant that when Michael left, he'd be taking a bit of her with him. And that made losing him a little less painful.

Michael closed the door and leaned with his back against it, triumphant, exhilarated. He had her! He hadn't even been trying, had barely set in motion the plan he'd concocted, and had hooked her anyway. Crossing back to the table, he walked around it, eyeing the progression from sketchy idea to nearly finished product. There was every possibility they could use Tory's elevating towel enclosure. The concept was sound and imaginative, but that was a bonus. She was hooked, involved in a way he would never have envisioned.

A night of walking the floor, for which he was paying now, had left him convinced that the only way to gain Tory's cooperation was to see that she became emotionally involved—with him. He would leave, give her space. She thought he was a gentleman; he might as well let her go on thinking it. But he had to devise a plan that would throw them together as often as possible, and the idea of using her business had been the most logical way.

The narrative she'd be working on had indeed been part of the bid proposal submitted to and approved by the ad hoc committee months before; they were well into the second stage of the process, awaiting the signature of the senior partner to make it official. But the narrative was the only thing he could think of to use that would serve his purpose. He would butcher the draft from which the finished product had been typed, make it so difficult to understand that working closely with him would be a necessity. The more frequent the contact, the easier it would be to reshape the relationship into one that would make her more malleable.

And she was fascinated by the man who'd masterminded the housing complex. That interest could be used, played for all it was worth. But would that be enough? Lee as a strong enough lure to be his own savior, making her want to help find him, would be an ideal solution, but an unlikely one. He would still need all the ammunition he could bring to bear.

She liked him, he knew, and as angry as he was at having been deceived, he liked her and, yes, he wanted her. He pulled one hand from his pocket, stared at his open palm, remembering how precious her small breast had felt with his fingers nestled around it. And her hands. There was magic in them in more ways than one. She had sent his blood racing with her touch alone, etching desire along the length of his back, across his chest. She was as hungry as he was, and he'd have to use that. He'd feel like a rotten son of a bitch, but he'd feed that hunger, make love to her, listen to her cry out with passion, do it again and again, until she loved him too much to deny him anything he asked.

The whole rotten scheme left a sour taste in his mouth. He went to the kitchen sink, drank a little water. It didn't help. He'd have to get used to it. Something told him he'd carry that taste with him the rest of his life. For Lee.

Perhaps Tory's skewed thinking was right, after all. Love could indeed drive you to lie, cheat, abuse trust. The irony was that the person on the losing end of this plot to save his oldest friend was also the first woman with whom he *knew* he could fall in love. That was a trap he had to avoid. You didn't misuse someone you loved. And he would use Tory Shelton. He had no choice.

Chapter 8

Thursday. Michael drew an X through Day Six of his calendar and tossed it into his briefcase. Six days of getting together with Tory at the end of her workday, scanning the pages she'd finished, making minor editorial changes. Six days of sitting on her deck or Jake's afterward, of talking about the housing complex or Lee, of seeing the excitement in her eyes. Tory had become completely engrossed, with no help from him, in the nuts and bolts of seeing Woodland Rise come to fruition.

He'd been lucky so far and he knew it. With so much time on his hands, he had, in fact, begun to wonder about the part coincidence had played in this whole scenario—the way he'd wandered into Tory's backyard right off the bat without knowing it, losing his tie clip, and now discovering that the work he'd been doing for years touched a segment of the population for whom she felt great empathy. It was eerie, reminding him of his mother, God bless her, a great believer in, among other things, fate.

"If it's in your stars, Michael, it will happen and there's nothing you can do about it," she'd warned him. "I was meant to meet your dad, rascal that he was, and somewhere out there is some poor lass with your name written in a secret compartment of her heart, and hers in yours."

He remembered laughing at her, especially as, at that point, he thought girls were a pain in the behind, but her wise smile nagged him now. The whole fabric of his beliefs seemed to be fraying. He had filed what he'd learned at the Wayland Institute for Parapsychology Research in a mental niche entitled "I'll Believe It When I See It," and as a result had arrived in these mountains with his cynicism intact. Tory's unwilling demonstration of her ability had blown that out of the water, so how could he be so cocksure about anything else, fate included? If Tory was that woman his mother had spoken of...

"Shape up, Gallagher," he said aloud, as the kettle began to whistle for attention. "You really are going around the bend." He removed it from the stove. This, too, had become part of their routine; she served lemonade or sparkling cider for their evening sessions. If they met here at the cabin, as they were scheduled to do in a couple of hours, he made iced tea or coffee. He put the tea bags in the kettle, set it aside and began slicing a lemon, his hands on automatic pilot as he tried to gauge his progress with the other facets of his scheme.

There were only three days left before he ran up against the arbitrary deadline he'd given Tory. The time remaining weighed heavily on him, because as well as the business relationship was going, their personal relationship was still struggling to get out of the starting gate. He'd thought Tory would be a pushover, that if he played his cards right, she'd fall into his arms. Not only had she failed to do that, she appeared to be going out of her way to discourage personal interaction of any kind. If the subject under discussion veered too far from the narrative, the housing complex or related issues, she steered it back or brought the work session to an end. He'd dated one or two women who'd played hard to get, but Tory had refined it to an art, as elusive as quicksilver from a shattered thermometer.

He nicked his finger, swore, and tossed the knife into the sink, sick of lying to himself. The truth was that the hours he spent waiting to see her in the evenings stretched into small eternities. The truth was that the sun didn't rise on his day until he'd seen Tory's face, the way her smile bounced light into her eyes, making them dance; there was nothing as satisfying as hearing her laughter begin as a throaty chuckle before it exploded into uninhibited hilarity. The truth was that he loved to watch her catch her bottom lip between her teeth when she was thinking, to see the frown of irritation whenever her thoughts outraced the ability of her mouth to express them. He had kissed that mouth only once, yet still felt the imprint of her lips on his. Tory might be hooked on Woodland Rise, but he was hooked on her.

The key rattled in the door, and Michael jerked toward the sound. It was too early for Tory and, as far as he knew, no one else had a key except—

"Jake!" he bellowed as his friend opened the door. "Am I glad to see you! When did you get back?"

Jake Burnside stepped in, pulling the key from the lock, a grin stretched from ear to ear. Stocky and muscular, he looked like a boxer or a professional wrestler and had the face to match. It took most people a good while to see past the heavy brows and off-center nose to the gentle heart and creative mind underneath. That Jake made little effort to disabuse those willing to judge books by covers had a great deal to do with it. And despite the coarseness of his features, women especially were mysteriously drawn to him. He returned the feeling with gusto. Whoever first coined the phrase "ladies' man" had Jake Burnside in mind, as well as "love them and leave them," which he did on a regular basis. Jake was the quintessential bachelor and enjoyed his freedom.

They shook hands, pummeling one another with good humor and genuine affection.

"Brother, will you look at that tan! Florida agreed with you. How's your dad?" Michael asked.

"At home raising hell again, which means he's fine. He sends his regards. I have a tremendous thirst." Crossing to the refrigerator, Jake rooted in the bottom for a beer. After stepping out of his loafers, he flopped down on the love seat and propped his feet on the coffee table. "Leslie told me about your misadventures. You okay?"

"Fine. Stitches out, leg twinging now and again, but otherwise doing great. The whole business knocked me on my can for several days, but I'm back to about ninety percent now. I've started taking walks to get the kinks out."

"Well, don't rush things." He locked his fingers behind his head and waggled his brows. "Tell me about the sweet young wench you damn near killed yourself for. According to Leslie, she's a winner."

Michael took the matching chair and leaned forward, elbows on his knees. "It's her, Jake. I. V. Shelton, only she calls herself Tory now. She was the second person I met here."

Jake's jaw dropped. "Well, ain't that a kick in the head." He peered at Michael, his expression sobering. "I take it she says Lee's dead, since you're still here."

Michael shifted uneasily. "I haven't asked her yet."

"What?" Jake's feet hit the floor. "Why the hell not?"

Michael grimaced. "It's a long story."

"Tell it. I'm just here to check on you, not to stay, but you can bet your bippy I'm not leaving until I hear the whole thing. What's been going on?"

Playing for time, Michael went to the front door to make sure it was locked. He wasn't looking forward to laying out his plan to Jake, knowing precisely how he would react. Jake didn't disappoint him, his expression becoming more grim by the minute as he listened, flipping through the copies of the articles Ed had sent.

When Michael had finished, Jake asked, "How long have we been buddies, buddy?"

"Six years."

Jake nodded. "Right. As far as I'm concerned, that entitles me to call you a class-A bastard. Don't bother to tell me the end justifies the means. It doesn't. If you want proof, just ask yourself how Lee would feel about this."

Michael winced, but stuck to his guns. "If we don't find him, we'll never know, will we? I'm not enjoying it, Jake. She's...she's unlike any woman I've ever known. I keep asking myself what might have happened if I'd met her before all this. She's..." He shrugged, unable to find the words.

An expression of malicious glee brightened his partner's eyes. "I'll be damned. You've fallen for her, haven't you? Michael Gallagher, man about town, is smitten. Good! Because if you go through with this, as soon as she finds out what you want her to do, she's going to walk out of your life, and that's just what you deserve. I only hope she kicks you where it'll hurt the most before she leaves. For God's sake, forget it, Michael. Be straight with her now, before it's too late."

"Why? Was she straight with me?" Michael shook his head doggedly. "She's gone to one hell of a lot of trouble to erase any trace of her early life, and the whole town's backing her, lying through their teeth to protect her. The only reason she wound up finding the kid was because his mother forced her hand, literally. I figure I—" He stopped, his head coming up. "That's her car. I had a feeling she'd be early. Jake, look, I know you don't agree with—"

Jake stood up and went to get his shoes. "Don't worry, I won't blow it for you. Considering the number of hearts I've broken, I have no right to throw stones. You're my friend, right or wrong, and this time it's you who's wrong, for a change."

"I'm not denying that," Michael said, going to the door and opening it. "All I'm saying is that I have no other choice. Damn! Do something with those articles! I'll stall, but make it fast." He stepped out onto the porch, the waiting over. The afternoon was suddenly brighter, sunnier.

Tory, a thick envelope under one arm, hopped out of her car, eyeing Jake's low-slung Ferrari. Still in work attire— sans gloves, her feet clad in high-heeled sandals more strap than shoe, she approached the cabin, an uncharacteristic hesitancy about her. "You have company. I know I'm awfully early. I can come back later."

"No need. Come on in and meet Jake."

"Mr. Burnside is here?" For some reason, this seemed to increase her uncertainty.

"Relax," Michael said, an arm around her shoulder. "He doesn't bite—until he gets to know you better." The fact that she didn't immediately move away from him was proof positive that she found the prospect of meeting Jake unsettling.

He ushered her in. The articles were out of sight. Jake was at the sink, removing a second beer from the refrigerator, his eyes already taking Tory's measure. "Victoria Shelton, this is my partner—and friend—Jake Burnside."

"It's Tory, please. I'm glad to meet you."

"Same here. And I'm Jake. Forgive the icy hands," he said, extending his. "But you know what they say about that."

"Cold hands, poor circulation?"

Jake barked a laugh. "Clever. I'll remember that. Michael showed me the terrific job you're doing with the narrative. I thank you. My secretary thanks you. Whatever you're charging, we'll pay double."

Tory placed the bulky envelope on the table. "I should get that in writing, especially considering what I have to say. Or perhaps... Michael, is it possible for me to meet Mr. Varnum?"

."Why?" Michael dispatched an anxious glance at Jake, who looked away and became very busy opening the can of beer.

"I realize I'm probably overstepping my bounds, but he's the one I should talk to."

"I hope you'll be meeting him soon," Michael said, his heartbeat slowing toward its natural rhythm. "In the interim, run whatever's on your mind by us. We'll probably react in much the same way he would."

"Okay." She took a deep breath. "I'd like to ask him—and you two—to rethink the slant of the concept. Something about it had been bothering me since I first saw the drawings, and I just figured it out today." She squared her shoulders, and Michael realized that she was really nervous about this.

"What is it?" he asked, encouraging her.

"You've got all the people with like problems lumped together—one section of the development for the visually impaired, one for the deaf, one for those in wheelchairs. You're setting up segregated enclaves."

"Well, I wouldn't put it quite that way," Jake responded, on the defensive, but the crease across his forehead meant that she'd made him think.

"The houses are in groups of fours. Why not mix the residents—no two with the same disability in a quad, unless it can't be avoided."

"Why, Tory?" Michael asked, forcing himself to focus on what she was saying, rather than the determined jut of her chin, which he found charming.

"So they can become sensitive to the challenges of people whose problems are different from theirs."

"I'm not sure I understand."

"When you have a disability or something that makes you feel different from everyone else," she said, "it's so easy to become self-absorbed. I set up a buddy system in my typing class, pairing a blind student with one in a wheelchair or a kid on crutches, just to get the class started on time. I made them responsible for helping each other into the room and to their places in front of the computers. They were uncomfortable about it at first, but after a while they began to get a kick out of the fact that they could help someone else."

"Interesting," Jake said, his expression intent. "Tell me more."

"One of my favorites, a dynamite kid, has spina bifida and he admits he never gave a thought to what it's like to be blind. I can't tell you the difference it's made in his attitude. His sense of self-worth has shot up, and he genuinely enjoys being able to make a contribution."

Michael glanced at Jake. "What do you think? The interiors are your territory."

"You're talking about children, Tory. We're dealing with adults who've outgrown the self-centered stage."

Tory didn't respond for a second, her eyes glued to his face. She checked her watch. "Do you have time to make a run with me? It's not far, but I think it's the only way I can prove my point."

"Am I invited?" Michael asked, feeling left out.

She turned a startled look toward him. "Of course. Well?" she said, rounding on Jake.

"This is really important to you, isn't it?" he asked.

"Not as important as it'll be to the people who'll live in Woodland Rise. Can you go or not?"

Jake's grin was a clue that he liked what he saw. "Feisty little lady, aren't you? Sure, I can go. Who's driving?"

"I am. Come on, we'll have to hurry." Leaving them, she trotted out to her car to clear the back seat of assorted gear.

"What do you think of her?" Michael asked as he waited for Jake to lock the door behind them.

Jake eyed him coolly. "Her, I like. You, I'm liking less and less. Move it. The lady's waiting."

In silence, Michael followed him to the car. Jake's response had stung, but what could he say? If the truth were told, he didn't like himself all that much either.

"This is what I call a dessert," Jake said later as the waitress at The French Connection eased a bowl of trifle in front of him. The popular restaurant was only half-full for the moment; after dusk, tables would be hard to come by, when the lights were lowered, candles were lit and the pianist at the baby grand crooned tales of loves won and lost. It was Tory's favorite eating place, but she rarely came after a certain hour. She didn't mind dining alone most of the time, but after dark, surrounded by couples, the romantic atmosphere and the empty chair across from her could trigger the onset of melancholia.

She'd agreed to come this time because it was still early and Jake had been insistent. He was as voluble as Michael was silent; Michael had been uncharacteristically subdued all evening, and stirred his coffee now with lackluster enthusiasm. He maintained that he felt fine, but Tory had her doubts. Something was wrong. She longed to lace her fingers through his, if only as a gesture of comfort, but after almost a week of keeping things strictly business, to relent now would be foolish. It was difficult enough sitting in the booth beside him arm-to-arm and thigh-to-thigh. There'd been no choice; Jake left little room for a seatmate. He wasn't overly tall, but he was built like a Mack truck.

"So what do we do now, pardner?" he asked Michael. "Tory's right. It would never occur to me that senior citizens would go for that buddy business, but it obviously fills a need. The woman I talked to—God, what a flirt!—said that helping someone who couldn't walk at all made her forget the arthritis in her knees, that until the staff insisted that they pair off, she was a miserable, self-centered, cranky old broad—her words."

"Muriel Simon," Tory said, recognizing the description. "She wasn't kidding. She used to rain on everybody's parade."

"Well, she's sunshine and roses now. Even if we can't pull it off with Woodland Rise, we'll sure as hell remember it the next time."

Tory forgot her concern with Michael's strange mood. "Why couldn't you do it now? You think Lee—I mean, Mr.

Varnum—would disagree? Bring him here and let him see for himself."

Michael stirred, as if struggling to pull himself out of his lethargy. "He'd agree hands down, Tory. That isn't the problem. The problem is time. We're about out of it. It's too late to redo the detailed drawings."

"What you submit now ties your hands for all time? You can't make any changes at all?"

"No major changes," Jake said, "but we may be able to work something out. An addendum to the narrative? Let me sleep on it."

"Promise?" Tory asked, seeking reassurance.

Jake's hard-boiled features softened. "You're really into this, aren't you? I promise I'll sleep on it, but I can't promise anything else. I never let my mouth write a check that my...uh...butt can't cash."

"A man after my own heart." Helen Stiles stood at Michael's elbow. "Do I need my eyes checked or did I just see you three leaving Silver Acres?"

"Hi, Helen. This is Jake Burnside, Michael's partner. I took them over to show them the buddy system in operation," Tory explained.

"It's a good thing she didn't tell us where she was taking us," Jake said, rising just enough to shake Helen's hand. "Get more than two old folks in a room with me and I get the willies."

"What's the matter, sonny?" Helen asked. "Feel the Grim Reaper breathing down your neck?"

"Me?" Jake was agog. "How old do you think I am, anyway?"

Helen sniffed. "Not nearly old enough to be interesting. You're still damp behind the ears."

Jake seemed truly insulted. "Listen—what's your name? Helen? I can give you a list of fifty women who'd tell you otherwise."

Tory watched, mesmerized by the exchange. There was a subtle difference in Helen she'd never seen before. She was as plain as ever, as angular as ever, her salt-and-pepper hair coiled in its usual haphazard knot atop her head, but the difference was still there. Sultry was a word it would never have occurred to Tory to use in a description of Helen Stiles, but it was the closest she could come. Helen was suddenly softer somehow, a dozen times more feminine, and oozing pheromones.

"Babies." She wrote off Jake's conquests in a single word. "Innocents. I know a grown man when I see one, and you've got some growing to do yet. You even wear a digital watch. Excuse me, there's Millie with my Brandade de Morue. Nice meeting you, sonny." She gave Michael a wink and moved across the room to a table where a single place was set.

"A digital watch!" Jake spluttered. "What the hell's that got to do with anything? Where'd she go? I've got to talk to that woman!" He pried himself out of the booth and steamed toward her, full sail. Glowering at her, he yanked the empty chair away from the table and sat down, hard. Helen raised one brow elegantly and, ignoring him, began to eat her cod.

Michael's eyes danced with laughter. "My God, he left his dessert. I have never seen Jake react to a woman that way. She really got to him. How old is she?"

"Forty-eight," Tory said, shaking off her shock. "Forty-nine at the most. How about Jake?"

"Forty-five in August. God, she played him perfectly, hooked him right in the ego. Who'd have believed it?"

"I shouldn't have been surprised," Tory responded after a moment's thought. "She said she's seen Jake a couple of times when he was here on the weekends. She just didn't know who he was. He reminds her of her husband—he's been dead for years—same build or something."

His smile broadened. "In which case, my man is a goner. Brother, you mountain women are dangerous!"

Tory wasn't sure how to respond to that, but was saved by the approach of a waitress named Carla Ransom, her skin as rich and brown as the chocolate mousse she carried on a tray. The youngest of eight daughters and two sons, one of them Phil Ransom, Carla had been born in a house a mile from the one in which Tory had lived as a child.

She introduced Michael, and Carla nodded. "Philly told us about you. Nice to meet you, Mr. Gallagher. Tory, Mom asked me to check and see if you'd been up home recently. I was gonna call, but since you're here . . ."

"I was there the end of last month." Tory felt a stab of alarm. "Why? Is something wrong?"

"Mom's not sure. That windstorm raised Cain with the trees. She thinks one might have come down across your roof. Daddy would check, but he's not supposed to drive anymore, and Mom can't handle a stick shift. I could see if Clayton—"

"Never mind. I'll run up there myself. Tell your mother I said thanks. How are classes going?"

She wrinkled her nose. "Summer school's the pits, but I'll graduate in December and head right for grad school to get it over with. I'd better go before this mousse turns to mush. See ya." She smiled at Michael, and became the efficient waitress again.

"You have another house?" Michael asked.

"A cabin—but not like Jake's. I mean a real log cabin. My father went through a series of jobs and finally lost the house he and Mom were living in. The only place they had left was the cabin Dad used when he went hunting. That's where I grew up. I go every so often, spend a weekend sometimes when I want to get away. I guess I'd better see about it." Michael would have to leave Sunday to turn in the proposal the next day, she reflected, and she'd probably need some time to herself once he was gone.

"How far is it?" he asked.

"About ten miles, as the crow flies. Driving, it takes about half an hour. Narrow winding roads."

"Then let's go check on it. It won't be dark for a while yet. We can make it."

Tory shook her head. "It can wait. Besides, it's too late. It's going to rain."

Michael leaned over and peered above the half curtain covering the window. "Not a cloud in sight."

"There will be. I can smell it. I'll go in a few days." She sipped her coffee, hoping the discussion was at an end.

"You promised to show me around," he reminded her. "I won't be here that much longer. As soon as you finish the narrative—"

"It's done. I didn't get a chance to tell you, because I had the other thing on my mind."

"That's great, Tory. You're worth twice what you charge. But if it's finished, there's no reason for us not to go now. Please. I'd like to see it."

"What about your leg?" It was her last hope.

"The leg's coming along fine. I need all the exercise I can get. Any other excuses you can think up?"

Tory gazed into eyes as blue as approaching night. He might even leave before Sunday. "All right. We'd better get Jake."

Michael chuckled. "Are you kidding? Look at them." Jake had moved from the chair opposite Helen to the one on her left and sat, elbow on the table, listening as if fascinated by her conversation. "I'll ask if he's interested in coming with us, but I doubt he is." He slid from the booth, helped her out, and picked up the trifle. "Something tells me this will go to waste if I don't take it to him. The way he looks, it may go to waste anyhow. I'll be right behind you."

Praying that Jake would come along, Tory escaped to the car, grateful for the time to herself. She had to be emotionally ready if Michael exited the restaurant alone. He did.

"God, give me strength," she prayed, and leaned over to open the door for him.

Chapter 9

The tree had missed the cabin by inches, but the back steps lay flattened under it, a stack of splintered boards. Grateful that there was no other damage, Tory dismissed it. "I'll call Carla, and Clayton—he's the youngest—can come and chop up the tree," she said. "The Ransoms can use it for firewood this winter. This is what I want you to see." She led him around to the front.

Michael stood and gazed down on the valley below. "This is the most beautiful view I've seen yet."

"Yes, it is. It made up for a lot. We had practically no money, and the only time I ate meat was when Dad managed to shoot something—rabbit, wild turkey, occasionally a deer, but living here made me feel as if our front yard extended as far as I could see."

"I can understand why. It's remote, but I'm surprised you didn't move back here."

"I considered it," Tory said, "but it would be impractical. The businesses I depend on—and who depend on me—would be too far away. And I could be marooned up here in winter.'' She smiled. "I'm glad you like it. Dad hated this place. All he could think about was moving back down there, which is why he bought the house I'm in now.''

"How could he be blind to all this?" Michael asked.

"If you think this is pretty, you should see it from up there." Stepping out into the yard, she turned around and pointed to a spot above the cabin. "Look just above the top of that tree. There's another ledge. I spent many a day in that tree just sitting and looking. I could have fallen climbing from the ledge onto the branches, but it was worth it.''

"Let's go then."

Tory's head snapped down. "You can't be serious! I don't climb trees anymore. Besides, it's an uphill walk all the way, and there's no path or anything. Your leg may be better, but that would be pushing it, Michael. And I told you, it's going to rain soon.''

"You keep saying that, but I don't see any sign of rain. Let me worry about my leg. If it gets to be too much, I'll let you know, Scout's honor.''

He seemed set on it, and a small part of her was glad he was. Even now she considered the ledge her secret sanctuary, and nothing would please her more than sharing it with him. "Okay, but don't say I didn't warn you.''

The woods were thick and the undergrowth heavy, slowing their progress. Tory's high-heeled sandals were a hindrance as well. It was a twenty-minute hike and the sun hung low over the valley by the time they reached their goal. Tory, giving in to a whim as they were about to clear the trees, said, "Humor me, Michael. Give me your hand and close your eyes. I want to lead you to just the right spot.''

"At your command, m'lady." He smiled, acceding to her wishes.

She led him out onto the ledge, as far as it was sensible to go. "All right, we're here.''

Michael opened his eyes, then his mouth, in awe. "My God," he whispered. The panorama at this point was at least a mile wider in each direction. Cedar Hollow, Chestin, and other small towns whose names he'd never know nestled against the horizon, the occasional church spire pointing toward the sky, a glistening exclamation point.

The mountains in the distance were gentle hillocks growing slowly darker, and the sun, a ball of molten bronze, painted the valley in a wash of auburn. Watching the wonder in his eyes, Tory knew that what little contribution she'd made toward the design of Woodland Rise would not be the only thing of hers Michael would take back to the city with him.

His arm slipped around her shoulder. Unresisting, she moved closer, permitting herself this one small liberty. They remained in that position for an endless time, the only reminder of the passing minutes the soft dark shadow spreading across the valley.

"This place has always been my secret," Tory said finally, wanting him to know. "You're the only person I've ever brought up here."

"Am I?" He looked down at her, his eyes almost ebony in the dusk. "Thank you. I'll never forget it. It's..." He broke off, listening. "What the hell is that?"

Only then did Tory realize why his eyes had appeared so dark. She looked above the rugged rocks that lined the face of the mountain behind them. Even as she watched, a boiling slate-gray cloud eased over them, heading out over the valley, dragging sheets of pelting rain in its wake. Thunder rumbled, and the sky turned black. In a matter of seconds, they were drenched.

"Come on!" Tory yelled over the beating rain. Grabbing his hand, she struggled toward the rocks.

"Where are we going?" Michael shouted. "We came from the other direction!"

"Too late! It's going to get worse! Mind your footing!" she warned, as she stepped out of her sandals and tossed them aside. Pulling him along, she climbed, groping for purchase on boulders treacherously slick with rain, until she reached her destination, a deep grotto several yards above the ledge. She was just in time. Lightning streaked across the sky and landed in the valley, a white-hot arrow, its tip embedded somewhere below. Scrambling into the dim recess, she turned and reached down to help Michael over the last hurdle. He heaved himself up into the mouth of the cave and collapsed on his back, gasping for breath.

"If you say 'I told you so,' I'll deck you," he said, when he could finally speak. Sitting up, he scooted away from the opening to place his back against the rough stone wall, and gave a yelp of pain.

"Your leg?" Tory asked, inching over to him.

He shook his head, drops of water flying in an arc around him. "My butt." Leaning to one side, he removed the small sharp stone on which he had sat and hurled it out into the rain.

Tory tried not to laugh, having landed on a burr or two in her day. "If we move farther back, there'll be leaves we can sit on. The wind blows them off my tree right in here."

He got up and followed her toward the rear of the niche, where the ghosts of the previous autumn lay in a heap against the back wall of the cave. Michael knelt, felt them, as if testing their texture, then with several sweeps of a long arm, spread them until they carpeted the hard earth like a patchwork quilt of reds, oranges and browns.

"Well, it's not goosedown," he said, "but it's better than nothing. Here, let me—"

Suddenly the interior of the cave came alive with blinding light, along with a sharp, explosive sound of such volume that the whole mountain seemed to vibrate. The air crackled, sizzled, and the stench of charred matter slammed into the cave. Just outside the opening, the top of Tory's favorite tree burst into flame. The trunk opened lengthwise, exposing its viscera to the elements, shuddered, and with a heartrending groan, died as gravity pulled it down over the edge and out of sight.

"My God," Michael said. "That's about as close as I ever want to be to that much power. If we'd still been out there..."

Tory stared at the empty space where the top of the tree had once sheltered the mouth of the cave, tears blending with the dampness on her cheeks. Another childhood staple gone. Her life seemed to be coming apart, piece by piece. She turned aside, her face taut with pain that had nothing to do with the death of her tree. In a matter of days, she would suffer the most agonizing loss of her life. She moaned without realizing it.

Michael misinterpreted the sound, wrapping his arms around her protectively. "It's okay now. There's nothing else on this ledge for it to hit. Hey, you're shivering." Shifting her a few inches, he unbuttoned his shirt and pulled it off. "It's as wet as you are, but it might help to have something covering your arms." He wrapped it around her and pulled the collar up under her ears. "It swallows you. Lord, you're so tiny, so..."

Tory glanced up and saw his face nearing hers. Before she could move or voice a protest, her words were sacrificed to the pressure of his lips, his mouth seeking hers eagerly, his tongue seeking entrance. No! she thought, and placed her hands against his bare chest to push him away. But the jackhammer pace of his heart under her palm beat off all thought of further resistance. He wanted her!

He mouthed her name, his voice barely audible above the rising wind and lashing rain. Her fingers closed, snaring his nipples in a tender trap, and his reaction was immediate, decisive. Time began playing jokes, squeezing minutes into seconds. She was clothed and then she wasn't, without having lifted a finger, her dress, slip, bra, panty hose gone, in a heap behind her somewhere. Tory stood nude before him, despairing that she couldn't see him clearly. She had no way of knowing whether his face wore disappointment or approval. Michael, with less to remove, skinned his slacks and briefs off in one motion, rolling them into a ball and placing them within the circumference of the cushion of leaves. Tory watched, longing for sunlight, candles, a torch, anything. She wanted to see him, all of him, memorize every detail, etch the picture of his body on her retinas so that no matter how long she lived, his image would be at the center of everything she saw.

Finally satisfied with the placement of his slacks, he stood, turned toward her, then, inexplicably backed away, fists clenched, the cords of muscle in his neck visible even in what little light there was.

"Tory, I can't do this. I can't."

She heard him but refused to credit her ears. "Why?" Her anguished cry echoed against the hard rock walls.

"Don't ask me, Tory. I just can't."

On his final word, a bolt of lightning cut a jagged path across the darkened sky. Michael stood illuminated against the flare of ten million candles, like Thor rising out of the storm and the rain, his long, muscular legs planted as if he stood with his feet riding the waves of separate oceans. It had lasted a fraction of a second and was gone, but in that sliver of an instant, Tory had been granted her wish. She saw him clearly.

There was no mistaking the hunger in his eyes. And he could say what he would with his voice, all she'd had to do was lower her eyes to see that his body put the lie to his words. Everything that was male about him was centered in the juncture between his thighs. Erect, proud, demanding, its vote carried more weight than any statement he made to the contrary.

Tory reacted out of the same primal need that had gripped her that day on the porch of Jake's cabin, when he'd opened the door and she'd seen him, real, vibrant, virile. She had wanted him from that moment and would not be denied now. She hurled herself at him, felt the hard planes of his chest against the soft mounds of her breasts, the rigid presence between his thighs against the slope of her abdomen. He stood frozen, his breathing hissing between his teeth.

She molded his shoulders, his back, his buttocks between her palms as if he were clay. Her hand skirted his hip, slid between their bodies, seeking and finding velvet, iron and heat, throbbing, pulsating with life. Her fingers closed around him, and he inhaled sharply, his nostrils flaring as she drew her hand along the length of him, let her thumb glide across the silken moisture bathing its head.

Something deep inside her screamed with impatience. She'd waited long enough. Raising her arms, she wrapped them around his neck and pulled herself up his body, climbing him until, her legs circling his thighs, she could feel the smooth, hot knob wedged between lips swollen with hunger. Outside, the wind moaned, the sound not unlike the one that escaped with Michael's shuddering breath. "Oh, God," he said, his arms coming around her.

Her face now level with his, Tory pushed her advantage and drew the shape of his mouth with the tip of her tongue, teased the inner tissue of his lower lip, nipped and nibbled, ever mindful of the increasing heat building at the point where firm, smooth muscle butted against soft, honey-damp tissue.

She caught and held his gaze. "Now, Michael," she said, steel hardening her voice, but she couldn't sustain it. "Now," she said again, and it was a plea, raw with need. Ankles locked together, she tightened her grip around his hips. "Please." The word was lost in the hiss of violent rain.

"Tory," he said huskily, "I'll hurt you. You're so small."

Her eyes bored into his. "Am I? How do you know?" she asked, drawing the question out, each word a challenge.

He growled deep in his throat, and his strong hands gripped her waist and lowered her slowly onto his shaft, his gaze riveted on her face. Tory gasped as she felt her body yielding, opening, inviting sweet invasion. She was being stretched, filled, her journey to the base of him and his to the peak of her taking an eternity of ecstatic sensations which he orchestrated with marvelously controlled strength. When she was finally, firmly seated, her yearning pink pearl embedded in the coarse black hair that covered his groin, Tory melted, became soft wax, overwhelmed by a sense of completeness. She sought and found his mouth, her tongue craving the rough texture of his, her ears ringing with the sound of her pulse.

Mouths and bodies still joined, Michael lowered himself to his knees and leaned forward until Tory, clinging to him, lay on her back, her head on the pillow he'd made of his slacks. He settled atop her, and Tory gave a silent shout of joy, his weight a prize she'd hungered for, the reality beyond her capability to imagine. He broke the contact with her lips, and smoothing her hair from her temples, looked down at her, a question in his eyes.

"Yes," she whispered on a sigh.

"Tory, I love you," he said, holding her face between his hands tightly. "No matter what happens, I want you to remember that. I love you."

The despair in his voice blunted her joy. Did he think he was alone in how he felt? Didn't he know? She opened her mouth to shout that she loved him, too, and had from the moment her hand had closed around a small, gold tie clip. The words never came. He shut them off, his first deep thrust taking her by surprise as thunder rolled down the mountain, reverberating against the walls of the grotto. He moved slowly—at first—each withdrawal bringing him dangerously close to loss of purchase, each forward glide taking him to the mouth of her womb where its lips greeted him with a kiss of welcome. He was expert, thorough, deliberate—at first—in its way a well-rehearsed performance. He took his time, as if experience had taught him the necessity of urging his partner to respond. He was wrong.

Tory whimpered, her hips rising at each and every stroke, every muscle straining to participate. Her hands traveled the landscape of his back, squeezed his buttocks, and she gasped at the feel of the power driving him forward. She tested the spring of the curls at his groin, felt the dew—hers—pooling at their roots, eased her hand even lower, spread her fingers so that he slid between them, hard, her touch seeming to shatter his rigid control. His pace quickened, his plunge deepened. His hands, cradling, cupping her breasts, massaged her nipples between his fingers, and Tory began to rocket toward a dimension of heightened sensation.

Flame danced along her skin, burrowed into her pores. She strained toward him, seeking to hold him fast inside, to prevent his escape, yet reveling in his retreat, knowing that a lunge would follow, again, again, again. The leaves crackled beneath them, the wind moaning like a lover in the throes of ecstasy. The rain flailed the earth, thrumming with a steady insistent beat, but still no match for the storm which raged at the site where Tory and Michael were joined.

She had been watching his face, bathed in intermittent flashes of harsh yellow light, memorizing the smoldering passion in his eyes, but his increased rhythm had become too demanding of attention. She gave herself up to it, let it become her master and was given a hint of the reward for her obedience. She felt herself expanding, growing beyond the bounds of her corporal being and gasped for breath, hoping for enough air to sustain her.

Suddenly the process reversed itself. She began to implode, all sensation compacting in a glowing fire in the pit of her stomach. Her back arched, and she reached for the light, for the heat, for Michael, who drove toward her center, watching, watching her, his eyes dark with desire.

"Now, Tory!" he commanded, his movement quick, short, hard, and she cried out, spasms racking her small frame, her voice rising above the rain and wind. Her nails raised welts across his shoulders, her contractions rolling through her like thunder across the sky. Suddenly he came into her with a thrust that carried him beyond sanity, and Tory screamed his name.

He inhaled sharply, his muscles rippling through his torso, through his pelvis, and the engorged sheath embedded in her erupted in a hot, swirling tide. His face was buried in her hair, his muffled groans in her ears. She held him until he quieted, praying that he would never withdraw, never leave her, knowing that sooner or later he would. For the space of several minutes, however, he remained firmly lodged, softer inside her, but there, his respiration slowing. Still, he didn't move, but she did, responding to reawakening hunger, her internal muscles gripping, releasing him, urging, demanding.

His head came up and he looked at her in surprise. She offered no excuse, her legs lifting to enfold him, to increase the pressure, an offer he would be unable to refuse. Accepting it, he pushed into her gently, and their lovemaking continued. Outside, beyond the mouth of the cave, the rain slackened into a muted shower. Then it was over.

"I refuse to take you home looking like this," Michael said, unlocking the door of the cabin and hitting the light switch. "Your reputation would be shot. Jake has a dryer, so let's use it."

"I don't much care about my reputation anymore," Tory responded. "Besides, it's almost dark. Who'd see me?"

"Tory, that's not the point." He crossed to close the draperies. "You're the one who lives here, remember? In a place as small as this, the line between your personal and professional lives is probably not as clearly defined. I'd hate to have your business suffer because someone got the impression—"

"That I sleep around? That I'm a woman of loose morals?" She chuckled, the sound hard, with a bitter edge. "I don't and I'm not, and everyone knows it. Don't forget, you're a local hero and I'm probably the envy of any number of women who'd love to be in my ruined shoes." Moving to the trash can in the kitchen, she removed her sodden sandals and dropped them in. "Sixty dollars down the drain."

"I'll replace them. After all, I didn't listen when you said it would rain." Spotting a sheet of paper on the table, the letters across it big and bold, he picked it up and read it, a smile easing across his face. "I told you. Jake left this. 'I'm in love,' he says. 'See you whenever, but definitely not tonight.' I don't know Helen that well, but from what I saw today, I'd say she's good for him. Is it something in the air, or are all the women up here as enticing as you two?"

"I'd say just the opposite. We aren't enticing enough."

He shot her a probing look. "Having regrets already?"

"No." Now that she knew she needn't be concerned about Jake walking in on her, she shrugged out of her dress and tossed it into the compact dryer, setting the timer for twenty minutes. "How could I regret today?" she asked, her back to him. "It's tomorrow I regret, next week, next month."

He was silent. She heard his footsteps, and after a moment his arms came around her from behind. "I'm really sorry about that. I'm not usually so irresponsible, but making love to you today wasn't something I planned, and I'm not the type of guy who carries protection around in his wallet."

Tory shook her head. "I'm sort of glad to hear it, but that wasn't what I meant. I'll miss you, Michael. I'll hate to see you go."

He pulled her back against him. "You talk as if I've already packed. I'm in no hurry."

She turned around in his arms, confused. "But the narrative, the proposal. Aren't you leaving to turn it in?"

"Haven't you ever heard of the U.S. mail? Actually, for something this time-critical, we use a messenger service. It'll get where it's supposed to go."

Collapsing against him, she buried her nose in his damp shirt, relief weakening her knees. "How long will you stay?"

"I have to be honest, Tory— I don't know. It depends on someone else. A week more, maybe two. At this point, I'm fairly fluid." His eyes narrowed. "In fact, I have an idea. I'll look over the narrative one last time and stick Jake with it. His secretary can type the addendum about integrating the units. Can you take some time off?"

"Oh." Tory backed out of his arms. "Why?"

"Let's go away together. You pick the place." He smiled. "I'd like to get to know the woman I love a little better."

She hesitated, feeling all breath leave her lungs. "That's the second time you've said that."

"There's something *you* should know, darling," he said solemnly. "It's the first time I've ever said it to anyone, and to be honest, I hadn't planned to say it at all. It's a bit rough on a man's ego to fall in love with someone who doesn't love him."

"Doesn't..." Wide-eyed, she stared at him. "You couldn't tell from the way I acted in the cave? I'm not an easy lay, Michael. I don't go for one-night stands. If I didn't love you, I would never have let you so much as touch me."

"You didn't say it."

"You never gave me the chance. I love you, Michael Gallagher. I'm embarrassed to tell you how long I've loved you. But, to paraphrase, it's a bit rough on a woman's ego to fall in love with someone who isn't going to be around."

"God. We've got a lot to talk about, haven't we? Let me get out of these damp clothes, and then... Well, we'll see. The extended weekend sounds like a must for us. Think about it. I'll be back in a flash." He left her and went bounding up the stairs, disappearing through the bedroom door on the left. The day's activities had clearly had no harmful effect on his legs.

Tory slumped against the counter, hugging herself, pinching her arms in disbelief. Things were happening so fast. This morning she'd awakened thinking she had a few more days of keeping herself at arm's length. In the space of fourteen hours, she'd climbed his body, lain under him, held him inside her, screamed his name. He loved her, wanted to go away with her. Knowing he was not the kind of man to take such things lightly, she felt a flicker of hope for the first time since his arrival. But only a flicker.

She couldn't imagine him staying on in the Hollow on a permanent basis, no matter how she tried. And she couldn't imagine herself in the city, any city, where skyscrapers rose from the earth like concrete and brick tombstones, where the emanations of strangers might grind her down under their petty problems, stifling her spirit. Despairing, she turned toward the miniature stove top and saw the kettle, the labels of the tea bags hanging around the rim. She might as well finish what Michael had started.

She removed the bags, found the glass pitcher and set about keeping herself busy. Opening the refrigerator to get a lemon, she gaped at its contents. Lying atop a six-pack of beer was a large brown envelope and several sheets of paper, their corners curling inward. Thermal paper, she noted, on which copies of newspaper articles had been printed. Why would anyone put them here?

Sliding them out carefully, she placed them on the counter behind her and returned to the opened refrigerator, when the headline of the short article on the top sheet registered, the words a branding iron searing into her mind. "Psychic Child Finds Missing Husband."

Whirling around again, she picked it up, scanned the first few sentences, put it down. She flipped through the remainder of the loose ones, emptied the envelope and examined the rest. The memory rose like a phantom before her eyes. This was the envelope Marty had delivered the week before, the envelope that Michael had alleged contained the news about the change in deadline for submitting the proposal. The envelope about which he had lied. He had known who she was since then! And today he'd made love to her.

The pain came first, a blue-white pilot light of anguish, then a blind, unreasoning anger—unreasoning in that it was she who'd set the precedent, she who had lied first, had been lying every day since in not admitting who she was. She knew she had no right to play the role of wounded party, but her anger was beyond bending to the rules of logic and justice. He had been buttering her up, seducing her into being used again, and ah, what a magnificently effective seducer he was. She could still feel her body rocking under his, and she bent over double, her hands clutching her abdomen.

After an excruciating time, the pain subsided, but the hot rage of moments before had been replaced by one of arctic temperature. Her head cleared. She felt razor-sharp, lucid, in control. Snatching open the door of the dryer, she grabbed her dress and pulled it on. Then, gathering the treacherous papers from the counter, she took them to the dinette and placed the sheets one by one around the perimeter of the table, and the envelope in the center. She finished just as the bedroom door above her opened.

Michael, pulling a polo shirt over his head, stepped into the doorway, too far back to be able to see her.

"Tory," he called, "I should have asked—would you like to take a shower?"

"No, thank you." The timbre of her voice was sharpened by ice crystals. "The kind of soil I'm wearing will take a year of scrubbing before I'm clean again."

Puzzled by her choice of words and her tone, he stepped out and crossed to the railing to look down at her. His eyes took in the scene, and the blood drained from his head, leaving him slightly faint for a few seconds. She stood at the end of the table, gazing up at him, with all the evidence laid out before her. Her anger was a palpable force, filling the room, buffeting him. He looked down into her eyes and knew that nothing he said, no lie, no truth, would matter to her now.

"Tory, think back," he said, taking the steps at a cautious pace. A minute before he'd felt like Atlas, strong, sound. Now everything seemed to hurt. "I told you I loved you, and asked you to remember it no matter what came later."

"Oh, I haven't forgotten. I'll never forget it, *never*. And neither will you, because at bottom, you're not normally a liar. Just this time." She was fire and dry ice. Either would have rendered her untouchable; the combination was like a force field he dared not try to breach.

"I meant what I said," he protested, feeling the first nips of anger himself. "But speaking of liars . . ."

"Yes, I lied to you," she said, her voice grating. "It's the only protection I have against the users—people who have no idea how much misery they expose me to, people who wouldn't care, even if they knew, as long as they got what they wanted. You came here to be a user, so I lied."

"That's not fair, Tory. I needed your help—"

"No." She rode right over him. "There's nothing you can say to me. I sensed you were a man of deep-rooted integrity the moment I picked up your tie clip. With the kind of mind you have, once I knew you were looking for me, I realized you must be desperate. You must have hated it, but you came anyway and I respected you for that. But it never occurred to me that you would mangle your integrity, prostitute yourself to get what you wanted."

That couldn't have stung more if she'd slapped him. "I told you I hadn't intended for today to happen."

"Then when was it to happen? What was the schedule? Tomorrow? Friday? You could have had my body any day you picked, Michael, with no strings. I wanted you just that badly. But to play the old 'I love you' game, that's what gets me. You must have detested yourself for pulling that stunt. So that's my retribution, letting you live with that, and letting you find whoever you lost with no help from me." Grabbing her purse, she turned, and in her bare feet, walked out of his life.

Chapter 10

Tory eased her car alongside Helen's vintage VW Beetle with an inch to spare. It was after seven; Helen should have left hours before, especially as it was Friday and Jake would be arriving this evening. Helen's presence was a complication she didn't need. She had a call to make—a private call. Cutting the engine, Tory removed the key from the ignition, set the emergency brake, but did not get out. She sat, leaning against the door, and examined the front of the house.

She spent as little time at home as she could these days, even during office hours, doing more of the legwork while Helen handled the rest. This was how she had avoided being there on the occasions when Michael had driven up to try to see her. But it wasn't just for that reason that she was ducking him. How was it possible that the brief presence—and permanent absence—of one man could make such a difference in the feel of a place? She'd brought him here on Sunday, he'd gone back to the cabin the following Friday, and her house hadn't seemed the same since. Neither had she.

She couldn't even take the same satisfaction in lounging on the deck anymore without thinking of the late evenings they had spent there talking about Woodland Rise.

A month had passed since the day at the grotto, the day her relationship with Michael had reached its zenith and its nadir within the space of a few hours. It had been a long four weeks during which nothing had changed and everything had changed. Michael's presence still permeated the guest room; his cologne seemed to linger, even though she'd aired the mattress, vacuumed, waxed, oiled, tried everything. It was an aroma only she detected. When she'd complained and Helen had come up to check, her friend had sworn it existed in her imagination alone. Was she to live with the clean woodsy scent of him in her mind the rest of her life?

The legacy of pain and anger lingered, too, a permanent part of her existence, like a bad tooth aggravated by the persistence of a probing tongue. She bore it with stoicism. If she could recover from her years in the city, she would recover from this. The reminders were a constant problem, however, particularly in the specter of Helen and Jake; it was only a matter of time before they would be married. Helen emanated a serenity that Tory envied, but she couldn't begrudge her one moment of happiness; her friend had been alone too long. The thought that Helen might be moving away increased Tory's sense of isolation, even before the fact. The cocoon was slowly closing around her again, but leaving her with none of the contentment and companionship she'd enjoyed before.

Getting out of the car, Tory collected the bags from the hatch and, lacking even the energy to climb the steps to the front door with her groceries, headed for her office entrance. Helen opened it before she could turn the knob.

"Where have you been?" she demanded fretfully.

Surprised at her vehemence, Tory kicked the door closed. "What's wrong? I told you I had several errands to run. Why are you still here?"

"I was just worried, that's all. Here, let me take one of those for you." She reached to help with her friend's burdens.

Tory evaded her, unable to remember which bag the book she'd bought was in. "I can manage. They're not heavy."

Helen eyed the print across the brown sacks. "You've been all the way to Frederick?"

"I had to pick up the new font cartridge for the laser printer, so I figured I might as well shop there and save myself a stop on the way home." Tory bustled up the steps, wondering how to wangle the privacy she'd need to unload the bags. The trip to Frederick had been intentional; she could go to a clinic and see a doctor without worrying about running into someone she knew. Had she gone to all that trouble for nothing? Why was Helen fluttering around her like a bird whose nest was in danger of invasion?

"Where's the bag from Frederick Computers?" Helen asked. "Did you leave it in the car?"

Tory slid the sacks onto the counter. "All right, Helen, what's up? What's going on?"

Helen made a three-hundred-sixty-degree turn, paced to the door of the deck, came back. "Oh, to hell with it. I told him I'd be no good at this sneaky stuff."

Tory frowned. "He who? Michael?"

"No, not Michael. Look, can we talk?"

"Sure, with the understanding that there's one topic that's off-limits."

"If you mean Michael, it's a deal. But he's not the only topic that's off-limits with you, and that's what I want to talk about." Helen's earnest expression made Tory realize the extent of her friend's concern. "Will you let me give you my honest opinion about . . . something?"

Tory's resistance was short-lived. How could she deny the person who'd been the closest to her these last few years? "Of course you can. Let's sit down. The groceries can wait."

Helen seemed to relax a little. Slipping into a chair, she folded her hands and waited for Tory to peel off her gloves and take the chair opposite. Focusing on her face, Tory wondered how she could ever have thought of Helen as plain. Her brown eyes sparkled, her skin was clear and glowing. She wore the same unkempt topknot, but there was a sheen to her hair that had gone unnoticed before. Love became her.

"I've never asked what happened to you in the city that would make you come back and squirrel yourself away up here," Helen said. "I'm not asking now. But if there's an eighth deadly sin, Tory, it's wasting one's ability, and you're committing it. I think you're being very selfish with a God-given talent."

Tory stood up and walked over to the window, shaken that Helen would plead Michael's cause, even by indirection. There was only one way to make her understand. It was simply a question of how much to tell her. "I bought a new keyboard for the computer," she said.

"I saw it. I wondered why you'd buy it and then stick it in the closet, but what's that got to do with what we're talking about?"

"Everything. I use the word processor most of the time—you use the computer almost exclusively. A couple of weeks ago Rich Stoddord dropped off his budget projections and I started setting up his spreadsheet—on the computer. That's when I realized there'd be a problem. I went out and got the new keyboard the next morning. I've been using it ever since."

"But the old one's connected when I arrive every afternoon," Helen said. "I must be missing something."

"I didn't." Tory turned to face her. "I sat down at the old keyboard that Rich left, and got it all—the sadness you felt at saying goodbye to your husband's memory, your relief at not being alone anymore, your passionate love for Jake, your concern that you may be a passing fancy for him because you're older than he is, and you think you're not pretty.''

Helen had turned pale as Tory began her list of emanations from the keyboard. Now her cheeks were flushed. "Oh, God, I'm mortified!" A dawning awareness made her features go slack. "And so sorry. I've been trying not to talk about Jake and me, which has been hell, but I didn't want to make you feel any worse than you do. And all the time you've known...even things I probably wouldn't have told you."

Tory nodded. "You're in a muddle about a lot of it, but the bottom line is that you're in love and deliriously happy. And I'm really, truly happy for you. I told you about the keyboard to help you understand. Unless I'm on guard, for all practical purposes I'm a soul reader. That's where people keep their innermost secrets, their most intense emotions. People don't want you reading their souls, Helen. *I* don't want to read their souls. I have enough trouble with mine."

Helen frowned. "I didn't realize that's the way it works. I guess I was thinking of the glamour, the personal satisfaction of finding someone who's lost."

"Personal satisfaction?" Tory, after a silence spent weighing a very important decision, shoved her hands in her skirt pockets. "Helen, I've never talked to anyone about this. About four or five months before I came back to the Hollow, Dad and I were in Baltimore—the reason isn't important—and we stopped at a corner grocery store on the outskirts. As Dad was paying, I saw a teddy bear lying under the vegetable stand. The only other people in the store were a lady with a little girl, and I assumed the little girl had dropped it, so I got down on all fours to pull it out. As soon as I touched it..." She hesitated and shivered, remembering.

"It wasn't the little girl's?"

"No, it belonged to a little boy. You have to understand, Helen. If I'm holding something that's precious to someone who's under a great deal of stress, I...in a way I become part of that person, feel everything he does, see whatever he does. What I got from the teddy bear sent me into hysterics. The child was confused, terrified. He was trapped somewhere. All, I— I mean, all he could see was a sliver of daylight, and a tall, brick building with tiny balconies on each floor, as if he...as if *we* were looking outside through a crack in a door. Everything was deadly quiet, no sounds at all. And I couldn't sense his name. It was as if no one had ever called him anything."

"But you could tell where he was," Helen said.

Tory, caught up in the memory, refused to be rushed. She had to insure that Helen understood the reasons for the choices she'd made with her life. "Dad called the police, who kept insisting no one had reported a child missing. Meanwhile, the boy kept slipping in and out of consciousness. He—we were shivering, so cold. It had been a wicked winter. It was maybe twelve degrees that day. I knew we had to hurry, that he couldn't last much longer, but no one would listen.

"Finally I ran outside. There was a vacant lot directly across the street, and in the next block beyond that, six tall, dilapidated apartment buildings around a center courtyard. You could tell that most of them were empty. They were moving people out because they were going to be torn down. I knew that was where the child was, and I didn't wait for Dad and the policeman. I took off running."

"But you found him." Helen leaned forward in her chair, her arms wrapped around herself.

"I stood in that courtyard and looked up." Tory stopped, swallowed. This was harder than she'd expected. "They were all alike, Helen. Look at one and you were looking at the others. I simply couldn't tell which apartment building he was in, which building he was seeing from his vantage point. Something told me that he was too cold to be inside, he had to be on one of the balconies. Half of them were full of debris and trash—he could have been on any of them and would never be seen. I ran into the nearest building, crying, ripping in and out of vacant apartments, banging on the doors of people who still lived there. When I could get onto the balconies, I could see what he saw—there, and there, and there." She turned, pointing to imaginary structures. "All, just alike.

"I ran through three of those buildings, Helen, from bottom to top. I was frantic, because I kept losing touch with him. The cold was so agonizing, he had to have been outdoors for hours and hours. It was like being cut with a thousand little razors."

"Tory, stop, please." Helen held up her hands. "I've heard enough."

"No. You haven't." Pausing, Tory took a deep breath. "I was heading for the fourth building when . . . when he died. I went through it all with him, Helen, felt the slowing, the brain gasping for breath, the body shutting down. I don't remember the rest of that day—or the month, actually."

Helen, her face talc white, her eyes filled with tears, bit her lips.

"He was a deaf-mute who lived in one of the buildings and had gotten himself trapped in a discarded upright freezer on the balcony of a vacant apartment. The catch on the door was defective. The people who'd left it said sometimes the catch would release and other times it would hang so you could only open it a crack. That's what had happened. No one was sure how long he'd been there—one of those cases where his mother thought he was with his grandmother, the grandmother thought he was with the baby-sitter, and vice versa."

"My God, the poor baby. It must have been awful for you, too."

"I broke, went to pieces, checked out on reality and missed Christmas altogether that year. By the time I got out of the hospital, the forsythias had bloomed." She sat down again, dry-eyed, her throat tight with strain. "Dad took me to our plush high-rise apartment, and I packed my bags. I told him I was going home. He came with me, but only because he thought that sooner or later things would go back to the way they'd been for the past nine years, with little Tory playing bloodhound to please him and fill his pockets."

"He charged people?"

Tory nodded. "Raking in all the market would bear, which I didn't find out until after he died. But I swore when we left for the Hollow that I would never put myself through anyone else's agony again and never chance that kind of vicarious dying again. If that makes me selfish, I don't care. And I stay out of Washington and Baltimore—any big city—because I still have nightmares about running through those buildings. The sight of a high rise . . ." She shuddered. "Some people experience vertigo looking down from a tall building. For me, it's looking up at one. I can't tell you what it does to me."

"Oh, Tory." Helen got up and hugged her. "Forgive me. I had no right. I never dreamed . . . But why didn't you explain to Michael?"

"I've never been able to talk about it. If we'd had enough time together, I might have, but it's too late now. There's too much garbage between us."

"So toss it in the can where it belongs."

Startled, Tory jumped up, sending her chair crashing to the floor. Jake stood in the doorway, having come up from her office. "I didn't knock," he said apologetically, "because I thought I was expected."

Helen crossed and kissed him quickly. "She got home late, and I didn't get a chance to tell her you were coming. He wanted to talk to you, Tory. I was suppose to butter you up so you'd listen. The plans have changed, honey. Leave her alone."

"Why are your eyes red?" he demanded.

"Because I've been crying, and the reason's none of your business. Come on, we're going."

"Can I at least say hello, for God's sake?" Jake asked with a wounded expression.

"Hi, Jake." Tory smiled, but her heart wasn't in it.

He swaggered over to upright the chair and peered at her intently. "You look pretty good, a helluva lot better than Michael. Honey," he said over his shoulder to Helen, "mind waiting in the car?"

Helen's brows came down. "I'm serious, Jake. The little chat's off. There's a damn good reason for everything she's done, and we need to leave her alone and respect her decision."

"Maybe when I know the reason, I'll be able to do that. This is too important for me to walk out of here without having said what I came to say."

"You won't take my word for it?" Helen asked, her color high.

Tory knew a fight brewing when she saw it. "Wait a minute. I don't want to be responsible for a lover's spat. I'll listen, Jake. It won't do any good, but I will listen."

He yanked a chair from the table, turned it around backward and sat down. "Do you love Michael?" he demanded.

It wasn't a question she'd anticipated, but there was no reason to lie. "Yes. I do."

"Then this is stupid. You're hurting, he's hurting. You can't tell me there isn't a middle ground you could meet on."

"There isn't. If he's hurting, it's because he failed in what he came here to do. He'll get over it. He'll have to, because I can't help him."

"You mean you won't." Jake's eyes hardened with anger. "What if I told you that he's given up on Lee and—"

Her hand, playing with a saltshaker, froze. Salt poured freely, forming a tiny white mountain. "What do you mean? Did they have an argument?"

Jake's head shot forward on his thick neck. "God Almighty. He never told you? You didn't either?" He turned on Helen, then back to Tory. "It's Lee he wanted you to find."

"Lee? Michael said he was away, and I assumed he meant out of town, out of the country. He didn't talk as if the man was missing."

"Well, he is. Went sailing almost three months ago and disappeared. Michael's been eating guilt three times a day because he was supposed to have gone with him and canceled at the last minute. He's blown thousands of dollars paying a private investigator who hasn't come up with so much as a whisker. I feel partly responsible for what happened up here because I'm the one who talked him into looking for you."

Tory rounded on him, astonished. "You?"

"I'm going," Helen said. "If I stay, I'll kill him. I'll wait in the Ferrari."

"How long ago did I ask you to do that, huh?" Jake yelled as she left, slamming the door behind her. "God, she's terrific!" He grinned, then returned to the subject. "My Dad and I remembered you from way back. It was a farfetched idea, but we figured it was worth a try. Michael had come to the end of the line. That's the only reason he agreed to try to find you."

All of Tory's muscles went slack and she plopped into a chair. "But the plans, Woodland Rise. I don't understand."

"That's another reason Michael wouldn't give up. This is Lee's baby, but without his signature on the detailed drawings before the end of the month, Woodland Rise is so much paper and nothing more."

"But all that work, all that effort..."

"Tell me about it. I have to be honest, Tory, I think the man's dead, otherwise nothing would stop him from getting back to see the project through. So it's finished. Michael's my concern now. He doesn't care anymore—about whether Lee's dead or alive, about Woodland Rise, about anything. All he cares about is you."

"Jake," Tory said, fixing him with a steady gaze, "Lee will always stand between us, in one form or another. If his body turns up, Michael will never forgive me for not confirming that he was dead. If Lee walked in the door tomorrow, says he decided to sail around the world, Michael will never forgive me for not confirming he was alive."

"Yes, he would. Damn it, Tory, the man loves you! I know him!"

"And I," Tory said, "know him in a way no one else ever will. Lee's part of him, and he'd do anything to find him, *anything,* even if it meant ... Never mind. I can't help him, Jake. And that's what he really wants from me." Getting up, she wiped the salt from the table. "Don't believe for a second that Michael's given up hope that Lee's alive. Nothing else is acceptable to him. As long as he has that, his guilt that he didn't go with Lee is manageable."

"But what if he is alive?"

Tory turned to face Jake. "He just might be. Did it ever occur to you that Lee might have disappeared intentionally?"

"No. He wouldn't do that. Sabotage Woodland Rise? His baby? Not Lee."

"You're speaking of the same man who sabotaged his daughter's first job, one she'd found on her own, one that would give her true independence."

"You're joking."

"Michael told me. I'm sure Lee felt he had a good reason for doing it, but Leslie was his baby, too, literally, and he sabotaged her. He wouldn't let her go. All I'm saying is that you never know what influences people to do anything. It's possible he just walked, or sailed away for reasons he feels are valid."

The expression on Jake's face made it clear she'd hit a nerve. Jumping up, he walked away, came back, running his thick fingers through his hair. "He wouldn't," he muttered to himself, clearly agitated. "That's too incredible to believe."

"What, Jake?" Tory asked gently, knowing that his thought processes were causing him a good deal of discomfort.

"Michael was leaving the firm as soon as construction began on Woodland Rise. Lee's known his plans for a long time and tried his best to convince Michael to stay." He stopped pacing. "Tory, Lee's a great man with a big heart, but he is possessive as hell. Would he pitch Woodland Rise and everything else out the window, pull a stunt like this, just to keep Michael on board?"

Tory pulled in a deep breath. "All I can say from painful, personal experience is that people walk away for reasons that seem bizarre to someone else. I sincerely hope he's not trying to take advantage of Michael's loyalty. It will do an incredible amount of damage."

"You're telling me?" He gazed down at the floor for a long moment, then shrugged hopelessly. "Well, regardless, I tried. You definitely won't change your mind?"

"About helping to find Lee?" Tory shook her head. "Ask Helen to tell you why, but I want your promise that you won't pass it along to Michael. He's wearing enough guilt, and this might make it worse. I'd just as soon he thought of me as a heartless, selfish bitch. I can live with that."

Jake closed in on her and clasped her in a bear hug. "What a mess. Well, let me go make up with Helen." He started out, hesitated, and then turned around. "By the way, Michael left a Waterman fountain pen and pencil set up here somewhere. They're in a leather case, the kind of thing a man sticks in his shirt pocket. If you come across it, give it to Helen or just drop it in an envelope and mail it to the office. Don't touch it with your bare hands or you'll have blue fingers for weeks. It leaks."

"Thanks for the warning. And thanks for caring about Michael. He's lucky to have a friend like you."

"That's debatable. Take care, Tory." He trotted down the steps, and a minute later the Ferrari roared to life, followed by the familiar clackety-clack of Helen's Beetle. They drove away, and Tory became aware again how loud silence could be. She unloaded the groceries, put them away and took the book she'd bought, *Nine Months of Miracles,* into the bedroom, closing the door behind her. She had a call to make, to the clinic for the results of the test she'd had taken this morning. They'd promised an answer by this evening.

As far as Tory was concerned, verification was simply a matter of form, a case of making it official. She already knew, had known from the second Day One had ended. Miss Regular as Clockwork, who had never been late or missed a period since the onset of puberty, was pregnant.

Michael crammed the last of his books into the carton, sealed and marked it, and shoved it against the wall. He'd spent the week packing, and now it was all done. After satisfying himself that he hadn't missed anything, he stepped out onto his balcony. It was almost dark, but Washington was still sweltering, the July heat and humidity trapped below the clouds. After only a minute outside, his face gleamed with perspiration. Manhattan could be just as stifling, but he would miss the Potomac-scented mugginess.

He hoped Jake would forgive him for ducking out without saying goodbye; he hadn't even mentioned that he was packing, but then he hadn't mentioned much of anything the past couple of weeks. It was over—Tory, the job, Woodland Rise, the years with Lee. Lee was dead. Period. He'd been stupid to hang onto a futile hope for so long, stupid to let it cloud his thinking so much that he would risk the love of the only person who'd come to matter more to him than the old man.

He had called, left messages on her answering machine, which Helen—via Jake—said she'd cut off as soon as she recognized his voice. He'd driven up there three times, twice to encounter Dobbins standing guard at the end of her block, promising to shoot him if he drove a foot farther, once to find her gone, the house unlocked and empty. Taking the main chance, he'd scoured the guest room and office trying to find the Waterman set. It wasn't there. He'd left a note for Helen, but she hadn't been able to find it either. Perhaps it was just as well he'd lost it. It put an end to things. Now he was leaving. This was his last night in Washington, and the way things were stacking up, it would be a long, last night.

He and insomnia had become bosom buddies since his return from the mountains. If he closed his eyes, she was there, writhing under him, purring with ecstasy, her small, tanned body rising to meet his in perfect synchronization, as if she already knew the pattern and rhythm of his movements even before they were executed. With that kind of memory alive in his mind, sleep was impossible. What was the point of stretching out on the sofa to stare at the ceiling all night, when he could just as well leave the key with the manager so she could let the movers in tomorrow? He could toss a couple of bags in the car and head north. There was nothing else to keep him here.

His belongings would be going into storage here until he found a place in New York. Except for Jake and Leslie, both of whom were crazy in love, which made them difficult to be around, there was no one else to say goodbye to. Why not just cut the cord and go? Why the hell not?

Tory stood on a step stool, replacing the bug light outside her front door and grumbling at herself for having forgotten to do it earlier. It could have waited until morning, but closing up the house for the night, she'd felt the weight of darkness more keenly than ever before. A full, bright moon didn't seem to help. She felt vulnerable and alone, and the only immediate remedy was to push the night a few feet from the house with the help of the light she should have replaced a week ago.

She gave it one last twist, reached inside, turned it on, and smiled bitterly to herself. A light bulb working as it should was the one good thing to have happened today—a sorry state of affairs. She climbed off the step stool and placed it inside, still not ready to lock herself in yet, even though it was nearing eleven. She sat down on the stoop, elbows on her knees, chin propped on her fists.

How would she fill this weekend, keep herself busy? She'd cleaned the house and office soon after Helen and Jake had left, telling herself she might as well get an early start, knowing all the while that the point of the exercise was to search for Michael's pen again. She had done it first, fairly superficially, after she'd arrived home to find the note he'd left for Helen, had known even before she'd seen the handwriting that he'd been there. His cologne hadn't been a figment of her imagination that time. She'd been more concerned with ridding the house of his fragrance than searching for a pen she would surely have seen by then, and it had taken two days with the air-conditioning off and the windows open before she could no longer detect his essence. This time, however, she had made an exhaustive search for the Waterman. If it was around, she wanted it out of her house, out of her life. She had all the reminders of Michael Gallagher she needed. And search she had, guest room, bath, kitchen, living room, deck, office—every place she knew he had been, even her car. She'd found nothing to match Jake's description.

Sitting on the front steps now, the cool night air fanning her arms and legs, Tory made a vain attempt to relax. The conversations with Helen and Jake had drained her, and the results of the call to the clinic had added to her emotional fatigue. If she could just relax, let everything go, she might be able to sleep.

Cricket song and the sighing of the wind became a lullaby, and after fifteen minutes she was ready to head for bed. She stood up, stretched, heard distant thunder and knew with sudden certainty where the pen was, the only place it could be. The grotto. If it had been in a pocket of his shirt or slacks, it could easily have fallen out and become buried under the leaves.

Tory covered her face with her hands, snatched them away, jumped up and dashed inside.

She couldn't do it, she couldn't go back there.

Yanking off her gown, she rooted in a drawer, found a T-shirt and pulled it on.

She'd said goodbye to the grotto a month ago. It held too many memories, the last more vivid than ever.

Upending the hamper, she found the jeans in which she'd cleaned the house earlier and stepped into them.

What difference did it make anyway? Jake said it leaked. Why keep a pen that leaked, for Pete's sake?

Tory tied the laces of her running shoes, grabbed purse and gloves from the hall table, the big utility flashlight from its hook beside the circuit breakers in the kitchen, closed and locked the front door, and fifteen seconds later, was roaring out onto Arbor Road.

Once she'd reached it, Tory didn't remember the drive up to her cabin, except for the brightness of the moon, the only illumination on the narrow mountain road. She took the flashlight, the denim jacket she'd left on the back seat the week before, and almost strangled herself trying to get out of her seat belt.

She had no hesitation about taking the path to the higher ledge in the dark. This was her domain; she could have made the trip blindfolded. She arrived in record time, sending any number of night creatures scurrying for cover. On the ledge, she used the flashlight to survey the lay of the land now minus the tree that had been her landmark to find the cave.

This is crazy. There's no reason this can't wait until morning. If you fall, you might never be found. This is your secret place, remember? No one ever comes here but you.

Shining her light on the boulders she'd have to climb, she began her ascent, checking each handhold for a secure grip before pulling herself up. She'd done this, too, visited her rocky nest at night, especially in summer when the heat in the cabin had driven her to take sanctuary in a place where Mother Nature supplied the air-conditioning. She made it to the mouth of the cave with no trouble, hesitated, then, with flashlight lit, walked into the grotto.

At first the silence was as she remembered it from her childhood—the only sound that of her own breathing. After a second, however, she could hear it, if only in her mind—her soft cries, the crackle of the leaves beneath her back, the luxuriously wet sounds as their bodies met, separated, met again. Michael's groans, her name on his lips at the explosive moment of his climax. It was still here, trapped in the rock walls. And it hurt to hear it, a hurt that surpassed any pain she'd ever experienced. She had to find the pen, get out of here and never come back.

There was no way to miss it. The wind had scattered the bed she and Michael had shared, pushing it back into the rear as they'd first found it. The slender leather case lay in plain sight now. She considered wearing gloves to retrieve it, but saw no point in that now. It was six weeks too late. Stooping, she picked it up and went rigid with shock. It wasn't Michael's pen. It was Lee's.

"Damn you!" Tory screamed, hurling the case against the wall. "Damn all of you!" She sank to her knees and began to sob, still swearing—at Michael for being so easy to love, at Jake, for playing the game and not mentioning that the pen in question was not Michael's, at Lee for having induced such fierce loyalty in Michael, at Lee for being alive. She hadn't gotten much from the narrow kidskin sheath, just enough to reveal his living, breathing presence. A bubble of hatred welled in her throat. How could he have done this to Michael? Why couldn't he have let him go, as fathers should their sons? And how could she live with his treachery, knowing how firmly guilt was now embedded in Michael's soul?

What should she do? It was obvious he had no idea where he had lost it. He had undoubtedly brought it for her to use for this exact purpose, but it was also probably as precious to him as the tie clip. If she sent it to him, he would know she had handled it, would know she had the answers he needed. Marty. She'd ask Marty to send it with a note saying he had found it. That would get her off the hook.

It took her several minutes to find it again; this time it was truly buried among the leaves. Since the damage was already done, she slipped the pen from the leather sleeve and held it tightly, curious to see if she could verify her suspicions about Lee's reasons for disappearing. She wanted to be right, wanted a valid reason for hating him.

That was her second mistake of the night. As soon as it settled into the creases of her palm, she knew she had run out of choices. Lee was alive, yes, but he was also alone, weak, in pain. Wherever he was, he couldn't move. Lee Varnum was very close to dying.

Tory put the pen down and let the darkness surround her. The specter of sharing a second death closed in on her, burrowed through her pores, gnawed at the marrow of her bones. She was terrified, remembering the last time. How could she go through that again?

But how could she abandon Lee, knowing what she knew now? His memories of Michael, even more so than of Leslie, had sustained him all this time. He was counting on Michael to rescue him. Could she live with that on her conscience? But telling Michael what she sensed might do more harm than good, because for the first time in her experience, she had no idea where the person whose soul she had invaded might be. Not only was he far away, his surroundings were completely alien. How could she tell Michael that Lee was alive, but that she doubted she could find him? And if by some miracle she did but they were too late, Michael would truly hate her, with good reason.

Tory retrieved the pen and slid it back into its holder. She had to tell him. She had to try. She could no more turn her back on Lee than she could have left Danny Baggett to drown. But she had to hurry. There wasn't much time left.

She made it back down to the car at a reckless pace. There was no reason to stop at home, she reflected as she buckled herself in. She knew Michael's address; he'd left it in the note. The note! Her hand froze on the key in the ignition. The note had been addressed to Helen, the instructions very pointed: Helen, not she, was to look for it. Helen, not she, was to wrap it and send it to him by mail or by Jake. He hadn't wanted her to touch it, and she'd assumed he was so angry at her that he didn't want her handling any of his possessions again. He hadn't meant that at all!

If she'd found it, she would have inadvertently done precisely what he had originally wanted her to do, and he'd tried to make sure it didn't happen. Jake was right. Michael had to care about her far more than he did about Lee. But if Lee died now...

Tory headed for Washington, playing havoc with the speed limit. She wasn't really sure where she was going; she hadn't been to Georgetown in years, but she knew the general direction. The highway was the easiest part of the trip and, oddly enough, she found the suburbs of Washington more claustrophobic than the city, once she crossed into it; outside the capital, apartment buildings rose like brick monoliths whereas in Washington, with its unyielding height limitations, the buildings were lower, less threatening.

Her sense of being up against a deadline became more and more oppressive, leaving her hands sweaty, especially after she realized that the urgency to beat the clock related to Michael, not Lee. She grasped for reasons; she'd never experienced this kind of dread before.

By the time she reached Georgetown, Tory was lightheaded with panic, a foreboding clutching at her heart. Her sense of Michael's presence, which she had perhaps taken for granted, was growing fainter. Was he in his car, speeding away from her, or had he severed his emotional ties with her so completely that she had no signal to home in on? How could it be happening at all? She held nothing of his, and Lee's pen was in the pocket of her jacket.

Paying no attention to street names, traffic signs, directional signals, Tory barreled toward an apartment building sitting high on a hill along the C & O Canal. Braking to a halt in front of it, she scrambled out with just enough presence of mind to turn off her headlights and lock the car.

The glass doors to the lobby remained firmly closed, and she pounded on them, startling a dozing security guard. He opened it, his brows lowered in consternation.

"Don't you know you could have broken the glass?" he barked, perhaps to put the lie to the sleep in his eyes. "Who do you want to see, anyway?"

"Michael Gallagher," she said breathlessly. "Please, which apartment is he in?"

He rocked back on his heels. "That's confidential. The way it works, I call on the intercom and ask if it's all right for you to go up. In this case, I won't have to bother. He's gone. The manager said he told her he was leaving and to let the moving men in in the morning—this morning, that is. Sorry, miss."

"He can't be gone!" Tory cried. "Not yet. I'd know it!"

He gave her the kind of look that clearly indicated he thought he was dealing with a mental case. "Well, I'm sorry, but—"

The elevator door on the right opened, and Michael stepped out, a suitcase in his hand. He saw her and stopped, surprise arcing around him like a force field. "Tory!"

She darted past the security guard. "He's alive, Michael! Lee's alive! But he's sick or hurt or something, he's just barely alive. And oh, God, Michael, I don't think I can find him!" Unable to control herself, Tory burst into tears.

Michael dropped the bags, pulled her into his arms, and held her, not as a person offering comfort but as a man bursting with elation at seeing the woman he loved. He wiped her tears with his thumbs and kissed her even as she sobbed.

"Watch my bags, will you, Harry?" he said over her head. He pushed the button, the elevator door whispered open, and he took her upstairs to his apartment.

Megan Gallagher, Michael decided, was right. His mother had believed in miracles. So, now, did he, he reflected, feel-

ing the warmth of Tory's small body against his. All night
he had delayed leaving, eyeing his bags beside the door. All
night something had been building, a tension, a sense of
anticipation, the unreasoning conviction that he should
wait, that something was in the wind. Not once had he associated the premonition with Tory, not even, if he were
truthful, with Lee. He hadn't been able to pin down the
source of it and finally, disgusted with himself, had picked
up his luggage, locked the door behind him and had said
goodbye to his old life.

Lee alive? Now that he knew, his relief was total, months
of anxiety flowing from his body with the pulsating force of
arterial blood. His insistence that if the old man were dead,
he would know, had been justified. That it mattered so
much that his instincts had been right proved something
about himself he had yet to understand. For the moment,
however, he needed to concentrate on Tory.

Her tears slowed. With nothing available except toilet
tissue, he dabbed at her eyes and sat her down on the couch,
a finger pressed against her lips. "Before you say anything,
I want to say something for the record. I love you, Tory. I
set out to make you fall in love with me and got caught in
my own trap. From then on, you were more important than
Lee."

"I know," Tory said. "Oh, Michael, I do love you. I'm
so sorry about everything, and I'll explain later why I lied
to you, but now—"

"Don't feel you have to do that, darling," he cut her off.
"After I thought about it, which I admit I didn't do until it
was too late, I realized you had to have a very good reason,
and I tried my damndest to find Lee's pen so you wouldn't
come on it accidentally. I even searched the house that day
I left the note for Helen. Where was it?"

"In the cave. Michael we—you and I—can wait. Lee
can't. He's hurt—something about his leg—and very weak.
I think he's close to dying, Michael. The problem is, he's so

far away. His surroundings are completely unfamiliar. I...I don't think I can find him."

"His surroundings? You can see what he sees?" When she nodded, he was again reminded of his mother. Tory was a miracle in itself. "Describe what's around him."

She held the pen, her eyes closed tightly, then opened them. "He's asleep now. All I can do is tell you what I saw in his memory. Water—not deep, because, there are reeds and cattails growing up out of it. Lots of trees, some I've never seen except in pictures and I can't remember what they're called. The roots are above the water."

"Wait a minute. Let me get a sketch pad." He found the appropriate box and ripped it open.

Tory looked around, apparently noticing the cartons for the first time. "I thought the guard downstairs was handing me a line. You really are moving?"

"Yes, to New York," he said, found a mechanical pencil and took it to her. "Try to draw the tree. It might give us a clue."

"New York," she said softly, some of the sparkle fading from her eyes. Lowering her head, she began her task, Lee's pen in her left hand, the pencil in her right.

There was more of the artist in Tory than she realized. Michael recognized the genus immediately. "That's a kind of cypress."

"Lots of them, and there are others I've never seen around here either. They remind me of palm trees, except their trunks are different." The pencil darted, danced, the lines taking shape as he watched.

"Palmettos?" He frowned. "That's odd. It means he's a damned sight farther south than I would expect him to be. Anything else?"

"Wait." Tory's voice coarsened with stress. "He's waking up. Michael, he's in such pain. Oh!" She stood up suddenly, her eyes wide and staring into the distance. The sketch pad slid to the floor.

"What is it?" He watched, fascinated by the process.

"A searchlight?" Her brow furrowed. "No. A lighthouse! The beam is horizontal, sweeping in a circle."

"A lighthouse? Palmettos and cypresses? Where the hell is he? Florida? No, wait a minute. Lee used to own a summer house in South Carolina, on the coast. I remember him talking about the mystique of a lighthouse he could see from the bedroom. But he sold that place years ago. I can't remember exactly where it was, though." Eyes closed, he massaged his temples, but finally shook his head. "I don't dare call Leslie. I don't want to get her hopes up if we are too late. Let me call a few of my sailing friends." He reached for the phone.

"Michael, it's after three."

"They can sleep late in the morning. From what you're feeling, we can't wait."

It took four calls and listening to a lot of imaginative swearing, but when he pushed the phone away, he had an answer. "The lighthouse is on Sullivan's Island, south of Charleston. According to Ray, Hurricane Hugo made a mess of the place. Even so, if Lee ran aground there, why wouldn't someone have found him?"

"No, no," Tory said. "The lighthouse is in the distance."

Michael felt a tightness across his chest. "God, I wish I could put my hands on my atlas, but I can't remember which box it's in. If we went down there, say, to Charleston, do you think you could home in on his location?"

"Maybe, but we've got to leave soon. I think his stamina's giving out. So's mine."

He saw signs of strain around her eyes and mouth, the sheen of perspiration across her forehead. "Tory, are you all right?"

She hesitated. "It's not me, it's him. Please, let's go. I'm not sure I can survive a second death."

"A second? Wait a minute. What the hell does that mean?"

"This is crazy. I haven't talked about this in ten years and I wind up telling it twice in one day. I was linked to a little boy I was trying to find. I was with him, I mean, *in* him when he died."

"No wonder you didn't want to do this. You don't have to, Tory. Now that I have some idea where to look . . ."

"Yes, I do have to. I'm committed now. When do we leave?"

"We'll have to fly—driving would take too long. A pilot I know owes me a favor. I think it's time he paid it. Why don't you stretch out until I've made the arrangements?"

Nodding agreement, she fell over sideways and curled into a knot, one hand massaging her thigh. Her face was flushed, her breathing shallow, her eyes slightly glazed, as if she were feverish. That this was what Lee was experiencing was bad enough; to see Tory sharing that agony was worse. This was what he had wanted to put her through? What would happen if Lee died before they found him? Would she die, too? He was too terrified to ask.

With a sick feeling in the pit of his stomach, Michael picked up the phone. If he lost Lee now, it would hurt him terribly, but he could take it. If he lost Tory, too, he would never be able to live with himself.

Chapter 11

Michael only dozed now and then, but Tory slept soundly all the way to the Charleston airport, her head in his lap. It did not appear to be a restful sleep; she moaned several times, frowned, and shifted her position awkwardly, as if she were stiff all over. Michael, who prided himself at being of the old school, attendance at which meant that men did not cry, blinked back tears now that he saw firsthand the effect this kind of experience could have on Tory. How she had withstood it as a child was beyond him, and he hoped that her father was turning on a spit in hell for having subjected her to such torture.

She awoke as soon as the wheels made contact with the concrete, and sat up, blinking. "We're here?" Leaning across him, she peered out the window until the small corporate jet had taxied to a halt, then hurried to the bathroom.

Michael watched her return with relief. Her color was a little better, but he noted that she walked with a slight limp, favoring her right leg.

"We're close," she said. "That way." She pointed toward the rear of the plane.

"South, toward the ocean. How do you feel?"

She was quiet for a moment, as if taking inventory. "Physically, he's no better, but the sun's up. His spirits are higher during the day."

"I meant you, Tory. How do you feel?"

"Oh. All right, I guess. It's hard to tell where I end and Lee begins."

He had to ask. It had been haunting him during the entire trip. "Tory, what happens to you if Lee dies? How does it affect you?"

Her eyes lost focus, as if looking into the past. "I don't know, Michael. The only time it's happened, I cracked up, and it took four months of therapy before I could face the world again. That's when I turned my back on what I was, what I'd been doing and everything associated with it."

The pilot appeared from the cockpit and began opening the door and lowering the steps. "End of the line, Mike. From this point, the meter's running and you'd better believe, I expect to be paid."

"Keep your shirt on," Michael said tersely. Scrutinizing Tory's face, the ravages of the night's experiences still etched in creases around her eyes, he made a decision that was nowhere nearly as difficult as he thought it would be. "Give me the pen, Tory."

"Why?"

"Just give it to me. I'll carry it."

She chuckled. "I bet you're a lousy poker player. I'll keep it," she said quietly. "It's the only way we'll find him quickly."

"We already know he's south of us," he argued. "Between what you've described and this man who's to meet us by the lighthouse and act as a guide, there's a good chance we'll find Lee. There's no reason for you to—"

She put a finger against his lips. "Not good enough, my love. Once I'd touched the pen and knew it was Lee's, I could have walked away and you would never have known I'd found it. I made a choice. We've come too far to back out now."

"Tory," he said, his voice breaking, "I couldn't stand to lose you twice."

She stroked his cheek. "I thought I knew you. I would never suspect that you were a worrywart. Let's go, Michael. Please."

Michael made quick work of buying a map, getting directions and renting a vehicle with four-wheel drive. In less than half an hour, they were rolling southeast on Route 26, blending with rush-hour traffic heading into Charleston, the temperature already in the high eighties. They'd been on the road less than ten minutes when Tory let out a squeal. "There's one, a palmetto! What a funny looking tree!"

"If I were you, I wouldn't pass that opinion along to a native," Michael warned her, an indulgent smile on his face. "In case you didn't know, this is the Palmetto State."

"Oh. I see what you mean." She clutched the pen, eyes narrowed. "Michael, I think Lee's southwest of us. I keep feeling a pull to the right."

Michael looked doubtful. "According to the guy I talked to, the island where the lighthouse is located is southeast of Charleston."

"It may be, but Lee isn't. You'll have to trust me, Michael. I don't know what else to say."

After a second, he nodded. "We'll pass that on to this Tom Gaylon. He's supposed to know the area like the back of his hand. Here, you take the map. Maybe you'll see something that might help."

Tory gave it a cursory glance, certain that she would find no clues there, but folded the map so that the section of coast between Charleston and Savannah were accessible. "I'm so thirsty, as if I haven't had anything to drink in days—which means that's how Lee is feeling."

Michael glanced up at a cloudless sky. "It's going to be sizzling out here by noon. If he hasn't had any water..." His lips thinned to a grim line, and he increased his speed. Tory, unaccustomed to being chauffeured, relaxed, dozed off without realizing it and came awake to find herself alone in the vehicle, the engine idling. Michael had stopped in the shade of a marvelous old oak, the branches of which stretched across a narrow dead-end street. He stood talking to the driver of a beat-up Jeep. She got out, reeling at the impact of the heat, and went to join Michael. He and the stranger behind the wheel of the Jeep, a reedy little man with skin the color of caramel, were embroiled in what appeared to be the kind of discussion that would go exactly nowhere.

"Mister," he was saying, "I'm as anxious to make a dollar as the next man, but how'm I to take you where you want to go if you don't know where that is?" Seeing her, he climbed out and removed his cap.

"Morning, ma'am. The name's Thomas Gaylon. Everybody calls me Cap."

"I'm Tory Shelton," she said, liking his eyes and weatherbeaten face. "Where are we?"

Michael answered. "Sullivan's Island. There's the lighthouse. It looks as if it's the only thing Hurricane Hugo left standing."

Tory took in the devastation she hadn't noticed until now. Despite over a year of cleanup efforts, the scars remained—jagged stumps of trees, crumbling foundations on which houses had once sat. Fully awake now, she held the pen tighter and became aware of a stronger sense of Lee's presence. "That way," she said, pointing.

"Ah." Cap smiled, pleased. "The little lady, she knows where you want to go, no?"

"Only the direction, and that's south." She closed her eyes. "There's lots of water, not all that deep because there are reeds and cattails sticking out of it."

"That could be anywhere, ma'am. This area isn't called the Low Country for nothing. There's marshland along the Intra-coastal Waterway, on most of the islands, and there's plenty of those, too. James Island, Johns Island, Folly—"

"The names don't mean anything," Tory said, shaking her head in frustration. "Lee doesn't know where he is." She pulled her focus inward. Filtering out everything except her connection with Lee, she catalogued what visual clues she could get from him. The lighthouse was nowhere in sight; he must be facing away from it. That was a problem. She had counted on using it to place him. Seeing through his eyes the angle at which the sun struck the lighthouse would lessen the amount of time it would take to find him.

"Wait a minute." Cap tugged at a long thin nose, his gaze flitting suspiciously from one to the other. "What exactly's going on here? You're looking for somebody?"

Michael nodded, rubbing his forehead as if it ached. "A very close friend. He went sailing and must have run aground somewhere down here."

"How long ago?"

"Back in April."

Cap shook his head. "Somebody would have seen his boat. Of course, if he got stuck back up in one of those creeks, say like on Johns Island, he'd be there until a good hard rain flooded the creek and lifted his boat up out of the mud. We've had plenty of that."

"What if he gave up and left the boat?" Michael asked.

"Depends on where he was. Unless he struck off in the right direction—and he'd have to know which way to head— he could wander around in water up to his knees for days, in which case he's dead. Snakes would get him, if nothing else."

"He's not dead," Tory said quietly, "but if we don't find him, he soon will be. He's weak and hurt, but he's alive."

Cap's hazel eyes locked onto her face. "You got the sight," he said, his tone full of wonder.

Tory's intuition told her this was one time she'd be wise to admit it. "Yes. I do."

He straightened, squared his shoulders and looked at her with open respect. "If that's the case, ma'am, I'm at your service. You just tell Cap which way to go, and he'll go. South, you say."

"Yes." Tory was a little off-balance. No one had ever re-acted to her in quite this way. "Oh, and wherever he is, he can see the lighthouse after dark."

"That's not much help, Miss Tory. He'd have to be blind not to. That's a twenty-million candle power light. You can see it for twenty miles."

"Oh. Well, can we just go, then? We don't have much time."

"I'm willing. The problem is whether we should use the Jeep or my boat."

"The boat," she said. "Definitely."

"Well, let's get moving. Just sit tight, ma'am. We'll use *Miss Lucky*. She's old, but she's perfect for shallow water, and she's never left me high and dry yet."

Michael looked startled. "Your boat is called *Lucky*?"

"I won her in a poker game, so the name seemed fittin'."

"Lee's nickname in college was Lucky." Michael gave a genuine smile for the first time since they'd arrived.

"Be damn," Cap said, shaking his head. "If that don't beat all. Well, ya'll just follow me." He hopped back into the Jeep.

By the time Tory found herself in a deck chair on the stern of the sturdy little boat, forty-five minutes had passed. It was her first time aboard a vessel larger than a canoe, and she was disappointed that she wouldn't be able to relax and enjoy the experience, but she would need all her concentra-tion to pinpoint Lee's location.

Without being asked, Michael assisted in helping Cap get underway by removing the ropes that tethered *Miss Lucky* to the dock. Cap, at the wheel, nodded his thanks, and before long they were rumbling south.

Michael came to stand behind her chair, his hands on her shoulders protectively. "Perhaps we should go below, Tory. Without tanning lotion or a sun block, you'll burn for sure."

"I'll be fine." Tory rested the back of her head against him and closed her eyes, the pen in her hand. Lee seemed to be in shade or shadow, but his body burned with an internal heat. He'd developed a raging fever which the ambient temperature would do nothing to ameliorate. Images flashed through his mind—and hers—a little blond girl in a swing, pushing herself higher and higher. Lee shouted at her to stop, and the picture changed. He was running now, on an indoor track, his lungs laboring for air. He crossed and turned, shouting encouragement to someone behind him— Michael, younger, neither as tall nor as broad-shouldered as she knew him to be.

"You used to run with Lee," she said, watching the scene, enchanted at the picture of the man she loved, as an adolescent.

"Yes. It's the only sport at which I could beat him. How'd you know?"

She squeezed the hand on her shoulder. "He's remembering." More accurately, Lee was hallucinating at a time when she needed lucidity and clear vision to see whatever he did.

Come on, Lee, snap out of it. We're coming, but we need your help to find you.

She felt a break in the continuity of the scene she was witnessing, then the onset of mental confusion of a different sort. He neither moved nor opened his eyes, but was now listening, as if he thought he'd heard something.

Good. He's coming to. Now if he'd just open his eyes . . .

Sunlight, bright, hot, appeared as spots of liquid gold through the lush growth of the nearby tree. He had done it. He'd opened his eyes!

Michael? Michael, is that you, boy?

The hope echoing in his mind was so poignant, so strong that Tory covered her mouth to avoid crying out in answer, then to avoid crying out in shock. Had Lee heard her?

"What's wrong?" Michael asked her.

"I . . . I'm afraid to say it. I think Lee can hear my thoughts. His eyes were closed, and I was thinking that he had to open them to help us find him. He did it, Michael. He's calling—thinking, I guess—your name. I'm a little scared. It never happened like this before, never."

"Tory." He kneeled beside her chair. "If I hadn't witnessed the things you're capable of doing, I would never have believed it. Now I'm ready for anything. Answer him for me. Just try it, see how he responds. Let him know we're trying to find him. Ask him to help. Swear at him. Nothing gets his attention like a woman talking the same way he does when he blows his stack."

He had no idea what he was asking of her. She wasn't just a little frightened, she was terrified. Had her psychic glitch gone through some sort of metamorphosis? Was she now also a mind reader as well as a soul reader, capable of communicating telepathically? That was not a comforting prospect.

Tentatively, she pushed the outside world aside, holding Michael's hands as if they were a lifesaver. Lee had subsided, his disappointment at not seeing Michael having a devastating effect. His eyes were closed again. This time he had truly given up.

Tory lost all hesitation about being ladylike. *Lee!* she shouted at him. *Damn you, don't do this! We're too close! You've caused a lot of people a lot of worry and me one hell of a lot of trouble! Michael's here. Don't you give up on us now!*

Again, a sense of him listening, or wondering whether what he heard was real.

It is, Tory assured him. *If it makes you feel any better, I don't understand it either. I'm not even sure I like it, but we're stuck with it, so cut the crap and help us. Open your eyes and keep them open.*

Sunlight scorched her sight. He'd heard her. Minutes and miles passed. He seemed closer, his presence stronger.

Tory opened her eyes. "Where are we?"

"I'll go find out." He returned in seconds. "The Intracoastal Waterway. This leg is the Stono River. That's Johns Island on our left."

"What's beyond Johns Island?"

"The Atlantic."

Tory jumped up and crossed to the port side, leaning out. Michael, perhaps fearing she'd fall over, hooked a finger into the back of her jeans. She squeezed her eyes shut. All she could see was the tops of trees, framed by... cartoons?

This didn't make sense. It wasn't enough, she thought. *Lee, if you're on your back, can you sit up? Look outside. I need to see outdoors.*

She felt his struggle to follow her instructions and the extent to which it sapped his strength. For some reason he seemed to be treating his right side with caution, but shortly the view changed, allowing her to see the trunks of the trees. He appeared to be looking out of a window down onto an expanse of marshlands, and in the distance a burned-out shack.

Tory spun around and ran forward to Cap, pulling Michael, his finger caught in her belt loop, along behind her. She described what she'd seen.

Cap's hazel eyes changed colors, becoming a deeper brown. "Land o' Goshen. It couldn't be."

"What?" Michael removed his finger, tension holding him in a rigid grasp.

"Crazy Zena. If he's on her property, we're in for trouble. She ain't called crazy for nothing. Meaner'n than a snake, too. Nawsir, he couldn't be. She'd have killed him."

"Who is she?" Michael demanded. "How do we get there?"

Cap ignored him. "Which direction is he, Miss Tory?"

She turned and pointed. "That way. A marshy area in front of him as far as he can see. He's looking down on it, as if he's elevated. Everything's . . . hazy—perhaps the window's dirty. The burned-out shack is to his left, nothing but charred walls on stilts. Does that make sense?"

"Yes'm, I'm afraid it does." He clamped a pipe between his teeth. "Mr. Gallagher, if you'll go below and look under the bunk on the right, there's a shotgun. Bring it and the box of shells. We may need them."

"Why?" Tory asked, as Michael left the bridge.

"Just want to be prepared, that's all. Now if you don't mind, little miss, I need some quiet time. Getting where we need to go is going to be tricky—and even trickier after we get there. I need to think."

"Of course." Shaken at this turn of events, she retreated to the stern again, and moved the deck chair over to the railing. She was only dimly aware of Michael's return and of the solemn conversation between them which she couldn't hear over the throb of the engine. Lee was on his back and hallucinating again, holding a conversation with a young woman who bore a startling resemblance to Leslie, but the hairstyle was from another time. That faded, until there was nothing. The screen was blank. Time was running out.

Tory opened her eyes with no idea how far they had come. The area was formidable, dark and thick with trees clogged with Spanish moss, which hung from their limbs and resembled dirty laundry. The water, too, was dark. Insects skated across its surface or hovered above the reeds like miniature helicopters, their iridescent wings the only color on a dreary waterscape.

Michael paced the sides, peering out. Suddenly the sound of *Miss Lucky*'s engines changed, became much quieter, almost purring. "Is that it?" he asked softly.

Had he not pointed it out, she'd have missed it. A soggy bank rose at a gradual incline on the right. The charred remains of a small house were sheltered behind a grove of trees from which the moss draped in thick, grimy curtains. Beyond it, perhaps fifty yards away and farther back on the bank, was the most rudimentary of shelters, a cabin of patchworked logs with a tin roof, the area around it littered with oil drums and the carcasses of wrecked boats.

It stood, like its nearest neighbor, on spindly stilts, high enough above the bank so that someone of Michael's height could have walked under it with no fear of bumping his head. There were no steps to reach it, but a ladder lay on the ground under what passed for a porch. There was only one window in sight, on the side nearest them, the glass coated with grime.

"Is that it?" Michael asked again, his voice a rasp against the silence. After a tight U-turn so that they now faced the opposite direction, Cap had cut the engine altogether.

"Yes. He's in there, barely alive." *Hang on, Lee. We're here.*

There was no answer. She felt as if she was on fire; her clothes were drenched with perspiration.

Cap addressed Michael. "You're sure you can handle him alone? I'm going to be pretty busy. Make no mistake, we are trespassing, and she'd have every right to take a shot at us."

"Hurry," Tory said, panting for breath.

Michael shook his head. "I can handle Lee. Cap, if you have any doubts at all about using that shotgun, I'll switch with you."

"No, you take care of your end of things and I'll tend to mine. I don't think we'll have a problem. Her boat's not here, and the ladder's not up. All we have to worry about is getting in and out before she gets back."

"Gotcha. Tory." Michael stood, his hands gripping her shoulders. "We'll be back as soon as we can. If you see or hear anyone coming, yell, and if there's trouble, hit the deck and stay there."

"Will you stop worrying and go get him out of there?" she said stridently. "He's this side of dead!"

With a terse nod, Michael lowered himself over the side and sloshed toward the bank. Cap followed awkwardly, the shotgun impeding his progress until he was in the water and could hold it above his head.

Tory watched, beginning a running commentary of their progress for Lee's benefit, hoping it might penetrate the nothingness she felt. Still, there was no response, even when she was able to shout that they had reached the shack and were maneuvering the ladder into position. Her only consolation was a sense of his presence, the flame of life burning so low that it was a pilot light, no more. Tory's heart thudded, and her mouth was dry, as if she'd eaten sand for breakfast.

Michael climbed the ladder while Cap stood sentry below. A second after he'd disappeared inside, a bellow of rage shattered the stillness, and Tory, staring into the black rectangle of the open doorway, clamped down on her bottom lip.

Centuries elapsed before Michael reappeared, a figure draped over his shoulder in a fireman's carry. She held her breath as he came down the ladder. As soon as he reached the ground, Cap took it down using one hand and pushed it back under the porch, never relinquishing his grip on the shotgun.

Michael slid down the bank and fought his way through the murky water, Cap hurrying after him, then passing him to climb the rope ladder up to the deck. He handed Tory the weapon, then leaned down to offer Michael what help he could. Lee, wrapped in something so incredibly filthy that it was unrecognizable, was deadweight.

"I hear something," Tory said, as Cap lifted Michael's burden, freeing him to climb the last two rungs quickly. The clatter of an engine sounded in the distance.

"Here," Cap said, shoving Lee into Michael's arms. "She's close. We've got to go." He hurried to the wheel, started the engine, and with a satisfying growl of power moved ahead.

Michael, cradling the wreck of a man as if he carried a baby, took him below, Lee's head tucked beneath his chin, a blend of tears and perspiration dripping onto thick white hair matted with blood and grime. In the cabin, Tory snatched the oilcloth from the table and spread it on a bunk before Michael put Lee down. Without being asked, she went back up on deck, giving Michael the time he needed to divest his friend of his filthy shroud and find something to replace it. When she finally went below again, he glanced up at her, his heart in his eyes. "Thanks, darling."

Lee was little more than skin and bones, and his right foot rested at an unnatural angle. A host of insects had fed on every inch of exposed flesh, and Tory swallowed the bile flooding into her mouth.

"He'll be all right, Michael, now that you're here."

Her words were a gesture, no more. The life force of the desiccated old man still emanated from him but little else. Where his thoughts had been was now a vacuum. There were no images, no voices, no emotions, nothing. Their victory, hers and Michael's—and Lee's—seemed hollow. For all their efforts, there was a distinct possibility that they'd found him too late. It was her fault. Hers.

Tory dreamed that she was falling and woke up in time to keep from rolling off the waiting room couch. She sat up and groaned, feeling as if she'd been in a championship wrestling match, which she'd lost in grand style. Everything ached. What didn't ache, itched. Her arms were peppered with insect bites and striped with welts from scratching them.

Michael, using the phone just inside the entrance of the emergency room, sagged against the wall, as if without its support he would not be able to remain upright. Seeing that she was awake, he waved, and after a minute, hung up. He was in worse shape than she was, both physically and spiritually. There were no marks on his face and arms; Tory knew that his wounds were on his soul.

"Leslie's in a meeting, but I got Yale," he said, and perched on the sofa beside her. "He'll bring her down on the first flight they can book. He's running off at the mouth about chartering a medical helicopter to fly Lee to Johns Hopkins or the Mayo Clinic. 'Only the best,' he's yelping, as if he's the one footing the bills."

Tory held her peace rather than remind Michael that he had wanted Lee taken to the closest big city hospital. The ambulance attendants awaiting their arrival, thanks to Cap's call from the *Miss Lucky,* had taken one look at the patient and had announced in no uncertain terms that if that's what Michael wanted, he'd be accompanying a dead man through the emergency room doors. Otherwise, he'd let them take Lee to Simmons Community Hospital, and if he didn't waste any more of their time, the man just might make it there alive. Michael had closed his mouth and let them do their jobs.

Tory glanced at her watch. Lee had been behind the double doors for an hour and a half now. There had been much coming and going, none, however, in their direction. The doctor, who could have been a double for Carroll O'Connor, had told them he would talk to them as soon as he could, and he had yet to reappear. Michael had prowled the waiting area, grumbling about the size of the facility, admittedly small, until Cap had apprised him of the average price of summer homes in the area. This was a small, well-to-do community, and as a result the hospital which served its residents ranked with the best in the state.

The doors from the outside swung open, and Cap came in. "Any word yet?"

"No. What the hell is going on in there?" Michael growled, frustration oozing from every pore.

Cap sat down beside Tory. "Count your blessings and keep your britches on. They know what they're doing here. I came to tell you I found you a place to rent. Four bedrooms right on the beach, practically across the street. It'll cost you, but it's a nice place, roomier than most, and there's a woman who'll come in and do the cookin' and cleaning, if you want."

"We'll take it. Where are the nearest stores? I'm set, but Tory needs a change of clothes."

"All Tory needs is a bath, a washer, a dryer, and a bed for a few hours," she corrected him. "I can't stay, Michael. I've got a business to run."

"Couldn't Helen—" He stopped, rising quickly. The automatic doors to the inner sanctum of the emergency ward had opened with a snap. The Carroll O'Connor clone strode toward them, his glasses pushed up into his hair like a headband.

"Sorry it took so long," he said in a decidedly non-Southern accent, "but there was a lot to be done fast. I'm Dr. Allen. That is one tough old man. They don't make 'em like that anymore."

"How is he?" Michael asked.

"Critical until further notice. Sunstroke, severe dehydration, renal shutdown and assorted topical infections, thanks to the local insect population and the filthy condition he was in. If we can get his kidneys operating, the next serious problem is his leg—a clean fracture of the right femur which was never set, so it's begun to knit improperly. We'll have to re-fracture it. He was lucky there—had it been his hip..."

"Will he be all right?" Tory asked.

"It's early yet. We'll have to see how he responds. His temperature's down to a hundred and two, so—"

"Down to..." Michael had paled. "How high was it?"

"A hundred and six. If you hadn't found him, I doubt he'd have lived till sundown."

"*She* found him," Cap amended. "Led us right to him. She's got the sight, she has."

Dr. Allen lowered his glasses to peer intently at her. "Is that a fact, or is Tom here angling for first prize at the Liars Club?"

Tory squared her shoulders, ready to fend off the usual put-down. "He's telling the truth. I'm psychic."

His smile was slow in coming, but when it arrived, it was the warmest, most kindly one she'd ever seen. "You're a finder? I've read about people like you, but you're the first I've met. You must be damned good at it."

A bit dazed by his receptive attitude, Tory said, "I couldn't have done it alone. Lee helped until the last half hour or so when he lost consciousness."

The doctor's eyes narrowed. "He helped? How?"

Tory dug her nails into her hand. She hadn't meant to say quite so much. "It's hard to explain. I could feel what he felt and see what he was seeing. He closed his eyes and I . . . I asked him—in my mind—to keep his eyes open so I could get what visual clues I needed to find him."

"And he did?"

"Yes."

"Young lady, you've just proven something, I just wish I knew what. That man's been unconscious for some time, at least a day, perhaps a day and a half. I hope I'll have a chance to talk to you later. I'd like to document this whole business. For the time being, if we're ever to hear his side of the story, I've got work to do. By the way, there are rope burns around his wrists and the ankle of his uninjured leg."

Michael stiffened. "Yes, I know. He was tied to a bed by one wrist when I found him."

"Then I guess you'll be alerting the authorities."

"When can we see him?" Michael asked, walking with him to the doors which announced "Authorized Personnel Only."

The doctor's mouth twisted to one side in thought. "Come back this evening. I don't want to move him quite yet, but he'll be going into our Critical Care Unit as soon as a bed is available. If we can clear the toxins out of his system, he'll probably pull through. Even then he'll have a long road back. Leave a number where I can reach you, just in case." He tapped a button set into the wall, and the doors slid open and closed after him.

Michael got the phone number from Cap and after a short exchange with the receptionist, walked slowly back to Tory, fatigue marking his face. "If Lee was kidnapped, why didn't anyone try to collect a ransom? Leslie ate and slept by the phone. No one called."

"Want I should take you to the sheriff?" Cap asked. "Or you could phone him after you get to the house, ask him to drop by. That may be better since after he talks to you, he'll want to come here and see what the Doc has to say. He won't have as far to go."

Michael rubbed a hand over his face and nodded as if his head weighed a ton. "Sounds good to me."

"Cap," Tory said, "I hate to ask—you've done so much already—but could you take me to the airport, after I've cleaned up, of course."

"Be glad to, Miss Tory, but..." He wore a pained expression. "Might be a good idea to wait until after you've talked to the sheriff, in case he...well, he might want to talk to you."

Tory was uncertain as to the implications of what Cap was trying to say. "I don't understand. Why would he want to talk to me at all?"

"Well." He shifted from foot to foot, clearly at a loss. "You found him. Zena's got relatives all over, and the police will want to be sure you aren't one of them and didn't have anything to do with him disappearing in the first place."

"Me?" Tory's eyes widened. "I never even saw the man until today! By the first time I'd heard his name, he'd been gone—" she turned to Michael for help "—how long?"

"Six weeks. Relax, you can prove your innocence. Stay anyway, until tomorrow, at least. By then we should have a better picture of whether he'll make it or not. Less than twenty-four hours, Tory. It'll give us time to clean up and rest, and maybe have a few moments to talk. We have a lot to discuss."

She wasn't sure they did. "All right, but I can't stay more than a day. I should call Helen. I didn't even tell anyone I was leaving."

"She knows where you are. I got Jake at the cabin, and she was there. He's driving down tomorrow. In fact, maybe Leslie and Yale can come with him. They plan to fly, but I've known Yale to get lost on his way to the airport. Let's get out of here. I'll phone them right after I've called the sheriff."

He folded an arm around her shoulder, and they left with Cap, who was as good as his word when he said the house he'd found was across the street. Tory plodded along between the two, wondering how many more times she would have to delay the inevitable. The news that he was moving to New York had killed all hope again.

To Michael Gallagher, New York meant Manhattan. He had confessed one evening to his adolescent fantasy of returning to his hometown a successful man, of moving into one of the posh condominiums overlooking Central Park. He had not mentioned then that he'd already begun making his fantasy a reality, nor had it occurred to Tory when Jake had said flatly that Michael was leaving the firm.

She had no right to feel betrayed; he owed her nothing. That they loved one another made not one bit of difference. In this case, loving wasn't enough. Her stomach heaved at the thought of the barrage of emanations she'd encounter in overpopulated, concrete-bound Manhattan, and she couldn't imagine Michael thriving in a three-by-five town like Chestin or Cedar Hollow. There was nothing he could say that would make her consider going with him, and she would say nothing to make him consider coming with her. She loved him, and in this instance that meant letting him go.

"I want them up before the judge for trespassing and for kidnapping my man. They had no call to take him. I took good care of him. He et when I did, possum, rattlesnake meat, good vittles."

Michael kept his head lowered, his hands gripping the arms of the ragged recliner. If he moved, if he so much as looked at the whining, unrepentant hag, he was afraid he'd lose it and kill her before anyone could stop him.

He'd been awakened from a sound sleep by a call from the police with a request that he and Cap meet them at Zena's house. She was insisting on pressing charges against them, and the police in her district, knowing they were dealing with an unstable character, were hoping to avoid a barricade situation—with gunfire. She thought the "trespassers" were being brought to her so she could supply positive identification.

The officer, named Millar, had looked uncomfortable when he'd met them outside the shack. "I'd heard a while back that Zena had found herself a man, but I figured maybe she'd lucked up on some damn fool who didn't mind living back up here on the creek. I 'preciate you coming. The chief thinks if we hauled her in first and asked questions second, she'd never tell you what you need to know."

Michael was almost sorry now that he'd agreed so readily, and even sorrier that he'd roused Tory. Zena Orry's shack was so disreputable, he doubted she was bothered with rats. No self-respecting rodent would be caught dead here, except as the entrée for her evening meal. There was no inside plumbing, and the ambient aromas were so pungent that Tory looked green around the gills. And it was obvious that despite her sobriquet, Crazy Zena wasn't the least demented. She was simply mean and eccentric by nature, and the thought of Lee at her mercy brought a return of Michael's murderous thoughts.

"You found him where?" Millar asked again. She had evaded the question the first and second occasions.

"Oh, for pity's sake!" She scowled, adding wrinkles to wrinkles. From an overflowing ashtray at her elbow, she picked through the butts, found one of lightable length and put a kitchen match to it. Michael watched as the flame singed the ends of the dirty white fringes that decorated her forehead in a semblance of bangs. "I was back up yonder Awendaw way—"

"On private property, you mean," Millar said.

"I was jes' passing through. And I seen this boat that had got itself caught good and proper—you know how Hugo flung things around, trees layin' every which way and nobody'd bothered to clean it out. That boat wasn't going nowhere, so I pushes alongside, and hear this moaning. Well, I got on her, almost killed myself doing it, and there he was, all bunged up. So I trussed him up real good and lowered him over the side into my Betsy, and I brung him home and took care of him."

"Miss Orry," Michael said, with barely contained anger, "that man had been missing for weeks. You knew he had to belong somewhere. Why didn't you notify the police?"

She picked an errant shred of tobacco off her lip. "Me and the sheriff, we don't get along."

"Didn't Lee ask you to call for help, call his daughter, call anybody?"

"He never did," she said adamantly. "Never did."

"Miss Orry." Tory's voice cut off Michael's protest, hard and cold, with a convincingly threatening edge to it. "Mr. Varnum's in the hospital, and we'll be talking to him tonight. What's he going to say when we ask him that question?"

Zena's pale brown eyes rolled toward Tory and evidently did not like what they saw. "He give me the money and wrote some numbers for me to call, but I just never got around to it. I was busy!" she protested self-righteously. "I had to do everything for him, dress him, help him to the privy in the corner there, cook for him, feed him practically. I didn't have time to be going way over to Weaver's store to call nobody. Besides, I needed the money to buy vittles."

"How long did you keep him here against his will, Zena?" Millar asked. "Don't bother to lie. The doctor noticed the rope burns around his wrists and ankle."

"Don't know how long. No calendar." Her bottom lip projected. She was a travesty of a sulky child. "And roping him was the onliest way I could keep him still. He wasn't supposed to be up on that leg. I did it for his own good."

"Let's go," Michael said, getting up. He'd had all he could take.

Tory placed a hand on his arm to delay him. The other hand she extended towards Zena. "We'll take his wallet," she said quietly, "with every single credit card and piece of identification he had. We don't expect the money back— you can keep that for your trouble. And if you say you don't have his wallet, I'll put a hex on you. You haven't suffered until you've been hexed by a witch from Cedar Hollow."

"Cedar Hollow? Where's that?" the old woman asked suspiciously.

"This side of hell."

Zena launched herself from her rocking chair as if it were a hot seat. She lifted a floorboard near a corner, felt around in the space under it and hurled the wallet at Tory, who caught it handily. "All I wanted was a little company," she mumbled. "That's all, a little somebody to chat with."

Michael hustled Tory out, wondering when she would stop surprising him. She passed the billfold to him by two fingers, then climbed into Cap's boat.

Crazy Zena stood in the door of her shack and waited until Cap started the engine. "I'm gonna get me a lawyer and sue! One of them palimony things, him leaving me like this."

"God Almighty," Millar, on the bank, said under his breath. "That's the closest I've ever been to her. It's a wonder your friend didn't catch something, living in all that filth." He gave Michael a sidelong glance. "I guess if you still wanted to have her arrested, I wouldn't blame you."

Michael had already given the matter serious consideration. The local law had been surprisingly cooperative, and Michael suspected they'd be more than willing to haul Zena Orry off to the hoosegow. She seemed to be a notorious pain in the neck in several counties. Even more to his amazement, the senior official had accepted the explanation of Tory's psychic ability without question, and had, in fact, treated them both with kid gloves from that point.

Now, however, Michael shook his head. "I guess not. It sounds as if she probably saved his life, so I won't push it."

There was no mistaking Millar's relief. "Thanks, Mr. Gallagher. I wasn't looking forward to taking her in. Chief'll be in touch with you. See ya around, Cap."

"The question remains," Michael said, once they were underway, "how did Lee get so far south of where he intended to go?"

"Well, if Millar finds Mr. Varnum's boat," Cap said, "we'll have a better idea. By the way, one of my boys will pick up your rental car and bring it here tonight."

"Good Lord. Thanks. I'd forgotten it. I need to square things with you, too. Why don't I pay you for two days instead of just one? I don't know how we'd have managed without you."

It was clearly a temptation, but Cap shook his head.

"Is everyone down here as nice as you are?" Tory asked. "You've really bent over backward to help us. Even the police were gracious."

She saw a blush creep across the back of his neck. "It's like this, little miss. It ain't every day you get a chance to rub elbows with somebody as blessed as you are. I figure anybody who puts herself on the line to find a lost sheep the way you do, if there's some way I can be of service, I'll do what I can. It was my pleasure, Miss Tory. My pleasure.''

Michael looked back at her, saw the pensive expression on her face, and warmed to the captain even more for the heartfelt plaudits he'd given Troy. He too would express his gratitude—and awe of her ability—but it could wait until they were alone.

He glanced at his watch. ''I guess it's about time we went to the hospital. Maybe Lee will be conscious. Why not? Miracles do happen.''

The captain smiled at Tory. ''Yes, sir, and if he is awake and kicking, it won't be the first miracle I seen today.''

Tory caught his gaze. With her features still softened by what appeared to be a deeply introspective mood, she curled up in the corner of the back seat and turned to look out the window. Michael watched surreptitiously. There were tears in her eyes, and he wasn't sure why.

Chapter 12

"Well, that's that," Michael said as he left the phones outside the Critical Care Unit. "Leslie and Yale will be here in the morning. The only seats available tonight would mean a two-hour layover in Atlanta, and they wouldn't get to Charleston until after midnight. There's no point in all that rushing, now that we know Lee's past the crisis point."

"What about Jake?" Tory asked.

"He's driving down, expects he'll be here around noon. Let's go get something to eat." He gave her a quick kiss, remembering how often over the last month he'd have given anything to do that. She tasted of the peanut butter crackers they'd shared to stave off hunger pangs until after they'd seen Lee. "Cap said the place at the end of the island's not bad. We can walk there—unless you're too tired, of course." She did look a little wan.

"I'm fine. A walk sounds nice."

Fingers laced, they strolled the length of the island in silence, perhaps because Tory seemed so subdued and contemplative.

The restaurant, Sherry's Sea Shanty, was a welcome surprise, with linen-covered tables on a screened veranda overlooking the ocean. Each table was illuminated by a miniature hurricane lamp, imparting an intimacy that Michael found suited his mood. They sat bathed in a small pool of flickering amber light which seemed to enclose them in a world of their own.

After they'd placed their orders, Tory glanced out of the window. "Look, Michael."

The setting sun squatted on the horizon, its last rays deep orange stripes against a pale purple sky, as gaudy as the colors in a kindergartner's drawing. The evening still clung to a remnant of the day's high temperatures. The breezes off the Atlantic, however, had washed away most of the oppressive quality of the heat, and now the air was pleasantly warm and scented with essences from the ocean. Gulls shrieked and wheeled, while at the water's edge sandpipers played tag with the tide.

"This is the kind of location I usually go to when I need to get away," Michael said. "But I miss the mountains. I've missed you, too." He looked at her closely, uncertain whether the shadows under her eyes were real or the effect of the lighting. "We should have gone back to the house. You're really beat."

She gave him an indulgent smile. "Will you stop worrying about me? It's been a long day. This time yesterday I was tearing up the house looking for the pen. I didn't realize where it probably was until almost midnight."

He gawked at her. "You went to that cave last night? In the dark?" His stomach flipped, remembering the climb over wet boulders to reach it. "Damn it, Tory, that was foolish! What if you'd fallen?"

"I didn't. And if I'd waited for daylight, Lee would be dead now. A good meal and a good night's sleep and I'll be fine, all right?"

He found it difficult to let go of the picture of her working her way to the cave, and finally blocked it out by watching the sun seem to lose a battle with gravity. Gradually the sky began a slow fade toward black.

"I'm glad we have some time alone," he said when it was too dark to see anything. "Once Leslie and Yale and Jake get here, that house will feel like an anthill, so I guess I should say everything I need to now while I can. Tory, I'm very, very grateful for what you did today. Lee—and I—owe you an incredible debt."

She pulled her gaze from the ocean. "Perhaps, but I can't forget that I came that close to costing him his life. I'm so relieved he's going to be all right."

"Me, too, but he's not going to bounce back from this overnight. He's been through too much. So have you, Tory. I had no idea the price you'd have to pay to find him. And to think you did this when you were a child..."

She seemed to shrug it off. "There were only a couple of times when it was as bad as it was with Lee. The truth is I shouldn't have been doing it at all back then. No child of nine should be exposed to the kind of emotional chaos I had to share with the people I found—teenagers running from abusive parents, husbands, wives running out of sheer hatred, to hurt a partner as much as possible, even the kids abducted because they were the grand prize in a custody battle. I did that for nine years. It took the death of a lost child and a complete breakdown before I had the guts to say 'no more.'"

"Tell me about it," Michael said, out of curiosity as well as a conviction that discussing it would help her begin to put it behind her. She launched into the fantastic tale of how a hair ribbon blown by a gusting wind had led her to the family whose plane had crashed and her subsequent move to Washington D.C. where her father could successfully market her strange talent. The arrival of their orders interrupted the flow only long enough for her to thank the waitress. She talked and he listened, a band around his chest becoming tighter and tighter as she related the human suffering to which she'd been vicariously exposed, with no support from the schoolmates to whom she was alternately witch and freak.

He learned things the articles hadn't told him, of the accusations of fraud by skeptics, of a police investigation into whether her activities constituted a scam. His throat closed with sorrow for her and the child she hadn't been able to save, and for the emotional collapse that followed.

"I still have nightmares about running through a maze of high rises that lean in toward me, as if they're about to fall," she said, her head lowered. "In my dreams I'm always looking for someone I never find, because the buildings are all alike and I can feel myself dying because the person I'm looking for is, too. That usually wakes me up."

"Tory, it sounds to me as if almost everyone's gotten some good out of your ability except yourself."

"Oh, I don't know. The little deaf boy who died gave me an appreciation for the problems of the disabled. Otherwise, I guess you're right. I probably could have handled everything if I'd been older, but not as a child. Perhaps one day I'll be able to forgive my father. But not yet. Not yet."

Michael had lost his appetite and pushed his shrimp from one side of his plate to the other. "What happens now, Tory? Do you go back to the way you were dealing with things when I met you? Are you packing your psychic talent on ice again, or what?"

She examined a clam and popped it into her mouth. She had long since swallowed when she responded to his question. "Or what, meaning I don't know what happens now. Things are different this time, perhaps because I'm older. When I was a kid, I picked up feelings from everything I touched. From the time I went back to the Hollow, I've worn gloves, even through college, and even after I'd taught myself how to short-circuit the process so I could survive around people and the things they touched without accidentally poking around in their lives. It worked, for the most part, but I always had gloves nearby, especially around strangers. Until the day I found your tie clasp, I had been alone in here—'' she tapped her forehead ''—for almost eleven years.''

''What happened, Tory? I assume you wouldn't have touched the tie clip if you weren't prepared to block out its vibrations... or whatever it is that comes through to you. What went wrong?''

She shook her head slowly. ''Nothing. I told myself that I took the risk because the Hollow had begun to smother me and I needed contact, any kind of contact, with the outside world. I knew the kind of person who'd wear that T-square had to be someone very special, and I was about crazy for a change in my life. Then when Sal forced my hand to find Danny, I rationalized that I had no choice, I couldn't have turned my back on my friends. That was true, but all the rest were lies, Michael, all lies.''

''How do you mean?''

She spread her gloved fingers and stared at them. ''There wasn't time to think about it while it was happening today, but sitting in that emergency room, I realized that I felt *normal* for the first time in years. I felt whole. And it had nothing to do with the fact that I'd helped someone—''

''And saved a life.''

''That either. What I've been doing for the last eleven years,'' she said quickly, her words spilling out as if they had been dammed up inside her, ''is exactly the same as a sighted person wearing a blindfold twenty-four hours a day, or a person with two good legs hopping around on one. This blasted thing in my head is a natural part of me, and I've fought like hell against using it, and letting it do whatever it's supposed to. I'm tired of fighting,'' she said, and peeled off her gloves. ''I've handicapped myself long enough.''

He captured a hand and kissed it. ''Tory, if you'd said that last week, I'd have said, 'Thank God, she's come to her senses.' But seeing what you went through today...''

''Let me tell you what I went through today, Michael Gallagher.'' She leaned forward, her eyes alive with an inner glow. ''A man I'd never met guessed, *guessed* that I was psychic and said, 'Here I am, lady. Tell me where you want me to go.' And he called me a miracle! Then a doctor, a man of science listened, reacted with excitement and said he'd like to document my link with Lee. A policeman sat across from me, said 'I'll be damned,' and showed not one iota of doubt or cynicism. They accepted me, Michael. That's also what happened to me today.''

Baffled and willing to admit it, Michael said, ''What's the big deal, honey? You live with people who accept you. Why else would they lie for you?''

''Because I'm one of them. I'm an uplander.'' She smiled, but it was one of sadness. ''And they like me. Some of them even love me. But accept me? I make most of them very nervous, and they make certain that I don't touch anything that belongs to them. Some of them are even afraid of me. Every community has its curiosities, and I'm the Hollow's resident freak. So today was rough in a lot of ways but in others it was glorious.''

Michael peered into the face he'd come to love, and stroked the back of her hand. ''You really have been alone, haven't you? Hell, the staff of the Wayland could have given you moral support, if nothing else.''

''Who?''

''You don't know about the Wayland Institute for Parapsychology Research? It's in D.C. Their sole purpose is to study psychic phenomena and to act as a point of contact for people with psychic gifts. They run tests, document various kinds of abilities, sponsor self-help and coping seminars, and support groups. If you like, they'll even take you on as a consultant. Anyone in need of a finder goes through them, and if they're legit, the Institute will give them your name. They refer police departments all over the country to the two on their rolls. Haven't you read articles or seen TV documentaries about psychics working with police?''

''No, intentionally. Don't you understand, Michael? That was exactly what I was running from. I didn't want to see or read anything about it. How did you find out about the Wayland Institute?"

"Jake. He's the one who suggested I try this route to find Lee, and since he knew I thought it was—forgive me—a bunch of bull, he recommended that I start with the Institute. They made enough of a believer out of me to make me come look for you when both their finders were unavailable. You took care of the rest."

Tory's eyes were locked on his face, but he could see that her mind was elsewhere. "I guess I have a lot to think about," she said softly.

"In spades. While you're at it, Tory, think about us."

That got her attention. "Us?" She focused on him, her expression taut with caution.

He poked her gently. "You. Me. Us."

She looked down at her plate, as if surprised it was still there. "This is delicious, but I've had enough. Can we go now, Michael? I'm tired of sitting."

It wasn't quite the reaction he'd expected. Was she intentionally avoiding the subject? "Why don't you wait for me outside?"

She hurried away as he signaled the waitress. He paid the tab and found Tory standing at the water's edge, holding the inexpensive thong sandals she'd bought in the hospital gift shop. His barefoot girl. He took the sandals from her and tucked them in a back pocket, amused that they were small enough to fit there. Hand in hand, they started back toward the house, walking along the beach.

The gulls had disappeared, or perhaps it was simply too dark to see them. The white sand was warm, strewn with sea oats, and they strolled in comfortable silence until they reached a pier that jutted out into the ocean. As if by prearrangement, they turned and walked to the end of it, where Michael lifted her onto the railing. He stood between her knees, his hands locked behind her back.

"Now, about us," he began.

She cut him off. "What happens to Woodland Rise if Lee doesn't regain consciousness in time?"

He swallowed his irritation at the change of subject. It was a legitimate question. "Leslie has agreed that I should apply for power of attorney. Dr. Allen, or whoever's attending if we move him, will attest to the fact that he's temporarily incapacitated. I'll have to check, but I'm pretty sure that will allow me to sign the drawings in his stead."

"Good. I'm glad."

"I doubt all that will be necessary. Since Lee's responding to stimuli, he could wake up any time. We're off the subject, which is us, remember?"

"I'm sorry. What were you going to say?"

The clouds parted, unveiling a full moon whose bright white light bathed Tory in silver. She seemed to shine herself. He took a breath to speak, and realized whatever had been on the tip of his tongue was gone. "I forget. Seeing you in moonlight knocked it right out of my head."

"Isn't that what they call blarney?" she asked.

"I meant it." He chuckled. "I can't wait for Lee to meet you. He always said that one day there'd be a woman who'd scramble my brains so thoroughly that I wouldn't know which end is up. Well, I have, and I love it. And you, too." He leaned forward and kissed her, feeling her lips part under his to afford him entry. It was she, however, who drew away from him well before he'd had his fill.

"First the talking," she said. "Then the kissing. This may be the only chance you'll have to say everything, remember? I really do have to leave day after tomorrow."

"You said you hadn't had a vacation in seven years. Take one now. Stay here with me, Tory. I don't know when we'll be together like this again, just the two of us. There's going to be a lot of Lee in my future."

"More than before?"

"Much more. I'll have to alter my plans, change everything now that he's back. I'm thinking that it'll simplify matters if I move in with him," he said, voicing his thoughts for his and her benefit, "especially if I'm to help with whatever therapy he'll need. Besides, when Leslie marries Yale—"

"That's still on?"

"Hot and heavy. I was wrong about him—he really seems to love her. God knows she's head over heels about him. Anyway, she'll be leaving, and Lee will be alone in that big house. It's a mansion in the old sense of the word, with guest wings, the whole bit, so it's not as if privacy would be a problem."

"It sounds like the perfect answer," Tory said, her tone sounding lighter than before.

"It is, but it's not quite the way I'd imagined things would go. It's like moving back in with Dad, and that's a step backward."

He felt a difference in her mood. She was suddenly much more relaxed. "He'll be depending on you for a lot of things. You won't mind?"

"The only thing I'll mind is that it'll cut into my time with you. I can't be two places at once." He pulled her closer and buried his nose in her hair. "Sometimes I can't quite believe the way things have gone for us. We met, what, six weeks ago? But the time we've actually spent together, today included, amounts to less than two."

"A lot can happen in two weeks," she said, an odd timbre in her voice.

"Tell me about it. I find a mysterious young woman, fall in love, really in love, for the first time in my life and lose her in the space of ten days."

She pulled back. "The first time? I'm supposed to believe that?"

"It's true. There've been lots of women, I won't deny that. But I had no trouble doing my work after I'd met them. None of them distracted me to the point where I found myself sketching their faces in the corners of a client's blueprints. They never reached me, Tory. As my mother would say, their names weren't written in my heart. Yours is. Ina Victoria Shelton." His fingers traced her initials across his chest.

This time when he kissed her, she didn't move away. Her arms stole around his neck, and she met his embrace eagerly, avidly, as if drawing sustenance from his mouth on hers. It reminded him of the way she had shinnied up his body in the cave, placing herself in such a position that he couldn't have resisted her if it had meant his life. The memory, and the movement of her tongue against his teeth, evoked an immediate response. He knew there would be no stopping it, that he had no wish to.

"Tory," he warned her, "we'd better get back to the house. Making love on a beach might be fine for a movie, but in real life it'll probably get us charged with indecent exposure and being a public nuisance."

She sighed and hopped down from the railing. "Too bad. I'd enjoy making love with you under the stars. The sand would be a perfect bed, even better than leaves."

"Hush," he said, and scooped her up. She laid her head on his shoulder, and he carried her off the pier, past four large beach homes to the fifth. It, like the others, sat well above the sand on concrete block columns. On his way up the steps to the deck, Tory began unbuttoning his shirt. He opened the sliding door to enter the living room and, still in his arms, she tugged his shirttail free of his slacks. By the time he'd reached the top of the stairs, she had unbuckled his belt with one hand. He nudged open the door of the bedroom he had chosen earlier in the day, bumped it closed with his rear and put her down.

The room contained the basics and no more, a king-size bed, nightstands attached, a triple dresser, and one chair. Full-length mirrors paneled the folding doors of the wall-to-wall closet and the connecting door of the bathroom. The furniture was arranged to pay homage to the focal point of the room: the view. The wall on the ocean side was floor-to-ceiling glass doors which opened onto a smaller deck. Not quite the same as making love on the beach, Michael thought, but damned close to it.

Tory unzipped his slacks with a single-mindedness that brooked no interference, holding them while he stepped free. She removed his shirt, then his briefs, easing them past his hips and thighs, then down his calves very slowly, her motions so seductively deliberate and deliberately seductive that it seemed she'd already begun the act of lovemaking when she had yet to really touch him.

He reached out to return the favor, but she backed away. Silhouetted against the moon, she removed her T-shirt, jeans, bra and bikini panties with the same languid movements. He detected no artifice or self-consciousness, only a fiercely sensuous enjoyment of what she was doing, an erotic dance without music. It reminded him of the morning mists rising to bare the beauty of the mountain behind her home, and wondered if she realized how closely her actions now mirrored what he'd seen then.

Finally she was as nude as he, a goddess in front of a scrim of shimmering moonlight. It was a picture he'd never forget, and he realized with sudden intuition that was precisely what she'd intended. He stepped toward her, and she toward him, and into him, her skin like warm silk against his as she rose up on her toes, her arms locking around his neck.

"Oh," he said, remembering. "My wallet. This time I'm prepared."

"No need," she murmured, and cut off his protest by sealing his mouth with hers. She clung to him, soft, firm, smooth, warm, and he responded to the miracle of her, holding her tightly, drinking in her scent, her breath, her moisture. She stepped onto the arches of his feet, still on her toes, and the downy nest between her legs meshed with his, her fleshy mound sliding against him. The liquid heat of her took his breath away, and he lifted his head for air, leaving her mouth, missing it immediately.

She pressed her lips in the hollow of his throat, stepped off his feet and let her tongue trail down his breastbone, then to each nipple, circling, nibbling. It was like gasoline on open flame. Already fully aroused and heavy, the action of her teeth and tongue across his chest pushed matters an extra mile. He could feel himself swelling even more until he wasn't sure his skin could contain him.

She pressed him further, igniting a trail of sparks down the centerline of his body, her tongue dipping into and out of his navel as she lowered herself to her knees. She fondled him, one hand around the rigid presence she had caused, the other reaching lower, cupping him in her palm as if testing his weight, her thumb moving over skin normally corrugated but now stretched tight across twin vessels.

She kissed him, sipped his nectar, then with an awkwardness he found touching, took him into her mouth. This was clearly a new experience for her, and that she was willing to do it at all humbled him. Her awkwardness was short-lived. Before long, Michael, his legs trembling, his teeth clenched, knew he had to stop her. Her mouth was ecstasy, her hands pushing him dangerously close to the point of no return.

Gently he pulled her to her feet and smoothed the look of concern from her forehead. "Thank you, my love, but this should be for both of us, not just me. Come." He led her to the bed and lowered her onto it, arranging her, testing her readiness with a soft touch. His fingers met a well over-flowing with honey.

He positioned himself above her, already anticipating the fiery massage, but held himself in check, knowing there was something he had to say, that there was no sense in putting it off any longer. "Tory, will you marry me?"

Her eyes became saucers. "Marry you? Marry you?" Her voice throbbed, full of emotion. "Oh, God, Michael!"

Her arms and legs whipped around him with a strength that caught him off guard, pulling him into her, her small body swallowing him whole. She was like a furnace, and he found himself gripped by walls that seared, yet soothed and aroused him. He had to freeze, hold his breath to prevent erupting even before either of them had moved. And she moved first, her hips pulling away from him. With a gasp, he plunged into her. She emitted a high keening cry that became a goad, urging him to begin a long, furious dance to the music of their bodies meeting, separating, coming together again in perfect harmony.

During it all, the forward charge and retreat, the gradual journey to the peak where Michael managed to wait for her, climb with her, he assumed that she was allowing her body language to speak for her, in which case she'd accepted his proposal with a resounding "Yes!" a chorus in which they both joined unabashedly, the syllable repeated again and again as they made the leap over the edge into the jaws of ecstasy.

The intensity of his climax shook him, leaving him weakened, lightheaded, delirious. If her name had been written in his heart before, it was now branded in the nucleus of every cell in his body. He settled in her arms as they drifted back toward mortal bounds, feeling sweet exhaustion seeping into his bones. He began to laugh silently, his shoulders jerking.

"What?" Tory asked, sounding sleepy herself.

Separating from her, he rolled onto his side and pulled her close. "It's just as well we'll have a private wing at Lee's."

He saw her slow smile. "Things can get a little noisy, can't they?"

"Yes, and that's a first for yours truly. That's what you do to me, Tory. Something tells me if I marry you I'm going to die young, but I'll sure as hell die happy."

She giggled, ran one hand the length of his torso before snuggling against him, her lips at the base of his throat.

He drifted off, awoke, reflecting on a life with this fiery little woman. "We'll have to practice making love at a lower decibel level, because apartments in New York have walls like tissue paper, unless we luck out on an older building."

She seemed to stop breathing for a minute. "You're still planning the move to New York." She sounded surprised.

"Yes, just not as soon as I hoped. I'm not worried. The firm in New York wants me whenever I get there. That means almost as much as knowing you'll be going with me."

"What about Lee?" she asked quietly.

"We wouldn't leave until he's back on his feet. That'll be a while. In the meantime, we'll spend every weekend we can in the Hollow. I wouldn't want you to sell your house. It could be our mountain retreat, like Jake's cabin. It'll also help Lee get used to our not being around. What do you think?"

It was so long before she responded that he thought she might have fallen asleep. "That I will always love you very much," she said, her eyes closed.

He propped himself on an elbow and gazed down at her. "You sound funny. Is something wrong?"

Her eyes opened. "Yes. I've changed my mind about that good night's sleep. You're wasting the only time we'll have together like this. Make love to me, Michael."

He obliged.

Tory, lying on her side, came awake slowly, started to stretch, then went rigid, feeling warm breath on the back of her neck and the weight of an arm across her midsection. Michael. She let her muscles relax and her mind recount the events of the last twenty-four hours. So much had happened, so much had changed.

Her psychological horizons had widened, and as a result, her world. What she would do, now that her telepathic whatever was out of mothballs, she wasn't sure, but just to know there were options to choose from was a jewel beyond price. The cord that had tied her to the Hollow had been cut. The irony was that now that she was free to leave, she wouldn't. It was a very good place for a child to grow up.

For a while tonight, she had made the mistake of hoping again, when Michael had talked about moving in with Lee and again when he'd proposed. The lovemaking that had

ensued had for her been an act of celebration and a conci-
liation to compromise. The thought of living in a city of any
size did not fill her with elation, but at least Washington was
a city she knew, and one where the buildings were low rises,
at best. For the most part it was open to the skies, and green;
there was no lack of trees. The Wayland Institute was there,
and the closest mountains an hour away. That scenario, she
felt, was manageable.

No sooner had the celebration ended when the reasons for
celebrating had all been snatched away. To Michael, the best
of all possible worlds was midtown Manhattan with her at
his side. He was still clinging to his dream of going home the
successful man, wanted by the most prestigious firm, holding his own in the most competitive city in the world. She
knew how much that meant to him. She had heard it in his
voice, had seen it in his eyes as he'd talked. She'd been
foolish enough to think that today's events would change
that.

Very simply, they lived in different worlds, never the twain
to meet. She could not survive in Manhattan, could not tol-
erate the prospect of existing with the stuff of her nightmares, high rise upon high rise right outside her windows,
outside her doors. Then there were the people, millions of
them, stressed to the limit precisely because there were millions of them in a space smaller than the Hollow and Chestin together.

The one thing she had learned over the past ten years was
that her mental block was no match for a person under
stress. When she was in the Hollow, sustaining that buffer
was tiring. In New York, how long would she be able to keep
it in place? Once it frayed, she would be barraged from all
sides, from elevator buttons, escalator and stair railings,
doorknobs and handles, all the places people touched without thinking. If she came behind them soon enough, she'd
be bombarded with snippets of anxiety, tiny sparks of anger, frustration and fear. Had she removed her gloves to-

day only to have to put them back on? Did finding herself
have to mean losing Michael?

Easing out from under his arm, she sat up and looked
back at him. He slept on his side, his breathing deep and
even, his features at rest. She watched him for a while,
memorizing the picture for future recall, until several of the
insect bites from the afternoon began to itch and she realized that's what had awakened her to begin with. The lotion Cap had brought for her was downstairs in the kitchen.

Shivering in the air-conditioned chill, she slipped into the
white cotton robe flung over the back of the chair. On Michael it was probably short; on her it stopped at midcalf,
and the sash wrapped around her waist twice. Barefooted,
she tiptoed to the first floor. The lotion provided instant relief, but she was now wide awake and knew if she returned
to Michael's bed, she would be restless. Crossing to a front
window, she knelt, elbows on the low sill.

It was almost two, and the neighborhood was quiet, the
windows dark. Down the street the lights outside the front
doors of Simmons Community Hospital threw pale amber
circles against the night. A dog trotted along the curb,
sniffed at something in the gutter, moved on. A small, dark
compact car drifted slowly down the street, hesitating in
front of several houses, then, like the dog, moved on. Several minutes later, it was back. This time it pulled over to the
curb at the house next to the hospital. The door opened, and
the driver got out and stood, looking back toward the medical facility. Something about his posture pulled Tory to her
feet. It was Yale.

His back was to her so she ran out to the curb and called
to him. He whirled around, and after a hesitation of several seconds, started across to her. Even in the dark his
classically handsome features were startling.

"Hi!" she said. "You decided to take the late flight anyway."

"That's the house? Talk about luck. How's Lee? Is he
awake yet?"

"No, but it could be any time. His kidneys have begun to function, so he's a lot better. Where's Leslie? Michael's asleep, but I know he'll want to—"

"No, don't wake him. I . . ." He seemed to run out of steam and glanced back over his shoulder.

For the first time, Tory noticed that he seemed very tense. "Is something wrong? Yale?"

He swung back to her, his white smile flashing quickly. "No. I'm just tired. That is the hospital, isn't it? It looks more like a school, a small one at that."

"It's a good facility, Yale. And we didn't have much choice. If we'd tried to take him into Charleston, he wouldn't have made it. You can talk to Michael about it in the morning."

"Forget it. I have no right to be critical. Which way's the ocean? I can smell it."

"Behind the houses on our side. There's a nice long beach and a pier. Why are we standing out here in the street? Poor Leslie must be tired of waiting." He didn't seem to be listening. Once again he was looking back over his shoulder at the hospital. "Yale," Tory said, shaking his arm.

Startled, he dropped his car keys, which disappeared in a thicket growing at the curb. Swearing under his breath, he pawed at the stubby branches.

Tory saw a glint. "I think . . . Yes, here they are." She picked them up by the ring and extended them to him.

He stared at them, then took them from her, but there was something different about his face when he raised his eyes to look at her. "Why did you have to do that?"

"Do what? Pick up your keys?"

"Everything's going wrong," he said, but she sensed he was addressing himself, not her. "Why does everything always go wrong with me?"

"Yale, what is it? Has something happened?"

He seemed to remember he wasn't alone, a frown of irritation tugging his brows together. "No. What are you doing out here, anyway?"

"I got up for something and saw you from the window. Yale, is there a problem with Leslie? Is she all right?"

"She's fine," he said, his manner suddenly abrupt. "In fact, how about giving me a hand with her? She's asleep in the back seat. You can walk her to the house while I get the bags."

"Be glad to. Let me get my shoes."

"The street looks okay. Any broken glass would show, even in the dark. Come on." He took her hand, rather more tightly than was comfortable, towed her toward the dark compact and opened the rear door.

Tory leaned over and peered in. The car was empty. Before she could react, Yale shoved her inside and climbed in beside her, shutting the door.

"Yale, where is she? Where's Leslie?"

He stared straight ahead as if he hadn't heard her. "Now what do I do? Everything was all planned. It would have worked just fine, the timing, everything." He turned his head, looked down at her. "If it hadn't been for you. You ruined it. You weren't supposed to be out here. It's your fault. You can see that, can't you?"

Tory felt the cold hand of fear on the back of her neck. She had no idea what kind of stress Yale might be under, but clearly it was winning and he was losing. He sounded perfectly rational if you listened to his tone and not his words, but his handsome veneer was cracking. She suspected she wasn't going to like whatever it had been hiding, and reached for the handle of the door.

"No. I can't allow you to do that." He yanked her into his arms and pushed her onto her back on the seat. Tory took a deep breath to scream, and his hand came down across her mouth, sealing her lips closed. With the other hand he whipped the folded handkerchief from his breast pocket and loosened his tie.

"I'm really sorry about this," he said as he crammed the white linen into her mouth and secured it in place with his tie. "You shouldn't have picked up my keys. Leslie told me all about this psychic business. You handled the car keys so now you know everything.''

Tory shook her head violently. She hadn't picked up anything from touching the keys. Yale, however, ignored her gesture of denial, yanking at the sash of Michael's robe. She kicked against the door, tried to squirm out from under him but he was too heavy, too strong. She couldn't even free her hands to hold the robe closed.

"It was all his fault," he said, pulling the sash free of its loops. The front of the robe parted, exposing her breasts. He didn't seem to notice. "I didn't mean to hurt him, just talk to him. But he laughed at me. He shouldn't have laughed at me." He used the long cotton strip to bind her hands and feet, talking all the while, but with the air of a person thinking aloud.

"It was my chance, the only one I'd have. Mike called and asked me to tell Lee he wouldn't be able to sail down to Virginia Beach with him—he wouldn't be back from his meeting with the hotshot architects in New York. I had to grab the brass ring while it was in reach, sail with Lee and use the time alone with him to convince him to let me fill Mike's shoes with the firm. Hell, Mike was running out on him, wasn't he? Lee's little dream of a dynasty—Mike marrying Leslie and taking over the firm—was going down the tubes.''

When she was thoroughly trussed, Yale sat her up, his expression intensely earnest. "You have to understand. Cross and Crosby weren't paying me what I was worth, nowhere nearly what Mike was getting. I was strapped. I had bills, the new car, the condo. Lee had to take me on.''

He stared straight ahead, his expression bitter. "He went for it at first, said he'd consider it. Then I told him how much I wanted. He laughed at me. At *me!* He said that was out of the question. I told him I'd do anything he wanted, even marry Leslie. I'd been dating her for a year, knowing Michael was leaving, just waiting to make my move. Why else would I bother with a woman who couldn't even see what I looked like?''

Tory recoiled from him, tried to squirm into the corner. How could she have been so blinded by his physical beauty? He was repulsive, a moral cripple, loathsome.

"That's when things went wrong. I don't know, maybe I shouldn't have mentioned Leslie at all. He told me to go ahead and marry her, but if I thought the job was the dowry that came along with her, I would be out of luck. I wasn't good enough for his company or his daughter."

Tory listened with one ear, trying to think. If she could just figure out what he planned to do with her, why he had come at all...

"I...lost my temper," Yale said. "I hit him, harder than I meant to. I knocked him out, and he fell against the ice chest. I heard his leg snap. It made me sick. I didn't know what to do. I didn't even know where we were—we'd sailed right on past Virginia Beach." He looked around, as if he couldn't quite remember where he was. "I guess I'd better move, don't you think? Drive around some. Yes, that's what I'll do. Maybe you'd better lie down. Right. Don't bother trying to get away. There are kiddie locks on the doors back here. You won't be able to open them."

He pushed her onto her back again and got out, moving so quickly that Tory missed the chance to do the only thing she'd been able to think of. Sooner or later, her opportunity would come again. Oh, Michael, she thought, and shoved him out of her mind. She had to concentrate, be alert.

He got behind the wheel, started the engine. "I carried Lee down to the cabin and laid him on a bunk until I could decide what to do. Nobody would ever believe I hadn't meant to hurt him. He'd have me arrested for assault, and I'd lose everything. I couldn't let that happen, could I?"

The car began to move, and Tory stared up at the stars. The more Yale talked, the less chance there was that he'd let her go. There was no point in hoping for a miracle; she'd used up her quota for one day. She would have to save herself, save her baby. Michael's baby.

"I turned the boat around and headed back, but we ran into a squall. Then the engine stalled, and wouldn't start again. So I went below to get the old man to tell me what to do. He wasn't there! I don't know what happened to him. There I was, stuck out in the middle of the ocean."

That was enough of a puzzle to distract Tory for a moment. Obviously he hadn't fallen overboard. Where had he hidden?

Yale's voice droned on. "I drifted until a couple of women came by in a speedboat. They saw me and pulled alongside. They were stinking drunk, wanted to know if I'd like to party with them. It was the first break I'd had all day. I told them the people I was with were stuffed shirts and I could use a party, so I climbed off and went with them. I figured Lee had fallen overboard during the squall and I didn't care what happened to his boat as long as I wasn't on it. I wound up spending the night with them in some two-bit resort on the Outer Banks of North Carolina. The worst part was I had to go to bed with them. Ugh. I felt ~~dirty~~ for days."

Tory shivered, astonished by his last statement. Either his priorities were skewed or he was completely unhinged. Under the circumstances, neither choice was reassuring.

"Weeks went by, *weeks* with no news of Lee's body or the boat. I thought I was home free. Leslie wanted a job. I got her a job. It proved I loved her. I'd marry her and get Lee's money and the firm. Farraday and Associates. It would sound so good. Now after all this time he turns up and spoils everything."

The car had stopped, and she sat up. She was fairly sure they hadn't left the island; there was only one way off, over a metal bridge that clattered loudly under the wheels of a car. If she was able to get away from him, she'd at least be in fairly familiar territory.

"Lee's unconscious. I've got to see he doesn't wake up. A hospital as small as that won't have much staff, and I can handle whoever's in my way." He turned around and looked back at her. "I shouldn't have said that, should I? Now you know everything. It's your fault, you know. You botched things for me." He cut the engine and sat for a minute. "Hurry up, Yale. You have a lot to do and a chartered jet waiting to get you back to D.C. in time to meet Leslie."

He got out and opened the back door. Tory, knowing the moment had come, was ready for him, her feet hitting him solidly below the belt, not, however, as low as she'd intended. He doubled over, blocking her exit from the car. When she aimed for him a second time to kick him out of the way, one hand, the fingers like iron bands, clamped around her ankle and held firm.

He hauled her out of the car on her back and she hit the ground hard, the impact knocking the wind out of her. She was spared the agony of trying to catch her breath, only dimly aware of Yale bending over her and even less of the large fist speeding toward her jaw. The explosive blast of pain from the blow made her forget there was no air in her lungs, made her forget everything. When the black hole of unconsciousness opened, she was in no condition to fight it. Her last coherent thought was of Michael and how much she loved him, how sorry she was that she hadn't told him about the baby and... The rest of it slipped with her down into the vacuum.

Chapter 13

"Tory?" Michael woke with a start. Something was wrong. The space beside him was empty. The bathroom door was ajar, but no light showed from behind it. Throwing off the sheet, he stood up. Her clothes were where she had dropped them when she'd taken them off, so logic dictated that she was somewhere in the house. He turned to get his robe, saw that it was gone and took momentary comfort in its absence; she must have taken it. But even as he searched the second floor, then the first, he knew she wasn't there. Still nude, he went out onto the lower deck. The beach was empty, desolate, the air cool against his skin. Where the hell was she?

Taking the stairs two at a time, he returned to the bedroom and grabbed his slacks and shirt. The fact that Tory's sandals were still in his back pocket sounded a warning in his ears. Why would she have left the house without shoes, wearing his robe and nothing else? She must be out here somewhere. The sand was light; so was his robe. It was possible he'd simply missed her.

As a precaution against overlooking the obvious, he opened the front door. She was not sitting on the front steps, and the street was empty except for a single car slowing to a stop just beyond the hospital. He closed the door and left by way of the deck, checking under the house, though why she'd be there defied his imagination.

He stood, debating which direction to go, and started to the right, jogging. He had gone perhaps fifty yards when he slowed, uneasiness creeping through his mind like an insidious vine. Where could she be? It was almost three. Tory was too levelheaded to... He stopped. Levelheaded? The same woman who'd climbed the side of a mountain after midnight? For you, he reminded himself. For a pen she thought was yours.

He turned around, looked back the way he had come. If she had decided to take a walk, she would probably head toward the northern end of the island, toward the restaurant, the pier—familiar territory. He started back, wondered if he'd make better time if he used the street where there was no sand to slow him down. The tide was coming in, and he wasn't sure how far up the beach it usually stopped. And if Tory was on the beach, he'd miss her.

He set off at a modified trot with an occasional glance between the houses, spotted the tail of the small imported car he'd seen before. The driver was in for a ticket. Granted, he'd pulled up in front of the house next door, but Cap had warned him that on-street parking was not allowed in this block in order to insure free access of emergency vehicles to the hospital. Either one parked under the house, or in the yard.

Michael caught a glimpse of the long driveway that led to the emergency entrance of Simmons Community Hospital. A figure in white moved in the shadows at the rear, probably, he thought, one of the nurses or orderlies getting a breath of air. Except...

He paused. Could that have been Tory? He didn't quite understand the mental link she had with Lee. Had she sensed that something was wrong? Would she have gone there barefooted, dressed in only his robe? Without waking him? He had to be honest; he could never be sure what Tory Shelton might do, so it wouldn't hurt to check.

Cutting through to the street, Michael jogged toward Simmons. The figure in white, moving quickly across the front lawn, angling toward the car was, to his disappointment, much too tall to be Tory. It was a man. Michael frowned. There was no mistaking that long stride, the blur of ash-blond hair, even in what little light there was. "Yale!" he called.

Yale whirled around, his attitude that of someone caught in the jaws of indecision. Finally he walked back toward Michael. He was not his usually dapper self. His jacket was rumpled, his pant legs wet.

"I thought you weren't coming until later. Where's Leslie?"

"She isn't here? I never reached her at home. All I got was her answering machine, so I figured she'd lucked up on a rush hour flight. Damn."

"Well, come on over to the house—that one—and you can call her. Wow, man, what happened to you? How'd your slacks get so wet? You're soaked from the knees down."

"Stopped to get something out of the trunk and didn't realize I was on the edge of a marsh. This place is dangerous at night."

"It does pay to watch where you're going. Did you get to see Lee?"

"At this hour? No. I just thought I'd check to see how he was doing, but there was no one at the nurses' station."

"That doesn't sound right," Michael said. "Maybe I should move Lee. Come on, let's check."

"No!" Yale's reply was sharp, strident. "I'd just as soon wait. You know me, I get the willies around sick people."

"We can at least find out what the hell the nurse in CCU is doing." Michael took his arm, and began walking toward the emergency room door. "Besides, I want to see if Tory's in there. She's not in the house, and—"

Yale yanked his arm away and was immediately contrite. "Sorry. Hospitals make me nervous. I'll see him in the morning. Right now, I'm more concerned about Leslie. I don't want her flying down alone. Think maybe Jake—"

The sound of a distant siren brought him to an abrupt halt.

"If that car is yours," Michael said, "you'd better move it. There's no on-street parking on this block."

"Yeah. Okay." Backpedaling, he turned and sprinted toward the car.

"Pull into the yard," Michael called. "The redwood over there." He watched as Yale got in, gunned the engine and took off. "Hey! This way!" But Yale was gone.

The emergency vehicle had cut its siren, but the revolving red and blue lights were visible the length of the street—a police car, not an ambulance.

The doors of the emergency room opened, and a man in the white uniform of a hospital attendant staggered out, holding a bloodied handkerchief to the back of his head. "Son of a bitch!" he moaned. Spotting Michael, he asked, "What'd you hit me for?"

"What?"

The police car careened into the driveway, and an officer scrambled out. "You all right, Wheeler? Central said there was an assault."

Again the double doors slid open. Dr. Allen stepped out, looking sleepy. "What's the trouble?"

Wheeler scowled at Michael. "I was at the desk, watching television—nothing going on in the ER—and somebody poleaxed me from behind. Knocked me cold. I don't know how long I've been out, but I caught this joker standing here."

Yale's sudden flight began to take on ominous implications. "I didn't hit you. Dr. Allen, is anyone on duty in CCU?"

"Mrs. Dooley. Why?"

"I have a bad feeling. Come on." Without waiting to see if they followed, Michael ran through the emergency room, took the stairs to the upper floor and burst through the doors of the Critical Care Unit. The nurses' station appeared to be vacant. Taking no chances, he ducked behind it. Mrs. Dooley had not left her post. She'd been stuffed under the counter, and an angry bruise decorated what he could see of her jaw.

Dr. Allen and the officer, gun drawn, came through the swinging doors.

"Under there," Michael said, pointing, and ran toward Room C, his heart pounding. The door was closed, the curtain drawn around the bed, the cubicle eerily quiet. Flinging the curtain aside, he stared down at Lee. The old man wasn't breathing. He lay in an awkward position, his chin to his chest.

"Damn it, Lee, what did he do to you?" He looked at the tubes snaking into Lee's arms. They had not been removed. Nothing seemed disturbed. Grabbing Lee by the shoulders, he held him, his eyes filled with tears, his vision so blurred that he almost missed the stains on the pillow. They were yellow, the color of the antiseptic smeared on Lee's face. Quickly Michael examined the back of the man's head. No antiseptic there. Yale, the bastard, had smothered Lee with the pillow!

CPR! Michael thought, cursing himself for not having thought of it sooner. He was feeling for a pulse when Dr. Allen came running.

He pushed Michael aside, found a pulse immediately. "Wheeler, get in here! Respirator, stat! Out, Gallagher. We've got work to do."

Tory's jaw ached, the first sensation to register when she came to. The next was wetness, water around her, then pain in her shoulders, arms, wrists. After a few groggy seconds, she remembered why. She was gagged. Yale. Where was he? Where was she?

She opened her eyes and frowned in confusion at a pattern that at first made no sense—a sliver of sky, then a stripe of darkness. A few inches over another sliver of sky and stars, another stripe of darkness. She was submerged in water chest-high. Yale had tied her to a center support under the pier.

Her legs were free, probably because the sash of the robe wasn't long enough to wrap around wrists, ankles and the piling, too. That was small comfort, however. No one could see or hear her unless they came out to the end of the pier. Unless someone came soon, it wouldn't matter one way or the other. The tide was coming in. If she was in water up to her chest now, that didn't bode well for where it might stop. By the time the sun came up, she would have long since drowned.

Oh, Michael, she thought. Why had things worked out the wrong way? Why was it she'd had a telepathic conversation with a perfect stranger instead of the man she loved? Yale was right; life wasn't fair.

It took the combined efforts of the officer and a burly orderly who appeared from nowhere to coax Michael from Lee's room. "Look," he said, turning on the policeman, "don't waste time with me. There's a man driving a small, dark compact, a rental, probably. I ran into him coming out of here. His name's Yale Farraday. Six-three, one-eighty, I guess. Blond hair, gray eyes, looks like a damned model. He did this. Why, I don't know. It has to be him. Otherwise, why'd he run?"

"Was that the car that pulled away from out front?"

"Yes. A Toyota, I think."

"Well, there's only so far he could go, heading south. If he's turned around, maybe we can catch him before he hits the bridge." He took off running, his portable radio glued to his chin as he barked orders.

Michael paced, a double dose of anguish flooding his veins. He was worried about Lee, of course, but his concern for Tory was now unbearable. She might, of course, be back at the house, wondering where he'd gone, but for some reason he didn't think so. Could she have seen Yale, too? If she had, it would have been before he'd gotten to Lee, and he would have had to... To what? Abduct her, hold her somewhere until he'd done what he came to do? Had she been in the car? In the trunk? That was the best of the scenarios he could think of. The worst made his legs weaken, and he collapsed in a chair.

Dr. Allen came out, perspiration glistening across his forehead. "He's back with us, breathing on his own. How much if any brain damage there is, I can't say, but I doubt he was without oxygen for very long. One thing we do know is that his speech center's functioning. He mumbled a few words. That's a good sign."

"He's conscious?"

"No, not yet."

"What did he say?"

"Nothing that made sense. He mumbled Miss Shelton's name a couple of times. And 'drowning.' At least that's what Wheeler thought it was."

Suddenly Yale's soaked pants' legs took on an ominous meaning. "I'll kill him. I swear I'll kill him! Find that cop! Tell him Yale's taken Tory somewhere. If he finds him, beat the hell out of him if necessary, but make him tell where she is!'' He left an astonished Dr. Allen and headed for the stairs at full speed.

The cruiser was gone, the street empty again. Michael barreled across the street and back to the beach, kicking off the thong sandals as soon as he hit the sand. The tide had made considerable inroads; it was several feet closer to the houses than when he'd seen it last.

"Tory!" he shouted, running north, his mind churning. Yale said he'd stepped into a marsh. There were marshlands on the west side of the island, but the water wasn't that deep. If Yale had seen Tory before going into the hospital, he probably wouldn't have taken her that far. The ocean was closest, but would he have simply thrown her in? He knew she could swim because of Danny's rescue. He would have to... to immobilize her so she couldn't swim or float.

Fear and adrenaline pumped through Michael's body, put rockets beneath his feet. He raced along the waterline, calling her name, praying, pleading, making promises to God. He ran all the way to the restaurant, his pulse a bass drum pounding in his ears. Nothing. Had he figured wrong? Had Yale taken her in the other direction?

Reversing his tracks, starting south again, he neared the pier, passed it, then stopped. He turned, his impulse to keep going, the muscles of his calves protesting at the sudden halt. There was no rhyme or reason for being rooted to that spot; he saw nothing, heard nothing, but he couldn't move, knew with certainly that this was where he should be.

He closed his eyes and emptied his head. *Talk to me, Tory. Tell me where you are.* There was no answer. He hadn't really expected one. Had he condemned her by not believing deeply enough? He moved on another yard, feeling as if he was pulling against some invisible rope being stretched to its limits.

"Tory!" he shouted. "Where are you? Answer me!"

Suddenly his senses seemed more acute. It wasn't that he heard anything specific, only a difference in the rhythm of the tide washing in, of the water slapping against the pilings. He backtracked, walked slowly onto the pier. Two thirds of the way toward the end, he felt it, a vibration underfoot. Then he heard it, a muted thumping—one, two, three. A pause. One, two, three.

He walked faster, trying to pinpoint the source, went all the way to the end and saw a flare of white billowing on the surface of the water. "Tory," he whispered, and jumped in.

She was a pale form floating on her back beneath the pier, her nose pressed against the planking with perhaps an inch or two of breathing space remaining. There was little time to spare; the tide wouldn't wait. He struggled with her bonds, tightened by her struggles, broke fingernails to the quick as he tried to loosen the knots. He had no success with the end tied to the piling. Abandoning it, he bobbed to the surface for air, submerged and attacked the ones around her wrists, eventually using his teeth to shred the fabric. He went up for air, went down, and pulling with all his strength against the weak spot, ripped it in two. She was free.

He pried the gag from around her head, lifted her onto the pier and pulled himself up beside her. She lay staring up at the stars, gasping for breath.

"Oh, God, Tory." Michael sat up and gathered her in his arms. She clung to him, her eyes squeezed shut.

"I'm not dreaming, right? You really are here."

"I'm here, I'm here."

"Yale..." she began, her voice roughened, hoarse.

"Shhh. I know. He tried to smother Lee with a pillow. They're looking for him now. I knew he must have done something to you. I knew it."

"Then you heard me," she said.

"Thank God, yes, I heard you. Your poor feet must be full of splinters, kicking the planks so hard."

She shook her head. "I mean, before that. I was calling to you in my mind, calling as loudly as I could. You heard me, you must have."

Michael gazed down at her. He'd gotten the first clue from Lee, but something had certainly paralyzed him after he'd run past the pier. Who was he to question her? "Yes. I guess I did hear you after all. Tory, let's get married right here, right now. I'm not going to chance losing you again."

"Michael—"

"I won't take no for an answer," he said, holding her tightly. "Say you'll marry me. I want you to be the mother of my children."

Tory looked up at him, the moon reflected in her eyes. "I've got news for you, darling. I already am."

A harsh burr blasted through Tory's dream. She turned over to see Michael standing beside the bed, hopping his way into a pair of slacks.

"What is it?" she asked, sitting up.

"Doorbell. Some idiot's been leaning on it for the last five minutes. I was hoping whoever it is would go away, but no such luck. Go back to sleep." He zipped, buckled and ran out.

Tory listened to his footsteps pounding down the stairs, considered getting up herself, but didn't have the energy. Settling down again, she began to giggle, remembering Michael's reaction to the news that he was going to be a father. He'd picked her up in his arms and had run, carrying her, all the way to the hospital, bursting in on Dr. Allen unceremoniously and demanding that she be examined from head to toe to make sure she and the baby were all right.

Dr. Allen had gone along, assuring him that the baby had in no way been affected by what had happened to Tory. If it would make him feel any better, she could come back in the morning, and someone in OB/Gyn would examine her.

Tory stretched, feeling loved, lazy, brand-new. There were still problems ahead—she would live in terror of the day Michael felt free to move to New York—but that was far enough away that she could follow Scarlett's advice and worry about it tomorrow.

It was already tomorrow. The sun was not yet visible, but the sky was that in-between hue, a light blue-gray, the last stages of the night stepping aside for morning's debut. For the first time, Tory began to wonder what was keeping Michael and who had been at the door at this hour. She'd give him five minutes and then go see. She drifted off again.

Consciousness returned, primarily because the air brushing across her face was warm and muggy. Opening her eyes, she saw the tall, broad-shouldered figure framed in the open doorway of the deck, the sky behind him only a little brighter than when she'd closed her eyes. The picture met her expectations except for one important difference. The hair was light, not ebony. Yale.

He stared at her, mouth open. "How did you . . . ?"

"Michael!" Tory screamed, leapt from the bed and hurtled toward the door to the hallway. Yale beat her to it by a second, slamming it shut. He spun her around and pinned her with her back against the door, one hand over her mouth.

"I don't know how you got away, but make a sound and I'll have to hurt you. I don't want to hurt you, Tory. Who's in the house? Where's Michael? In the bedroom next door? Quietly, now." He removed his hand, towering above her, the cloying scent of his cologne, triggered by his exertions, making her stomach lurch.

"You don't want to hurt me?" Tory hissed. "You tied me under the pier with the tide coming in and you don't want to hurt me?"

His eyes wandered from one corner of the room to the other, as if he struggled to make sense of what she said. "The tide?"

"If it hadn't been for Michael, I'd have drowned!"

242   *A Loving Touch*

"Michael." Yale's face tightened. "Always Michael spoiling things for me. He saw me, too. And the police are all over the place."

"Because you tried to kill Lee."

"Tried?" For the first time she sensed he was really listening. "Lee's still alive?"

"Yes."

"But . . . he was dead! I checked! He wasn't breathing!"

"Well, he is now, and the police are looking for you. Turn yourself in, Yale. Don't make things worse."

His face filled with panic. "How could they be any worse? Things always go wrong for me. What am I going to do?"

His mind was definitely elsewhere. He still had her backed against the door, but if she could just get away from him, get to the bathroom, put the door between them.

She started to move, and immediately his grip on her shoulders tightened.

"No. You ruined my plans first, so you'll help me get away." He nodded to himself. "Yes, that'll work. They won't shoot at me if you're with me. Michael won't let them. Where are your clothes?"

Tory, her mind paralyzed at the thought of being at his mercy again, pointed at the chair near the open door of the deck. He twisted her arm behind her, and she let out a shriek of pain as her shoulder protested.

"We're going over to the chair and you're going to get dressed." He backed across the room holding her against his front, one hand ready to apply the needed pressure on her arm to make her obey, the other clamped over her lips again.

Tory, having no choice for the moment, moved with him, her pulse pounding in her ears. Where was Michael? Why hadn't he heard her scream? She glanced at the items on the dresser as they neared the chair. All his keys were still there. Had he locked himself out?

"I'm going to turn you loose so you can dress, but I'm standing right here so you won't try anything."

"Michael's right downstairs," she said, when he removed his hand.

He gave her a blank look, then his eyes narrowed, glittering with a manic cruelty. "Yes, he is. And if he makes a move to help, if he so much as moves an inch in my direction, I'll kill him."

Tory froze, her T-shirt in her hand, wondering if he was armed. Her question was answered almost immediately, when he dug into the pocket of his jacket and showed her a small, shiny revolver. Obviously the weapon of a woman, it seemed dainty and incongruous in his big hand.

"I didn't use it before—guns are too noisy—but I'll shoot Michael, and that's a promise. If you want lover boy alive, you'll put your clothes on and go out with me the way I came in, and get me off this stinking island."

A door opened, closed downstairs. Michael! Ice formed in Tory's veins, clogged the valves of her heart. If he'd only stay downstairs long enough for her to dress so she could get Yale out of the house. But he didn't. The stairs creaked. He was coming up! She envisioned him opening the door, seeing Yale with her. He would try to save her, and Yale would shoot him. She had to do something before he reached the bedroom.

Her hand shot toward the dresser, seeking something with which she might wound, and her fingers closed on the keys. Her arm arced toward the ceiling, its journey halted solely by how high she could reach. Yale gasped, his eyes widening with shock. The left side of his face lay open from chin to temple, blood spurting to the surface, beginning a crimson trail down his cheek. He stumbled backward, his hand pressed against the wound. With a growl that came up from her viscera, Tory slapped both palms against his chest, fingers spread, and shoved with a strength fueled by a high-octane mixture of desperation and adrenaline. Yale was propelled backward through the open door, the deck railing momentarily slowing his progress before he tumbled over it and disappeared. He hit the deck below with a thud that snapped Tory out of her murderous rage. She rushed out and looked down. Yale had missed the lounger by inches and lay spread-eagled, blood still flowing from his cheek.

"What the hell was that?"

"Michael?" she called, astonished to hear his voice coming from below her.

"God Almighty, it's Yale!" Jake Burnside burst out onto the deck. He knelt at Yale's head and placed a finger at the base of his neck.

Michael appeared below, a telephone in his hand. "I need the police and an ambulance," he was saying when he glanced up and saw her.

"He said he would kill you," she wailed. "I thought I heard you coming, and I cut his face with your keys and pushed him over. I killed him."

"My God." He dropped the phone and disappeared inside.

"No, she didn't. More's the pity," Jake said. He looked up for the first time and grinned. "Ahem. Hi, Tory. Lookin' good."

Tory, belatedly remembering that she wore no clothes, gave a tiny shriek and backed into the bedroom just as the door was thrown open and Michael hurtled through it.

"Oh, baby, I'm sorry," he said, sitting on the end of the bed and pulling her onto his lap. "It was Jake at the door. We stayed outside to talk so we wouldn't disturb you. That's why I didn't hear anything. I don't understand how he got past us."

"He climbed up the deck somehow. I had to push him, Michael. I couldn't bear it if something happened to you."

"I know the feeling." He kissed her soundly, his thumbs wiping at tears she hadn't realized she'd shed. "Are you okay? Did he touch you, Tory?"

She saw the unasked part of the question in his eyes and shook her head. "No. I don't even think he noticed I wasn't wearing anything. He just wanted to get away, that's all."

She felt him relax.

"I guess I should check on him. You're sure you're all right?"

She nodded and stood up, watching nervously as he stepped out onto the deck and leaned over the railing. Whether it was self-defense or not, she didn't want Yale's death hanging over her head.

"Well?" Michael said to Jake. "How is the bastard?"

"Okay. I think the fall just knocked the wind out of him. His face is a mess, though."

"Pity. Tie him up or sit on him or something. I'll be down in a minute." Coming back in, he closed the sliding door and gathered her to him. "As much as I'd love to keep holding you like this, you'd better get some clothes on. The house will be swarming with police in a minute. They'll need to come up here to see how he got in."

"Oh, Lord." She slipped out of his arms and darted into the bathroom.

"We'll probably be tied up with them for a while." Michael continued talking from the bedroom. "You've still got your statement to make about Yale's confession last night. After that, we're going shopping."

"You and Jake go. Believe me, I'm not in the mood," she said, turning on the shower.

"I am not taking that thug with me to buy something for you to get married in. The clerk would never understand."

Tory stuck her head out of the bathroom door. "You're serious, aren't you?"

"Deadly." He stood at the foot of the bed, an uneasy frown on his face. "It occurs to me— I've asked you to marry me twice. I have yet to get an answer. Are you trying to tell me something without telling me something?"

"Hold on a second." She reached for the Merthiolate in the first aid kit Michael had purchased earlier and dabbed at herself awkwardly. When she'd finished, she stuck her head out the door a second time. "Ask me again."

He hesitated, as if uncertain of her answer. "Will you marry me, Victoria Shelton?"

"I think I'd better. It would be a little awkward marrying anyone else with your name written on my heart. Your initials, actually." She stepped out into the bedroom so he could see her impromptu artwork on her left breast. The reddish-brown *M* was fairly respectable, but the capital *G* tilted drunkenly, as if it might roll backward onto her nipple.

To her astonishment, tears glistened in Michael's eyes. "God, I love you," he said, scooping her up and depositing her on the bed. Crossing to the door in two long strides, he locked it. "The police will have to wait."

Epilogue

Tory locked the car, and with shopping bags dangling from both hands, hurried toward the entrance of the marina where two figures stood waiting for her, one white-haired and slightly stooped, but in complete control of the leash in his hand. On the business end of the line was a toddler with curls the color of newly minted copper coins, his dark blue eyes at their roundest. He strained against the halter that held him tethered to the elderly man, his chubby legs churning in place like a cartoon character going nowhere. "Mom-mee, Mom-mee!" he shrieked happily.

"Mikey, Mikey!" she mimicked him, her heart aglow at the sight of him. Except for the color of his hair, he was the image of his father. "Hi, precious," she said when she'd reached them. He held up his arms, and she knelt to kiss the soft velvety cheek and to receive and return a hug. "Did you behave yourself?"

"He has behaved exactly like you'd expect a precocious fourteen-month-old to behave," Lee said, tilting his jaw toward her; it was his turn for a kiss. He bore no relation to the wasted man he'd been two years before and, surprisingly, had no scars. His sixty-fifth birthday was behind him but he looked fifteen years younger, exuding energy and good health in much the same way Michael did.

"Is everyone here already?" Tory asked, running her fingers absently through her son's unruly mop of curls. Like her own, they defied brush and comb to swirl in any direction they liked on any given day.

"Practically. Jake and Helen are aboard and Michael's on his way. Leslie and Wayne were on time, for once. He threatened to leave her if she wasn't ready when he was, so there's hope for him yet. He's not bad, as sons-in-law go. No sailor, but he's trying. At least he knows there's storage space under the bunks, which is more than I can say for Yale. Never even looked for me there, thank God."

"Let's not talk about him." Tory gazed down the pier where Lee's new cabin cruiser glistened in the sun. "She's beautiful. Do you miss the other one?"

He nodded. "Sometimes. Whoever found her after Zena took me off has a good little vessel on his hands. If I hadn't run her aground..."

"It's a miracle you could run her anywhere," Tory reminded him, "considering the condition you were in."

"Well, my condition cut no ice with Jake. He's never going to let me forget I sailed all that way south thinking I was going north. That rascal brought me the biggest damned compass I've ever seen. You'll see it when you go aboard. Helen said he's had it for weeks, just waiting for the *Leslie II*'s maiden voyage."

A dusty pickup careened into the lot and Mikey jerked away from her. "Dad-dee! Dad-dee!"

Michael, lean and tanned, pulled into a space and hopped out. "Sorry I'm late," he said, striding vigorously toward them. "Had a meeting with the landscape architects. The east section of Woodland will be finished on time. Hi, boy."

He picked up his son and Tory smiled. Separately they were a handful. Together they were impossible.

He eyed her shopping bags and groaned. "There goes the budget." He squinted at them, spotting the names on them for the first time. "Tyson's Corner? Potomac Mills? That's where you've been?"

"In and out of two dozen stores," she said triumphantly. "Up and down escalators and elevators, in and out of rest rooms. Look, Pa, no gloves, and didn't pick up a thing."

Michael put his son down. "You're kidding!"

"No, I'm not. Walked around and shopped, touched, felt, darn near groped. I've learned how to block emanations when I want to. The Wayland said I could do it and they were right. I passed the test, Michael."

"Oh, honey." Michael grabbed her and hugged her, with a kiss for good measure.

"Congratulations, Tory." Lee squeezed her arm. "Michael, you've got yourself twice the woman you deserve. She did this for you."

"What do you mean, for me? She did it for herself."

"For both of us," Tory amended quietly. "With Lee acting as cheerleader all the way."

Michael turned on him. "Why am I the last to find out about this?"

"We didn't want you to be disappointed if it didn't work," Lee explained. "But it did, so now, if you still want to move to New York . . ."

"I'm ready," Tory said, stating a fact. "I can handle it."

Michael stared down at her. "Is that what this is all about? Tory, I don't need that any longer. Everything I want is right here and in the Hollow—you, Mikey, Lee, our friends. Haven't you been happy with the way things have gone?"

"Deliriously." It had worked well, at Lee's during the week, in the Hollow on weekends.

"If it ain't broke, don't fix it," Michael said. "We'll have to find our own place here and add a wing to the house in the Hollow, but that's it. We're here to stay. Now let's go find a cabin on the cruiser and make some more babies."

Lee shook his head, his eyes suspiciously bright. "He hasn't changed in the twenty-four years I've known him. Only one thing on his mind."

Tory went off in peals of laughter, happier than she sometimes felt she had a right to be. Michael picked up his son again and the four of them walked toward the *Leslie II,* Lee to launch his new craft and to spoil Mikey rotten, Tory to inform her husband that once again he'd been beaten to the punch. They could make love for the pure enjoyment of it; the second baby had already been made.

* * * * *

SILHOUETTE·INTIMATE·MOMENTS

NORA ROBERTS
Night Shadow

People all over the city of Urbana were asking, Who was that masked man?

Assistant district attorney Deborah O'Roarke was the first to learn his secret identity . . . and her life would never be the same.

The stories of the lives and loves of the O'Roarke sisters began in January 1991 with NIGHT SHIFT, Silhouette Intimate Moments #365. And if you want to know more about Deborah and the man behind the mask, look for NIGHT SHADOW, Silhouette Intimate Moments #373, available in March at your favorite retail outlet.

NITE-1

 *Silhouette Books*

Take 4 bestselling love stories FREE

Plus get a FREE surprise gift!

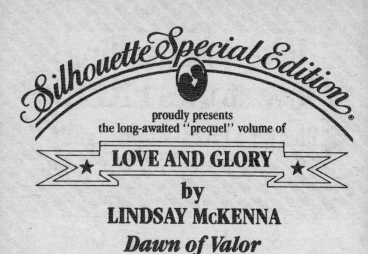

proudly presents
the long-awaited "prequel" volume of

★ LOVE AND GLORY ★

by
LINDSAY McKENNA

Dawn of Valor

In the summer of '89, Silhouette Special Edition premiered three novels celebrating America's men and women in uniform: LOVE AND GLORY, by bestselling author Lindsay McKenna. Featured were the proud Trayherns, a military family as bold and patriotic as the American flag—three siblings valiantly battling the threat of dishonor, determined to triumph . . . in love and glory.

Now, discover the roots of the Trayhern brand of courage, as parents Chase and Rachel relive their earliest heart stopping experiences of survival and indomitable love, in

Dawn of Valor, Silhouette Special Edition #649.

This February, experience the thrill of LOVE AND GLORY—from the very beginning!

DV-1

Silhouette romances are now available in stores at these convenient times each month.

Silhouette Desire
Silhouette Romance

These two series will be in stores on the 4th of every month.

Silhouette Intimate Moments
Silhouette Special Edition

New titles for these series will be in stores on the 16th of every month.

We hope this new schedule is convenient for you. With only two trips each month to your local bookseller, you will always be sure not to miss any of your favorite authors!

Happy reading!

Please note there may be slight variations in on-sale dates in your area due to differences in shipping and handling.

WRITTEN IN THE STARS

**Star-crossed lovers?
Or a match made in heaven?**

Why are some heroes strong and
silent...and others charming
and cheerful? The answer is
WRITTEN IN THE STARS!

Coming each month in 1991,
Silhouette Romance presents
you with a special love story
written by one of your favorite
authors—highlighting the hero's
astrological sign! From January's
sensible Capricorn to December's
disarming Sagittarius, you'll
meet a dozen dazzling and
distinct heroes.

Twelve heavenly heroes...twelve
wonderful Silhouette Romances
destined to delight you. Look for
one WRITTEN IN THE STARS
title every month throughout
1991—only from Silhouette
Romance.

STAR

Silhouette Books®